WEIRD TRAILS

A baker's dozen glimpses into a West that was more wild than we'd ever imagined, presented to us by

Happy Trails!
Michael Szymanski

Donald R. Burleson

Don D'Ammassa

Jessica Amanda Salmonson

C.J. Henderson

James Chambers

Clay and Susan Griffith

Keith Herber

Mollie L. Burleson

Mark McLaughlin and Michael Kaufman

Elizabeth Fackler

Michael Szymanski

Tim Curran

Mark Siegel

EDITED BY

Michael Szymanski

FOR

Triad Entertainments

2002

WEIRD TRAILS

The Blue Light People © 2002 by Michael Szymanski; *The Guardian* © 2002 by Mollie L. Burleson; *The Last Stand of Black Danny O'Barry* © 2002 by James Chambers; *Backlash* © 2002 by Elizabeth Fackler; *The North-West Monster Police* © 2002 by Clay and Susan Griffith; *All Around the Mulberry Bush* © 2002 by C.J. Henderson; *Battle on the Bridge of the Gods* © 2002 by Jessica Amanda Salmonson; *Salt of the Earth* © 2002 by Don D'Ammassa; *Sheep-Eye* © 2002 by Donald R. Burleson; *Skinning the Devil* © 2002 by Tim Curran; *A Treatise on Corporeality, or Jinn and Tonic, With a Whiskey Chaser* © 2002 by Mark McLaughlin and Michael Kaufman; *Showdown at Idiot's Rock* © 2002 by Keith Herber; *Death's Door* © 2002 by Mark Siegel

Cover art and Layout by Michael Szymanski

Address any questions or comments concerning this publication to:
Triad Entertainments, PO Box 90, Lockport, NY 14095, USA,
or by email at TRIADENT@hotmail.com, SUBJECT: Weird Trails

Triad Publication 0007, Published in 2002
ISBN 0-9719081-0-9
Library of Congress Control Number 2002090895

FIRST EDITION
1 2 3 4 5 6 7 8 9 10

Printed by:
Morris Publishing
3212 East Highway 30
Kearney, NE 68847
800-650-7888

THE WILDEST WEST

The wild and wooly west - a place of danger and hardship for some, a place of glory and adventure for others. For some, though, it could have been a place of dark terrors best left brooding in those lonesome sandstone wastelands where no human foot has ever trod. When the first trappers and prospectors ventured into the vastness of the American west, the land must have seemed as alien as the dark side of the moon; in such a land, anything was possible.

Imagine if you will the lone mountain man or the family with their entire lives bundled into a single wagon, huddled before a sometimes fitful and poorly fueled campfire that served as the only defense against an encroaching darkness and all the fearful mystery it may or may not contain. How did they feel, so far removed from all that was familiar to them, isolated from their fellow men in a land where only the self-reliant could survive, much less thrive.

What thoughts played through their minds on those chill evenings on the plains or at the foothills of some daunting mountain range that held its secrets closely beneath a veil of white? What visions did the strange sounds of the Southwestern night trigger within them, despite all of the cocky self-assurance that had been instilled in them by far-removed civilization?

And what of the people who had lived in these places for thousands of years, who knew full well the dangers of the wilderness and survived only by paying heed to that knowledge? So much of what they told the white newcomers was scoffed at and ignored, and only hard experience was to teach those newcomers the error of their ways.

What was real, and what imagined? Was the true shape of the western landscape darker and far more sinister than history has led us to believe? It remains for each of us to find their own answer to that question.

Within these pages are a lucky thirteen glimpses into that imagined landscape, where the subtlest quirk of fate or the tallest tale is all too possible, and very real to those who experience them within these tales. Perhaps in one of them you will find your answer, whether it be sublime, ridiculous, or a confirmation of something you've always suspected - that there really is something out there, just beyond the comforting glow of the fire. Something you fervently hope will *stay* out there.

Michael Szymanski

TABLE OF CONTENTS

ALONE BY THE FIRE

Well, friend, thank you kindly for letting me share your camp for the night. The fire's warm and the coffee's strong, so what more could a cowpoke ask for? 'Sides, it's a mighty big piece of country to be all on your lonesome in, ain't it? Fella's mind gets to playin' tricks on him and he starts imagining things that aren't there. A 'course, maybe they are.

It's a big land we chose to ride in, and a strange one too, if you spend enough time in it. A body spends a lifetime in the saddle, he tends to see things most other folks don't, and maybe that there is a good thing. The Old West has its dark side, and I don't just mean bandits, and gunslingers and New York lawyers. I mean the kind of thing you don't like to talk about in polite company, or think about when you're all on your lonesome out here on the prairie, with nothing but a campfire to hold back whatever all's out there in the dark. Maybe there's nothing at all, then again maybe, just maybe there's something just a' watching and a' waiting – for what, who knows? And do we really want to know?

There are stories I could tell you, friend, stories that'd curl your hair or turn it white, things that would make you hang up your saddle, put your horse to pasture, and never travel west of the Mississip for the rest of your born days. But you don't want to hear about none of that.

Or do you? I see you're curious, and I also see you think I'm pulling your leg. If that's what you think, why did you start looking over your shoulder all of a sudden like? Not all that sure of yourself, are you friend?

Well, I suppose there's a tale or two I could recollect if I think on it. Stories of injustice and comeuppance, of good and evil and all the shades between. Yessir, I could gab all night on it, but you have to get some shuteye before hightailing it out to the North Forty, don't you? So I'll just give you a few examples of what I'm talking about, and leave it to you to decide what's worth believing.

WEIRD TRAILS

White folks think the Injins were the first on this soil, but the Injins themselves know better. They know a lot of things we'd do well to listen to, and they know a lot more that's best left unsaid except to a few who've shown themselves worthy, like this fella I'm fixin' to tell you about.

There's things in the past that're best left there; but sometimes they come a'crawling out of their dark holes to pester good folk and bad, and that there's the time when a man's got to make a stand.

Take this fella name of Sam Hill. Like most cowpokes, he never looked for trouble, but trouble surefire could always find him. Well one day ol' Sam, he came up against a real snake in the grass, and it wasn't a meeting he's ever likely to forget.

The story goes something like this...

THE
BLUE LIGHT PEOPLE
BY
MICHAEL SZYMANSKI

It was getting on noon that spring day when ol' Samuel Clemens Hill rode into Coyote Junction, a dustbowl of a place out in the middle of the Devil's North Forty whose only claim to fame was that it sat square on the line between where you were and where you wanted to be; even so, it was still a far piece from either. The town had two reasons for being where it was: one, it was on the main East-West stage route between Fort Drummond and Antioch and two, it was in spitting distance of Old Man Teague's ranch - provided you were an experienced spitter, and you didn't rightly care what Old Man Teague thought about you spitting on his property.

And sure enough, almost anywhere you *did* spit it was most likely Teague's land. He had himself a mighty big spread out there north of town; place must have been big enough to run 200,000 head of cattle at the time ol' Sam rode into town. The story goes that Old Man Teague came out West with a few dollars in his pocket and the notion in his head that if you weren't with him, you were against him, and anyone who wouldn't sell out when he asked was definitely against him.

It was real interesting how anyone who stood up to Old Man Teague in those days wound up departing for parts unknown real sudden-

3

like, and most usually in the middle of the night. No one ever saw anything, either; even Teague's surly crew of hired hands, who were always traipsing around the countryside after sunset, "lookin' fer strays an' keepin' watch fer varmints." Yep, that was their story, and they stuck to it. Got away with it for so long that, by the time ol' Sam Hill rode in, Teague practically owned Coyote Junction.

Now ol' Sam, he didn't get to see as many years as he had by riding the range with his eyes shut. No sir, he was an eagle-eyed, cagey, quick-thinking cuss, and even as he and Brimstone rode onto the trampled sand that served as Main Street, Sam knew something was up.

Life in those parts was hard, damn hard, and it didn't offer the folks who chose it much to smile about, but Sam allowed as he'd seen more cheerful faces at a Comanche raid than he did in this town. Even the youngsters couldn't seem to get up enough gumption to cause their parents any grief; hell, even the mangy old mutt skulking in front of the dry goods store acted like he was sharing a cave with a grizzly.

Being a stranger in town and all, Sam expected that folks would take some notice of him, but the looks he got from the people he passed were more than curious; they were suspicious and, in some cases, downright nasty.

"Musta been a bank robbery lately," Sam figured to himself. "Best if I tread lightly an' be real polite." Well, that didn't work out all that well, so after a couple "Howdy's" an "'Mornin' M'am's," Sam just kept his mouth shut, figuring it would be smarter to find out what kind of nest of snakes he'd stepped into before dancing a jig in it.

As it happened, Sam did have one acquaintance in Coyote Junction, a Miz Abigail Pennifield, the one and only schoolteacher for a hundred miles around. They'd met that time Sam had helped guard Abby's stage through some mighty hostile territory a couple years back. It had been a rough time, and they all had been lucky to make it through with their hides intact.

These days Abby went wherever her skills were needed, and from time to time Sam would drop in on her to see how she was doing. He worried a lot about Miz Pennifield and he enjoyed her company, so he never once passed up a chance to stop by and chew the fat, along with a healthy portion of fried chicken and those sourdough biscuits that melted in your mouth.... Sam's stomach allowed as how it would be mighty agreeable to some of those biscuits right about now, so he rode on past the Snake Eye

Saloon and went searching for the schoolhouse.

Abby lived in a one-room cabin that looked like it had been pieced together from scraps and leftovers from other buildings around town, but even so she'd put her mark on the place. Sagebrush, yucca, cactus, and piñon pine sheltered the cabin from a lot of the sun's mischief, and even from a distance as he approached Sam could make out patches of color where a couple flowerbeds prospered under Abby's gentle care. As he got closer, he could see that the whole place was kept in first rate repair, but he didn't have much time to look things over, because at that moment the front door of the cabin opened and Abigail Pennifield stepped out onto the porch.

She was a fine figure of a woman, Abby was, a tall blonde with a proud posture, deep, sky-blue eyes, and lips made for smiling, as they were doing right now, their owner having caught sight of her visitor.

"Well, well," she greeted as Sam rode up. "It's been a spell since I've seen such a fine looking specimen."

Sam touched the rim of his Stetson in greeting. "Why, thank you m'am. Always nice to be appreciated."

"I was talking to Brimstone." They both of them laughed at that one. "How are you, Sam? I'd almost given up on ever seeing you again."

"Oh, no chance of that, Miz Abby; no matter where you hole up, I reckon I'll turn up there after a spell." Sam eased himself off Brimstone, taking a moment to get reacquainted with the ground. "Speakin' of which, whatever brought you to this unfriendly excuse for a town?"

Abby's smile faded a little at that. "It wasn't always unfriendly. But let's not stand out here in the sun; I've just made up a batch of lemonade, and I'd be honored if you'd test it for me."

Sam brightened up considerable at that. Miz Abby's lemonade was famous throughout the West; why one time a fella from back East tried to talk her into bottling her recipe and selling it at mercantile establishments and suchlike in towns all over the territory. Sam chuckled to himself as he followed Abby into the cabin. Imagine such a thing; folks going to the store to pay a nickel for a bottle of lemonade! 'Course Abby had laughed at the notion and turned the offer down; she had enough on her plate what with her teaching and all to be mixing up batches of lemonade for some back East dude.

There was mostly chit chat and catching up over that first cool glass, but on the second helping both had satisfied their thirst enough to get down to business. While Sam waited on her, Abby took a final sip and firmly set the glass on the table in front of her.

"Folks around here are scared, Sam. Things are happening out in the desert they can't understand, and that frightens them. Sadly, when they get frightened, they tend to get a bit... surly."

Sam barked out a sharp laugh. "I seen broncos with a burr under their saddle as had an attitude better'n them folks I passed in town. Must be somethin' powerful nasty to scare 'em that mean."

Abby agreed. "It's the fear of the unknown, Sam; if they knew what they were up against they could at least try to do something about it. But you can't fight what you can't find, and you can't find it if you don't even know where to start looking. I don't mind telling you, I'm more than a bit jittery myself."

Well now that startled Sam; he knew for a fact there wasn't much that could give Miz Abby a fright, so if whatever all was going on in and around Coyote Junction, it was for certain nasty. "Well now, Miz Abby, what all's exactly goin' on? Seems you're a mite spooked to even be talkin' about this, and that ain't like you."

"Isn't like me," Abby corrected automatically, always the schoolmarm. "And you're right, it isn't, so let's get to it.

"It started out at Lem Torkleson's place - or what used to be Lem's place. His son Jeb rode out one morning to check on their small herd and found their prize bull butchered and, well half-missing."

Once she got her fire up, Abby headed full tilt into the tale, speaking plain and clear in a voice which ol' Sam never tired of listening to.

Whatever had hit Torkleson's place came back the next two nights, killing and butchering two more head of cattle and throwing a fright into the rest. No one came out and said as much, but everyone figured it was Old Man Teague's boys seeing about opening up some new land for their boss. Well Lem, he'd had enough after losing three fine head, and decided as how he would spend the next night out on the range, "waitin' fer whatever varmint as shows itself."

Came next morning when Jeb rode out to the herd again, there was neither hide nor hair of his father to be found. Seems like Jeb saw something more out there, though he never said what it was; but the last time he came into town to arrange the sale of their place, Zeke Giles at the Land Office said Jeb was "pale as a bed sheet and looked like the whole Cherokee Nation was hot on his heels." The Torklesons left town shortly after, not bothering to tell a soul where they were headed. And that was just the start of it.

Other ranchers began loosing cattle all around Coyote Junction - then a couple of ranchers disappeared and folks started getting riled up. Resentment of Old Man Teague got near to the boiling point, when right about that time Teague and his boys rode in with a wagon filled with the remains of what was calculated to be a dozen head of prime steer. Teague was fit to be tied and working on a right fine conniption, yelling and hollering at Sheriff Beaufort to "bring the butcherin' sidewinders to justice, and damn quick!"

Well now it was clear to the townsfolk that Old Man Teague wasn't to blame, on account of him being so tight with a dollar that he'd never have done what was done to those cattle just to cover his tracks. And speaking of what had been done to those poor critters...

Doc Hagen, he'd taken a looksee at the remains that Old Man Teague brought into town, and he admitted to being right mystified. "I've seen a lot of wounds from a lot of different animals," he'd told Abby that night over lemonade on the porch, "but this has me stumped plain and proper. Only thing I know for sure, it *was* an animal of some kind, but it would have to be mighty big and mighty ornery to do that kind of damage to a full grown steer.

"Why, by the look of it, one of those poor creatures was bit clean in half, though no one ever found the other half; bit, I say! Even a full-grown Grizzly isn't about to stuff half a cow in its mouth and bite off the rest. I surely believe that whatever it is, it could scare the hide off a Griz."

And that wasn't the whole of it. "I don't know if Old Man Teague or anyone in town noticed, but while I was taking an up close looksee, I found what I can only say were bite marks in a couple of the carcasses. But the teeth that made them would have to be at least an inch thick and maybe ten long! And what's more, these particular wounds looked to be infected; I know I've seen marks like those before, but I can't quite place 'em. I wouldn't be troubling you with all this Miz Abby, but I figured you might have some thoughts on the matter, you being a schoolmarm and all."

Well of course Abby had never heard tell of such a critter, and she said as much to Doc Hagen, but a few notions did occur to her right then. "Doctor, do you suppose this animal might have had something to do with the disappearance of Lem Torkleson?"

That had made the Doc real uncomfortable. "I pray to God it didn't, because if that thing did for Lem, then it's not afraid of men; and there's a lot of families scattered out across the range." And though neither of them said it, they both knew that Coyote Junction was just as cut off as any of those ranches, and if something should happen to the town, help would be far too late in coming.

Abby finished her tale with a frustrated sigh. "We knew we should point all of this out to the Sheriff, or even Old Man Teague, but we knew they'd just think we were crazy. Now things have gone from bad to worse, and Mr. Teague has started laying blame on the Indians..."

"The injuns?" Sam was too startled to mind his manners. "Why, these parts is Novato territory, an' they're some of the most peaceful folk I ever did meet. They been pushed around considerable for it, too, but they never raised a hand to no man, save to defend their wives an' children."

Abby agreed with this. "It really doesn't make sense. Coyote Junction and the Novato Nation have lived side by side since the town was founded, and there hasn't been one recorded incident that was triggered by a Novato. Why they would turn so hostile so suddenly is a mystery I can't fathom, and I refuse to believe those people are capable of such monstrous savagery. But then, where does that leave us?"

Sam reflected on that for a spell. "Seems to leave us with some ornery critter roamin' the range, and a rancher with a gripe against the Novato."

"You don't think Mr. Teague is behind these attacks? That he murdered Mr. Torkleson and butchered his own cattle?"

Sam shrugged. "Not rightly, but this here Teague fella strikes me as the sort who'll take advantage of any opportunity he wanders across. I'd be willin' to bet if he's blamin' the Novato, then them folks has got somethin' he wants. It's just a matter of figurin' out what that thing might be. The smart thing to do would be to pay a visit to the Novato an' get their side of it; mebbe they have a take on the situation."

Abby looked uncertain. "That could be dangerous, Sam. The Novato may have been peaceful the last time you encountered them, but this business has raised bad feelings on both sides. You may not find yourself as welcome as you expect."

"Any other tribe, I'd allow as you might be right, Miz Abby. But y'see, Chief White Hawk and I go back a far piece, an' we became blood brothers when we were both still wet behind the ears. Then too, I helped White Hawk out of a scrape or two here an' there, so I'm an honorary member of the tribe; I don't 'spect they'll be lookin' to lift my scalp or any suchlike if I ride in."

Abby shook her head with a rueful smile. "You never cease to amaze me, Sam. Is there anyone in the entire West that you *haven't* helped out?"

Sam considered that. "Well, I reckon there's one or two mountain men who're just too consarned ornery to be helped. Then a'course there's Old Man Teague; an' whatever all he's up too, I doubt I'll be helpin' him at all."

"Well I'm in a mood to be helping you, Sam, and feeding you as well. What do you say to fried chicken, sweet corn and biscuits?"

Sam broke into a wide grin. "Well, Miz Abby, I say you can help me just about all you want!"

Funny, Sam thought to himself the next morning as he rode into the Novato camp, *folks are the same all over, no matter how much they claim they're different.*

The Novato were one of the most peaceful of the Indian Nations, past masters at dealing with other cultures and adopting new ways of doing things. They were a common sense folk who enjoyed life and all that the wide world had to offer, fighting only when their homes and families were threatened; Sam was proud to call many of them friend, and he had few that were better.

But as he rode into camp, the looks he got from the women and the braves could have moseyed on over from the folks in Coyote Junction. Suspicion and hostility didn't set right on a Novato's face, and it was a hard thing for ol' Sam to see. If he had doubted that something was up in these parts, just looking at the expressions around him would have told him different.

Mothers pulled their children into their tepees, elders glared, and braves stood stiff and tense, like they were fighting to hold back from calling him out right there, which is probably what they wanted to do. Though he didn't think he was in any real danger, Sam was still mightily relieved when he spotted a familiar face.

Spotted Feather had spent a year traveling with Sam back when they were youngsters, before his friend had to return to begin training as the tribe's next shaman, which by this time he was. Though his old friend was the picture of dignity and wisdom, ol' Sam had to rein in a smile as he recollected a young brave running full tilt for a nearby watering hole with a big swarm of riled hornets hot on his heels; Sam remembered that right clearly, seeing as how he was no more than two steps behind Spotted Feather at the time.

Now, years later, even though he was smiling, there was a mighty grim cast to his eyes, and Sam could see as how Spotted Feather had some mighty weighty matters on his mind, and he could pretty much guess what they might be.

"I see you, Long Rider," his old friend greeted, using his Novato name; that was a good sign. "It has been too long since we hunted together."

"I see you, Spotted Feather. I thought we gave up huntin' when the last critter we went after started huntin' us."

"We were young and foolish then. Now we are old and foolish; it should not take us so long to find trouble."

"Seems as how trouble's found you, and a few other folks 'round these parts."

It was clear Sam had entered territory which Spotted Feather wasn't hankering to ride through, but he'd come out here for some answers and he'd just have to see this through.

"It is not a thing we like to speak of, and never in the open where ears can hear. We will go to White Hawk's tent."

Chief White Hawk had grown from handsome warrior to distinguished leader in the time since he and Sam had fished in the nearby stream, doing more catching up than catching fish. White Hawk took to leadership like a longhorn sheep to the mountains, but today it was looking as if the chief was longing for that stream bank and a pole with no bait on it. He did manage to brighten up considerable on sight of Sam.

"Samuel," he welcomed with a gesture to have a seat. "I knew that I would be seeing you soon."

"Have yerself a vision on it, did ya?"

White Hawk grunted out a laugh. "Samuel, when there is trouble, are you ever long in coming?"

Sam considered that. "Seems to be the way my life's runnin' lately," he had to admit. "From what Miz Abby tells me I've come down right in the middle of it again."

White Hawk nodded, frowning. "It is a bad time. People are frightened; people of the tribe, people from the town. Even Teague is frightened, but he is one who knows how to use the fear of others for his own reasons."

"You think Teague is the varmint behind all this?"

White Hawk shook his head, but it was Spotted Feather who answered him. "Teague may use the fear, but he does not know what causes it."

"And do you?"

"Do you know of the Blue Light People?"

Sam thought on that a short spell. "Seems I recollect hearin' tell of some such. Part of a Novato legend, ain't it?"

Spotted Feather nodded. "They are from the story of how the Novato first came to this world. First Mother and First Father lived together many years in a land beneath this one, and they had many children. A time came when there were too many people, and First Mother and First Father decided it was time to look for a new place to live.

"They gathered together the tribe and told them 'We are too many, and if we stay here there will be much sorrow, much hunger and sickness. But there is another place, where there is light and food and water, and the land stretches on forever. We will go there.'

"Many saw this as a good thing and made themselves ready to follow First Mother and First Father into this strange new world, but there were a few who did not want to leave the old place. These few did not listen to First Mother and First Father, but instead hid away in caves and tunnels where the air glowed with blue light, and when the time came for the tribe to move into this world they could not be found, and they were left behind.

"Even though it was their choice to stay, those who remained behind grew to resent those who had gone on, and as the years passed, they came to hate their brothers and sisters who lived in this new land of sun and wind and rain. Their hate made them sick inside, poisoned their spirits. They turned from the True Way and began to worship false spirits that came to them from the bad places of that old world.

"The most powerful of these spirits was Great Snake. It was he that the Blue Light People worshiped, even though they had to sacrifice people to keep Great Snake from becoming angered. There have been times in the past when the Blue Light People have found a way out of the old world and into this one, and they came out in the night to take our people back to give to Great Snake. They are driven back when they are found, and the ways to their home sealed off, because they have become evil, and should not be let into this world.

"But still they find other ways, or are shown new paths by Great Snake and his children. There are even times when Great Snake himself comes out to feed on bear and sheep and men."

"And cattle?" Sam put in.

White Hawk nodded. "And cattle. This is a new thing, because the white men have made their homes on the land near where Great Snake can come out. It will not get better if more people come."

Sam frowned at the small fire pit around which they sat. "Well it don't seem likely that folks'll stop comin' out here, so it looks like everybody 'round these parts has got themselves a big problem. What does this Great Snake look like?"

"He is the father of all snakes," Spotted Feather told him, "so he can look like any serpent there is. Mostly, in these lands, he comes as One Who Rattles, and all his children obey him. He is playing with us now, my friend, but soon he will grow tired of playing. When that time comes, I fear for both our peoples."

Sam chewed on that a minute. "How is it this critter ain't caused trouble for you in all these years?"

"Our people live with the land; your people live on it," Spotted Feather told him. "We know the places where Great Snake roams, and we try to stay away from him. Your people go wherever they want, fighting the land, fighting the water, fighting Nature. They think that no person or creature is more powerful than they are, and they are too stubborn to admit this is not so."

"Or too desperate," Sam amended. "Some of them farmers an' ranchers out there just got no place left to go. Like it or not, if they want a better life for themselves, their last stand is right here. Seems like we should give 'em half a chance at it."

"It will not be easy," White Hawk advised. "Great Snake is angry, and the Blue Light People cannot control him, even if they wanted to."

"Well what's got him so riled up now, after all this time?"

"Teague. He has learned that there is much water here, far beneath the ground. His men found many caves in the canyons to the east. They used dynamite to break into places Nature never intended them to enter, and this angered Great Snake. Now he comes to punish anyone who lives nearby."

White Hawk made a disgusted sound deep in his throat. "Teague also knows that the water lies under Novato land, and that he cannot use it

12

without breaking the treaty with our tribe."

Sam nodded understanding. "So he starts blamin' the Novato for all the killin's, hopin' the government will come in and do his dirty work for him, maybe even change the borders of the reservation so the water is under free range, which he can buy up real cheap. He's a clever sidewinder, I'll give him that; him and the Great Snake got a lot in common, though I don't reckon either of 'em fits into the other's plans. An' seein' what kind of hombre he is, I 'spect he won't be willin' to lend us a hand, or even believe what we're sayin'. So I guess we'll have to handle this thing our own selves."

For a minute there, Sam found himself staring at a pair of mighty reluctant faces. White Hawk and Spotted Feather studied each other across the fire pit, and after a spell they seemed to come 'round to a decision. White Hawk nodded. "Great Snake is powerful, and the Blue Light People guard their secrets well. And you must know that no one from the town will help us."

"I know one that would, but I ain't about to be askin' her to do it."

"Wisdom Woman." Spotted Feather spoke with a smile. "She is a good woman, Sam, a woman who should not be lost to another."

Well now that just made ol' Sam plum nervous, so right quick he brought the talk back to its original subject. "Now how do we go about settling with this here critter an' them Blue Light folks?"

"That is simple," White Hawk replied. "We go to the place where they dwell and seal off the way into our world."

Sam grimaced sourly. "Yeah, pure-D simple." He brightened up right quick, though. "Well, I think there's somethin' Coyote Junction can do for us after all," he told his friends through a grin that was pure mischief and then some.

"Sure ya want two crates, friend?" the clerk at the dry goods store asked Sam some time later that day. "Aren't that many tree stumps around these parts, y'know."

"I reckon, but it's a mighty stubborn stump. Two crates'll do me fine, thanks." Sam glanced around the counter, scooping up what he needed. "An' these here matches. What do I owe ya?"

"Five dollars, and I'll throw the matches in for free. Need help carryin' the crates?"

Sam paused in his examination of the contents of one of the crates.

"Much obliged," he replied as he slid a couple items into the pocket of his duster.

A reception committee was waiting on Sam as he emerged from the mercantile; the roughest, meanest looking herd of range rats as you'd ever want to lay eyes on, every one of them hard and mean and looking like they were enjoying every minute of it. It didn't take much pondering to come up on the notion that these were Old Man Teague's boys come to pay a call.

The meanest of the pack was a tall, dark haired fella in a brown hat and duster, with a scar down his right cheek that made him look downright ominous. Just by his cocky swagger, Sam figured he was the leader of this bunch.

"You're that Sam Hill fella, ain't ya?"

"I reckon that'd be me," Sam replied as he scouted out the rest of the gang. They were typical hired guns, though none of them looked smart enough to jump in the river if their pants were on fire, so it was a sure bet they all followed Scarface's trail.

"Yeah, well don't go stickin' your nose where it don't belong 'round here, elsewise it might get cut off."

Ol' Sam, he pulls out a cheroot and real casual like lights up. "Well I thank you for your frettin' about my nose, friend, but I reckon I can look out for it pretty well myself, bein' so close to it an' all."

Scarface grinned, but you had to know he wasn't that amused. He was used to folks doing what he told them to, and it didn't set at all well with him when they up and didn't. "Makes no nevermind to me, saddle tramp; hell, I'd just as soon get it over with right here an' now." Scarface's right hand swept his duster clear of his holster, and you could see from across town he was itching for an excuse to go for his gun.

Sam, he moved real slow, so Scarface wouldn't get any ideas, keeping his hand away from his gun. "Well, I tell ya, we could do that, an' here's how it would go: You'd die first, with 'bout four, five of the rest of your boys. Then if I'd a mind to, I'd pick off a few more before they stopped runnin' an' went fer their guns. Right about then the law would show up an' take care of the rest."

Scarface snorted, spitting on the dusty street between them. "Pretty sure of yourself, ain't ya? An' how ya figure on drawin' down on the lot of us before we turn you to vulture food?"

"Not with a gun, pard," Sam explained as he brought up the stick of dynamite and touched the end of his cheroot to the fuse. "I 'spect I'll be usin' this."

Well now the range rats wanted no truck with dynamite, and they backed off right quick, disappearing down the alleys they'd slunk out of, leaving only Scarface and Sam.

The hired gun sneered. "You ain't got the belly for it."

Sam took a step forward. "Wellsir, you may be right on that." Another step. "But any way it goes, I'm surefire gonna have to get rid of this here stick, an' given the choice, I'd as soon get rid of it in your direction." With that he flicked the dynamite straight at Scarface.

Now the gunslinger might've been brave enough with a pack of men behind him, but he was no match for that stick of blasting powder; he broke, running full tilt down the street and out of sight around the corner, nearly running over the sheriff, who was coming to see what the ruckus was all about. For himself, Sam stepped into the street and retrieved the dynamite, wet his thumb and index finger, and doused the fuse with a quick pinch, leaving about an inch left over.

"Hate to waste this," he mumbled as he tucked the stick into the pocket of his duster. "Well, mebbe I'll find a use for it later on."

With the help of a shaken shopkeeper, Sam loaded up his two crates on the buckboard Miz Abby had loaned him and, calm as you please, he rode on out of town, back to the Novato reservation. So far, he thought, his plan was proceeding right well.

The canyon was a narrow slash cut deep into the sandstone of Shiloh Plateau, which left the canyon in dusky shadow for the better part of the day. The settlers had never named it, since the entire area was too inhospitable for them to bother naming, but the Novato called it Blue Light Canyon, for reasons that had already been explained to Sam. Because of the lack of sunlight, the canyon was cold, even when they first entered it, and it didn't get any warmer the further back they went; Sam kept telling himself that was the reason he was chilled to the bone and prone to the shivers now and then.

It was quiet in there, with only the echoes of their horses' hooves bouncing back and forth across the canyon, ricochet bullets of sound made all the louder by the lack of competition. Not even a turkey buzzard prowled the thin strip of sky peering in over the high lip of Blue Light Canyon, and even though he was surrounded by a band of twenty Novato braves, he had never felt so alone.

"You saw the riders." Spotted Feather's remark was more statement of fact than question.

"Yeah," Sam sighed. "Old Man Teague's men, sure as shootin'. That Scarface fella ain't up to facin' a man in public, but out here in the wide ol' lonely's a different story. He'll prob'ly follow us in; I showed him up pretty good back in town, an' I figure he'll be wantin' to settle the score."

"He is a fool," White Hawk grumbled. "This is not a place for fools."

"I 'spect you're right," Sam agreed as he glanced over his shoulder. "Mebbe he an' his boys'll learn a thing or two before the day's done. But I doubt it."

About a mile into the canyon, the trail was split by a sandstone pillar nearly as tall as the walls themselves, both paths leading into the deeper gloom of the canyon beyond. White Hawk motioned a number of his braves to take up positions in the rocky scree to either side of the pillar; quick as a blink they were so well hid you'd never know they were there.

"They will signal us when Teague's men pass by, then follow behind them."

Sam nodded. "Never hurts to have a few friends at the enemy's back."

The air grew colder as they moved deeper into the canyon, and after awhile it came to be pushed along by a stiff breeze wandering out from the end of the box canyon. It wasn't the clean wind of open spaces, either, but a damp, chilly breath of closed-in spaces that never saw the light of day; Sam didn't much care for it, and neither did his friends, by the look of them.

"Serpent's breath is cold," Spotted Feather grumbled as he brought his suddenly skittish mount under control, "and it is not healthy. Better to be gone quickly from this place."

White Hawk agreed with a nod, then pointed. "There is the way into the lands of the Blue Light People. You should know, Samuel, that we are the first of our nation to ever return to that place. To do this is not good for the spirit; we would understand if you did not want to go with us."

Sam shook his head. "This here critter's gotta be stopped, an' you all know I'm too lame-brained to run from a fight."

They left another small band of braves to guard the entrance to the caves, so in all the group that lit torches and squeezed through the narrow slit in the sandstone was about seven strong.

The interior of the cave near its mouth was carved out by Mother

Nature herself, a narrow, twisty passage with a thick sandy floor, open to the sun in a couple of places where the soft rock had been eaten away by water and wind. Farther in, though, where the tunnel began to slope downwards, the rock got harder, and darker, and not particularly friendly. The lights of their torches closed in around them in spite of the nearness of the walls, and there wasn't a man among them who would have dared set foot outside the shaky comfort of its glow.

The quiet outside got even thicker in the belly of the plateau, and the men spoke in hand gestures, the thought of what their voices might attract making them a might nervous. The sandy floor which muffled their footsteps deserted them, though it was only Sam's boots which made any amount of noise, which stopped when he took them off and put on a pair of moccasins Spotted Feather handed to him. Nodding his gratitude, he stuffed the trail-worn boots into the saddlebags slung over his shoulder and motioned for the others to move out.

The tunnel ran deep, deeper than Sam had expected. They traveled so far that he came near to believing they had really entered another world, the world of Novato legend. Just as he had that thought, Sam noticed that the dark beyond their torches wasn't as total as before, and was colored with a faint blue that made him real uncomfortable.

"We are very near," Spotted Feather whispered to him, and it was right clear he had noticed the light too. "This is as far as we should go, or Great Snake will know we are here."

Having no cause to argue the point, Sam looked around for a good place to plant his charges, and found just what he was looking for; two shallow niches the size of a man, roughly opposite each other across the tunnel. With the experience he'd picked up that time he'd worked the Lost Phantom Mine, Sam had no trouble setting the charges and laying the fuses to give them plenty of time to get back to the great outdoors before they went off.

The hard grip of Spotted Feather's hand on his shoulder stopped him just as he was about to light the fuses; he looked up, asking his question with a simple frown. His friend nodded on up the tunnel and put his hand to his ear. Sam listened, and after a spell he heard the sound.

It was like wind through the pines, or river water over sandstone; a quiet, hissing sort of sound that told him something was moving over the rocks of the tunnel, something mighty big that didn't walk like a man, didn't even walk at all but crawled on its belly like a...

"Time to hit the trail, boys," Sam whispered as he struck a match and set it to the end of the fuse, jumping back as the fiery cords lit up.

As he stood, Sam caught a shadow of movement out of the corner of his eye, only this was closer to something he'd had plenty of experience with - the sneaky little movements of a bushwhacker.

"We got company," he whispered to White Hawk. "Could be them blue light fellas are comin' out for a family reunion."

"It would not be a happy meeting," Spotted Feather sighed as he motioned for the others to high-tail it out of there. As they moved back down the tunnel they could hear a whole passel of sharp hisses and spits that sounded like speech, but this was no language they'd ever heard tell of. Even though the words couldn't be understood, their tone sure could, and it wasn't a happy one. Sam and his friends doubled their speed.

So hell-bent were they on getting clear of the tunnel that they nearly stampeded over the braves who'd been left to guard the entrance. "Teague's men," one of them growled as everyone got themselves organized. "They are coming down the tunnel, too many for us to hold."

"Can't get no co-operation from nobody today," Sam grumbled, scratching at the stubble on his chin as he gave the situation some hard thinking. "Right. There was a side tunnel a ways back; best we make tracks down there, let Teague's boys pass by, then run like hell, 'cause that there fuse ain't gettin' any longer."

Well they did just that, going just far enough down the side tunnel so that Teague's men wouldn't notice them. It was a mighty fine plan, but sometimes life just doesn't play along. They were just about to move forward into the main passage when the dynamite let loose, so close that the force of it knocked them right off their feet and a fair piece back down the side tunnel. Good thing, too, because those charges were a mite too powerful; instead of just blocking the main tunnel, they brought down a good quarter mile of the main channel, blocking off their escape route with a few tons of sandstone.

'Course, there was nothing for it but to follow the tunnel they were in and that's what they did; but this route led them deeper into the earth, where the air turned cold and damp, and nearly alive with a sickly blue light that made a man wonder just how long he could hold his breath. After a mighty long spell of walking a new sound came to them, and as it grew louder Sam was able to put a brand on it.

"Why, if that ain't a waterfalls, them I'm a mangy polecat."

Wellsir, Sam was no polecat, so when they all stepped out into one of the biggest darned caves Sam had ever laid eyes on, there was this rip-roaring gush of underground water over a hundred feet high, just waiting to say "howdy." But there were other things about this cave that pulled their attention from the falls, things that made them suspect that their fat had landed squarely in the fire.

That there waterfall was pouring from the mouth of a huge rattler carved right out of the cave wall, water boiling around black fangs taller than a man and near sharp as the real thing. And through the mist of the falls they could see that the wall in that area had been worked a lot of years, until the entire body of the snake had been chiseled out, right down to the wicked-looking rattles that stuck out into the lake at the base of the falls.

Right near those rattles a flight of stairs had been carved out, leading up to some kind of platform or altar that even from this distance looked to be stained with what Sam took to be blood, though it was hard to tell in the blue light that overflowed the lake and seeped from veins of some mineral he'd never set eyes on before - and wished he hadn't now. Beyond the altar they could just make out a huge, gaping hole in the floor of the cave, situated such that anything on the altar might be tossed into the hole real easy-like. Or maybe something came out of the hole to snap up whatever was waiting on the altar - but that didn't bear too much thinking on.

There was a smell in there, too; a heavy, musky odor that pretty near clogged the nose and made a fella mighty reluctant to breathe. Sam had smelt something like it before, when he'd come across this fissure in the sandstone that was home for three, four dozen rattlesnakes. This smell was like that but a far piece stronger, and it had this sense of age to it that spoke of something that went back a long ways into the history of the world, something that was waiting here, just for them.

"We are at the place of the Blue Light People," Spotted Feather whispered in Sam's ear. "This is where they offer sacrifices to Great Snake, and fan their hatred of those who dwell above."

"There are other tunnels," White Hawk broke in. "There, across the cave, and one there near the great hole. One of them may lead out of this place."

They crossed the cave without running into any trouble, but it was colder here than in the tunnels, and soon the men were shivering, their breath spewing out like smoke from a cheap cigar. And as they got closer to that hole in the ground, the cold, damp air was choked with a putrid stench so thick you could almost see it oozing out of the pit, an odor of rotting meat and...snake.

The first three tunnels they tried either dead-ended, or commenced to slope down at too sharp an angle for comfortable travel, and that brought them around to the opening near the altar, which meant they would have to pass by the pit.

Sam, being who he was, was the only one of the party who actually took a look-see down into the pit, discovering it to be not much of a drop into a circular tunnel about ten feet across, the walls, from what he could see of them, worn smooth by the passing of water - or something else. Pulling his eyes from the gloom below, he caught a faint movement in the rocks nearby and realized they weren't alone in the cave. He mosied over to White Hawk and filled him in.

"I spotted one of yer relatives skulkin' around the rocks by the lake. Pale, ornery-lookin' scutter, an' I 'spect he knows how to use the bow he's carryin', an' that he ain't the only one out there."

White Hawk nodded. "Then it is this tunnel or nothing. At least if we are inside they can only come at us from one direction."

The first of the party had reached the mouth of the tunnel when the attack came. Blood-curdling screams echoed off the cave walls, weird, almost inhuman cries of rage and hatred like nothing Sam had ever heard. Arrows began to fly, nasty-looking, barbed things chiseled out of some slimy black rock, and spears too, though most of them fell short. The arrows, though, had their range, and two Novato warriors went down screaming before the rest made it into the tunnel.

Again, Sam was the last one in, so it was him saw what came out of the pit. At first he thought he was drunk and seeing things, just imagining that that big rock carving had come to life to chase after him. The head was the same, except it was a pale, pasty gray-green, and the eyes glared red and when it opened its mouth the fangs dripped thick venom instead of just water.

Bigger than a locomotive it was; only reason it could squeeze up out of that hole by the altar was it had no skeleton to speak of. Its dry, leathery scales scraped against the rock with a rasp so sharp it cut right through the roar of the waterfalls.

More and more of it poured out of that hole and coiled up in the cavern, filling it up. The snake-stench was a solid wall now, and it knocked ol' Sam back a couple steps, and that movement drew some unwanted attention his way.

The head, big as a stagecoach, swayed in his direction, huge, ruby eyes pinning him with a gaze loaded with hate and hunger and - Sam shivered - an intelligence that was more than animal and surefire not human. Sam knew in his heart that the thing recognized him, and knew him for an enemy. Both stood frozen, like two gunfighters at high noon waiting to see who'd make the first play.

It hissed at him then, a sound he would have expected from a steam engine but not from anything living, hissed and lunged straight at him.

Sam threw himself back deeper into the tunnel, and was knocked off his feet by the force of the thing hitting the rock just outside. Spotted Feather was helping him to his feet when the Novato's grip on his arm tightened painfully; Sam was purely afraid to follow the direction of his friend's gaze.

The head filled the mouth of the tunnel, leaving enough room to spare for the critter to open up its own mouth far enough to swallow a man whole, and by the look of it, it was intending to do just that, because as Spotted Feather pulled Sam to his feet the Great Snake started coming down the tunnel after them.

They ran, just as fast as they could, and not caring much what lay ahead on account of they knew what was behind - and getting closer all the time. The others had gone ahead, so they figured it was safe, but that left only the two of them to deal with the beast.

"We cannot let him reach the surface," Spotted Feather panted as they ran. "He is angry, and he will strike out at everyone."

"Then he'll have to stay put," Sam responded as he dug furiously into the pockets of his duster. At last he clamped on to what he was looking for and brought it out; the one stick of dynamite he hadn't used. He held it up for his friend to see. "Damn short fuse on 'er," he commented, puffing rapidly on his cigar till the tip glowed cherry red.

"Then do not drop it," Spotted Feather advised as he put on a new burst of speed, getting out of his friend's way and letting him do what he needed to. He'd learned over the years not go get in the way of one of Sam's schemes, and that the safest place to be when they were played out was somewhere else.

What Sam did next was the hardest thing he'd ever done in his life, and up till then, he wouldn't have thought he was up to it. Stopping dead in his tracks, he spun around and faced Great Snake, stared down that big old gullet and stood his ground.

A roaring hiss blew over him, along with the stench of a hundred massacred souls, an icy cold blast of wind from the belly of a critter that had no right to be living in a natural world, a critter that was powerful mad, and powerful hungry.

So Sam lit up and fed it the dynamite.

He had about three steps before it blew, picking him up and shoving him down the tunnel faster than Brimstone could gallop. If there had been a curve in the tunnel just then, why he would've been slammed against rock so hard he would've burst like a melon at harvest time. But ol' Sam Hill, he had the luck, and it was with him that day in spades.

When he picked himself up, he saw that the tunnel behind him was completely collapsed, and more important, most of the rock back there was covered with big chunks of meat and all kinds of fluids that could've came from only one thing. Great Snake wouldn't be troubling the folks of Coyote Junction any more.

Well as luck would have it, the tunnel Sam and his friends had chosen did lead up and out of that hellhole, though fewer came out as went in, and that was a source of sadness as the group stepped out into the clean light of day. They found themselves one canyon over from where they'd gone in, and an hour later they'd found their horses and said their good byes.

"It seems so difficult to believe," Miz Abby opined a few hours later when Sam had told her the tail. "That horrible place, right under our feet. And that creature..." She broke off, shuddering at the thought.

Sam agreed. "But it's gone now, an' them Blue Light fellas are cut off from these parts forever, with only what's left a' Scarface an' his bunch fer company."

"I hope you're right, Sam, I truly do. I shudder to think of what might happen if there is a next time, and you're not around to save the day."

Ol' Sam, he chuckled at that. "Ain't a big thing, Mis Abby. All's a fella needs at a time like that is an ornery streak a mile wide, a long temper -- and a mighty short fuse!"

There are secrets most folk ain't supposed to know, and places they jus' ain't supposed to go. Fer good or bad, whatever protects those places don't take kindly to them who poke their noses in where they don't belong, or who think they can do exactly that and walk away with a whole hide. That could be fer the best, I'm thinking, but it's sure and certain hard on them as learns the lesson the hard way.

Now if someone tells me a place is bad and I shouldn't oughta go there, I tend to find another trail. But there's some who jus' can't pay heed to good advice when they hear it.

Now there was this fella one time....

THE GUARDIAN
BY
MOLLIE L. BURLESON

The mountains rose purple in the waning light as Jack urged his horse on. He'd been heading west all day from that little town where he'd spent the night. What was it, Sand Rock? Whatever its name, it was like all the others he'd encountered since he'd left Council Grove four weeks ago. A series of one-horse towns, each with a church, dry goods store, a string of saloons - the usual. At least, Council Grove was a city, of sorts.

Sometimes in these past few days, he'd wondered if he'd made a mistake, leaving his teaching job at the school, giving up his tiny rooms above the store, selling most of his personal belongings, buying Charlie, the saddle, and all the other things he knew he'd need on his journey west.

Journey? To where and for what purpose? But, the wanderlust had always been within him, ever since he was a child, the urge to travel, to see whatever there was to see. And, just a year ago, he knew that he'd make that trip out west to "find his fortune," as people said.

It's not that he dreamed he'd find gold or silver; he certainly wasn't cut out to be a crusty old prospector. But instead he'd gain a fortune in experience and knowledge that would outshine any precious metal he could ever find.

The sun had set, and the few clouds on the horizon had turned to flame. Jack thought he'd better make camp. Settling down for the night had become routine and he'd done it as easily as he used to turn down his sheets

24

and crawl into bed back home. He made his campfire from mesquite, its wonderful odor filling the night air.

What stars out here in the desert! Stars he never knew existed. And the air! So pure and so fresh, and now that he was so close to the mountains, the scent of juniper and cedar began to waft down upon him with a delicious aroma that made one glad to be alive.

How he loved it here. Why, he'd already garnered a fortune in experience and a thousand different sensations.

The warmth of the sun tickled his face, and he awoke. He stretched lazily, yawned, and got up to greet the new day. After breakfast, which consisted of coffee, beans, and the rest of the salt pork, he'd cleaned up and repacked the saddlebags, being careful to kick the remaining coals apart, covering them with sand.

"Howya doing, old boy!" Jack said, as he cinched the saddle tighter and patted Charlie's nose.

The horse snorted and tossed his head.

"Eager to be off, eh? Well, then, let's go!"

Jack mounted, and they rode off westward toward the mountains.

The mountains. He'd have to make a decision whether or not to cross them. Normally, there would be no decision at all to make, he'd just cross them, but after the other day in Sand Rock, well, he'd better think it over. Course, it would be silly to pay attention to what those old coots sitting on the porch of the hotel had told him. Crazy old buzzards, what in hell did they know? Probably told him the tale to get a rise out of him. Well, he'd been careful about his reactions, but still he wondered.

Those rounded mountains ahead were spotted with green, like leopard spots, he thought whimsically. They wouldn't be too hard to cross, and crossing them would save a whole two days of travel. Also, he'd be needing to replace his dwindling water supply soon, and rumor had it that there was a sparkling stream hidden in the canyon, filled with fish. How pleasant that would be, camping next to the singing water, surrounded by pungent pines, frying some delicious rainbow trout over his campfire. Made his mouth water, just thinking about it. Sounded like Heaven. All except for the persistent images in his mind of what the men on the porch said he might find in the canyon. Or what might find *him*.

Now the pines were closer, the ground rockier, and Charlie picked his way more carefully, maneuvering between larger and still larger stones. Mesquite had given way to masses of cactus, most of them blooming in shades of pink, red, and yellow. It was now or never to make the decision. Would he trek through the beautiful mountains and the canyon with its supposed dangers, or veer off toward the south, over a more sandy terrain, and face a couple of extra days' ride with his short water supply? He made his choice.

Charlie stumbled as the stones he was climbing over slipped under his hooves.

"Whoa, boy, easy," Jack cried.

The going was harder, but not too difficult, and already they were nearing the top of the rise. He could see the canyon below and had decided to make camp at the bottom. Even in full sunlight, it appeared dark. A solitary hawk flew low, his piercing cry echoing against the canyon walls. A chill ran down Jack's back, and he shuddered.

Making a fire from some fallen greasewood, he surveyed his domain. A pretty little stream bounced and sang its way toward the mouth of the canyon. Jack baited his line and tossed it into the swirling waters. Charlie whinnied and pulled at his tether, stamping his hooves in the damp sand

"What's the matter, boy? That old story scare you, too?"

He patted the horse, who finally bent his neck downwards and chomped on some fresh grass. Jack went back to his fishing, and after a while landed a large rainbow trout.

When every last morsel of delicate tasting fish had been eaten, Jack cleaned up, rolled a cigarette, lit it, and leaned back contentedly against the still warm canyon wall. *What a great life*, he thought, *and what a beautiful place this is.*

The last of the daylight disappeared as the sun slipped behind the rise, turning the canyon into a different place. Things began to lose their outlines, and the canyon became like a fathomless pit. It was now a place where the old gents' story came back in force, where pines soughed in the wind, which moaned low, eerily, like the cries of long-dead souls.

Jack shivered again, and wrapped his robe closer about him. Charlie nickered once and was still. One by one, the great stars appeared, cold and bright. From somewhere, the call of a coyote filled the air, starting low and rising higher, a keening sort of sound.

"Bull," denounced Jack, aloud. Charlie raised his head.

"Not you, old friend. That story the old men told is finally getting to me. I must be tired. Time for bed." He gathered fallen and fragrant pine needles to place beneath his bedding and settled down to sleep.

He awoke with a start. The moon was high in the sky, the stars were bright, and the wind had died down to a whisper. He looked around, threw some more wood on the fire, sending sparks upward, and settled back into his blankets.

But sleep wouldn't come. What *did* come were the images the old men's story had brought forth.

"The canyon is an ancient Indian burial ground, a holy place," the grizzled man on the steps had said. "And you can't go there. They wouldn't like it. *He* wouldn't."

"He who?" queried Jack.

"The Guardian," said the skinny, white-bearded old fellow.

"The Guardian?" What do you mean?

"Just, the *Guardian*," said the first. "He, *It* guards the graves."

Balderdash, thought Jack, but kept his peace.

"And what does this Guardian do to those who trespass?"

"No one really knows," said the skinny one. "No one's ever come back from the canyon. At least, no one we ever knew of. But from the stories we heard from the Indians 'round here, no one can go there and keep his head."

"Keep his head? You mean keep his wits about him?"

"I meant what I meant," said the crusty one on the steps.

Jack had left them then, but as he walked away, a cracked voice called after him.

"Remember, we warned you."

"The Guardian, indeed!" Jack muttered to himself now. But still....

A cloud passed over the moon, casting everything into darkness, a darkness barely relieved by the glow from the myriad stars. A bat circled, its wings flapping, its voice screeching.

Those old reprobates, like to scare a man. *Well, I'm not buying it*, thought Jack, as he turned over, his back to the fire.

A night owl hooted mournfully in the cactus, and Charlie pawed the ground. The wind picked up, swirling sand about them. But it seemed more than just the wind. The wind was coming from the south, and the sand came from everywhere.

Charlie's hooves were more insistent now as they pounded into the sand. His neighing became stronger.

Jack got up, moved Charlie to a more distant tree, secured the reins, and hobbled his front legs, just in case.

"Hey, boy, don't let the wind scare you."

But, *was* it only the wind that made Charlie's eyes wild and his nostrils flare?

Settling back into his blankets, Jack shivered again. Was he really letting the story of the Guardian get to him? Ridiculous. It was just getting colder.

He tried to sleep, and finally managed to nod off. His sleep was filled with dreams. Horrible dreams. Frightening ones.

A terrific blast of wind tore at Jack's blankets, ripping them off and tossing them aside. From the near distance, he could hear Charlie rearing and neighing, as if in panic. Grey clouds scudded across the moon and the fire guttered out.

And then he saw it. A massive figure seemed to separate itself from the canyon's walls. It was huge, and bipedal, but there its semblance to a man ended. It seemed to be clad in a shroud of sorts, but the most frightening thing about it were the two great spots of red where its eyes should have been. Like two glowing embers. It glided forward, and when it was within a few feet of Jack, it stopped.

The wind had dropped to a dead calm, and a dreadful silence ensued. There was nothing but the silence, the darkness, and those two globs of red.

And then it raised what should have been its head and howled. Loud. Long. The ululations reverberated in the darkness, rising and falling like a thousand souls in agony.

Jack screamed then and Charlie broke loose, running away as fast as he could, hobbled as he was. Ran away from the canyon, the sound, those two red eyes.

And then the howling ceased, and the thing took a step forward. And then another. Jack cringed in fear.

The eyes bore into Jack's, their redness now even more pronounced. A hand, or what *might* have been a hand, loosed itself from the stygian folds which covered it, and with unutterable slowness, stretched implacably toward him.

And touched him. Touched Jack's neck. Touched his throat.

Jack remembered no more.

The sun was high in the sky when he awoke. A hawk spun in the sky, searching for its meal, its shrieking call piercing the morning air. A red fox approached the stream, lapping the water while peering cautiously around. A cactus wren chirped high in a piñon.

Jack stood up, unsteadily at first, trying to get his bearings. There was the remains of his fire, there the blankets and saddle. Charlie! Where was Charlie?

Jack searched and called. To be without a horse here in these mountains was almost certain death.

As he made his way along the stream, he heard a neigh, and saw Charlie munching on some wheatgrass, his reins dangling from his bridle.

"Charlie! Charlie, old pal! Where've you been? Are you all right?"

Charlie nickered and nuzzled Jack's shoulder.

Jack scratched the horse's mane. "Boy, am I glad to see you!"

Grasping the reins, he walked Charlie back to the camp. Tying him up, Jack started gathering up his gear.

What a night *that* was! And that dream. More like a nightmare. *Should've never listened to those old fogies. How they'd laugh if they could've seen me last night!*

It wasn't until later, much later, that Jack knew. He had made it over the mountains to the town of Cottonwood Creek, and after stabling Charlie and getting a meal, he went up to his room, throwing his gear upon the chair.

Whew, am I done in, Jack thought, and eased himself onto the bed, dropping off to sleep almost immediately.

It was after six p.m. when he awoke, refreshed and hungry. Better clean up and get some food.

Lathering up his face, he began to shave. It was then that he noticed, then that he *knew*.

Those old men were *right* after all. It wasn't dreams he had, not nightmares, but *reality*.

Around his neck he saw those red blotches, those angry welts that started, even as he watched, to encircle his throat.

And the last thing he saw, before he could see no more, was his head as it toppled from his neck into the basin below.

WEIRD TRAILS

Sometimes, bad things happen to good people, and good things happen to bad people. Ain't sayin' it's right, it's just the way it is. If you lived in this ol' west for more than a day, you gotta know that's the surefire truth.

But sometimes, sometimes, bad things happen to bad people, and that there's what we call justice.

Now justice don't necessarily come from a judge, or sheriff or the like. Sometimes, it comes from a place that a man can't ride to in this life. Sometimes the bad he's done can call up something that's powerful as a thunderstorm over the mountains, and not half as forgiving.

Thinking about doing dirt to someone, friend? Well if you are, maybe this here story'll make you think twice on it.

The Barbary Coast has always pulled in bad folk. Some good, too, but mostly grifters, drifters, and sidewinders who'll as soon stab you in the back as look at you. There's lots of victims to be found there, and if you happen to be from China, chances are you're one of them victims.

The life is hard for them folk; harder still along the Coast, especially with men all too willing to make it harder. There's one fella I got in mind was just exactly one of them varmints. No matter how he tried, though, he couldn't outrun what justice had in store for him....

THE LAST STAND OF BLACK DANNY O'BARRY

BY
JAMES CHAMBERS

How Black Danny O'Barry came to be called by that name depends on whom you ask. Some say people called him black after his personality, and there's no doubt that Dan was one of the deadliest, nastiest and most ill-tempered prospectors ever to make it out of the Sierra Nevada with his hide intact and his fortune in hand.

Others say Dan earned the name by virtue of his appearance: a wild bramble of coal-black hair, a tangled weave of beard flowing around his chalk white face, an unvarying wardrobe of black clothing - and his almost religious avoidance of daylight. A few malcontents put it down to Dan's cynical philosophy and lurid sense of gallows humor, but that theory never held much truck with most folks.

I knew Black Danny personally. We struck up a rough friendship based on his steady patronage of a Kearney Street dive called Chesmire's where I tended bar, and it is my intention to preserve here a record of that unique rogue named O'Barry.

That Dan hailed from Ireland was obvious by his name and the deceptively charming lilt that was the vestige of the thick brogue he'd left behind him on his trail across the continent. His doings before he came to America remain shrouded in mystery, though there was talk in the past that he was a political man and a most wanted fugitive from the Crown, having refused to give up his home on the orders of an English landlord. Word had it that single-handed he stood off the Redcoats who came to persuade him toward compliance for better than a week, with more than a few of them finding that duty to be their last. Reportedly Dan spent three days in the Atlantic clinging to the underside of an American steamer, bound by a single rope and breathing through a thin reed in order to make good his escape. In the days when a fair number of folks still held first-hand memories of the most recent war with the British, that was a crime people could understand. In some circles it was an accomplishment much to be admired, and true or not, one can be sure Dan played the hand for all he could.

But once word of James Marshall's discovery of California gold leaked out to the world, there was no stopping Dan from heading west with the rest of the human throng to sample the wild climate of that far coast and seek his fortune.

One thing everyone knew for certain about Black Danny O'Barry was where to find him after the sun went down, for on any given night he was sure to be haunting Pacific Street, tasting whiskey at his favorite saloons, pinching the bottoms of dance hall girls and patronizing the local brothels. On a rare happy night Dan could be heard barking out a song the melody of which only he himself might rightly call musical. He became such a force for ruckus and debauchery that a night without him on the waterfront felt like a truce. It was commonly agreed that, should a stranger encounter Dan's pale visage while walking San Francisco's hard-packed streets, the wisest course of action was to step up one's pace, avoid his eyes and beat a hasty path to another part of town.

This especially when Dan was in his cups, which frankly was more often than not.

When drunk, he was at his most unpredictable and dangerous, and there's many an imprudent beggar who put the touch on old Dan and still bears the scar he earned for his trouble. There's not a few shopkeepers, too, who earned a tidy limp as reward for nodding politely in the wrong direction on their way home of an evening.

Even sober Dan was reputed to be more than a match for any ten men, and this reputation he guarded jealously against all those who cared to give him trial. He was blessed with an unearthly luck, a skin thicker than saddle leather and an ego that might just about have been contained by Mr. Jefferson's purchase from the French. It was the kind of attitude all too common among the roughneck gold hunters who fought not only the mountain wilds but each other for even the tiniest glittering morsel, but the difference was that in Dan's case it was a whole lot closer to the truth than usual, especially as supported by the story of how Dan came to be a rich man.

As it goes, riding down through the Sierra Nevada foothills, saddlebags full of gold, Dan led two men on his last prospecting jaunt when a band of rebel outlaw Joaquin Murietta's vicious followers rode them to ground. Murietta's men cornered them in a dead end branch off a narrow box canyon, and set to doing what outlaws and prospectors most often did to each other in those days. The battle began under the morning sun, and by the time it surrendered to the hot, afternoon quiet, only Black Danny was still standing on his two feet, having acquitted himself upon no less than twelve of the robbers. Of the other prospectors only one was still breathing when the dust settled, and so the story goes, Dan quickly put him out of his misery with the terminal cartridge in his Colt. Piling the sum of the previously divided gold onto two horses, Dan rode down alone and very free of financial worries.

Who knows what really happened? Mean and cold-hearted as he was, Dan might just have murdered those men for their shares of the gold, and it would not have been the first time it happened, and probably not even the first time the murderer got away with it. Dan did what he could to help the constable find that gully in the mountains, but somehow he never could manage his way back there, so that the bodies of Dan's party and Murietta's rebels, as well, were never recovered. This was in the days before the Mormon leader Samuel Brannan organized San Francisco's first Vigilance Committee, which made criminal acts a fair amount riskier, and the matter was dropped in short order, leaving Dan alive and wealthy and free to roam.

Now, the sensible person often wonders just why Dan, widely held to be as rich as a man can be, kept his digs just off Pacific Street in the heart of the most brutal district in town. That very thought once occurred to Dan himself, and around that time he set himself up in suites at the Hotel Le Marc (which had been built a mere six months earlier), began attending performances at Peterson's Opera (which took place in a tent pending Peterson raising the funds to build a proper opera house) and dining out on fine foods and wines such as they were. It wasn't but three months before Dan reached a pivotal conclusion - the bed in the hotel was too goddamn soft, the theater put him to sleep, and caviar, without fail, gave him a touch of looseness. What really clinched it, though, was the realization that, while usually a good deal easier on the eyes and a fair bit sweeter smelling, the whores of rich men left Dan feeling just about the same as the *chilenos* he used to patronize at a third of the cost up on Telegraph Hill.

It was back to the Barbary Coast for Dan and post haste, at that.

Back in familiar surroundings, it was a rare occurrence when Dan knew a moment's peace. Three things conspired against him: the need of drunken sailors to test his reputation as a scrapper, his own inflammatory disposition, and the talk that Dan's entire haul of gold was cleverly hidden somewhere within his quarters. Somewhere ingenious enough to keep it out of sight, but not so secure that the right man might not relieve Dan of the burden of his great wealth. Soon it reached the point where Dan began to lay booby traps about his quarters and took to sleeping with a loaded pistol beneath his pillow and a ready blade beneath his nightshirt in order to fend off those who slipped by the pitfalls. In those days quite a few would-be burglars learned just how light a sleeper was Black Danny O'Barry. Those that managed to crawl away, at least.

But it was Dan's own desires and ill-disciplined temper that led to the truly strange sequence of events that resulted in a night of otherworldly horror and the unforeseen inheritance of his gold by a handful of opportunity-minded neighbors. Like many of Dan's misadventures, this particular episode began in a brothel. This brothel, however, was no common crib or whorehouse, but rather a fairly unique establishment that featured a single whore, and operated under the innovative assumption that its customers would prefer quality to quantity. Unlikely as it may seem, the strategy worked thanks entirely to the rare beauty of the young Chinese woman whose presence and practices had become the constant subject of the whispers of lonely men.

"Go to the parlor two doors down from Black's Melodeon. Knock twice. Ask for Ling," they said.

Those who followed the instructions were promised pleasures of the flesh unlike any they had known before. Word spread, and once it reached Dan, it never occurred to him not to go.

One night he arrived on the front porch of the house, having polished off a prodigious amount of whiskey back at Chesmire's in order to develop a light alcohol buzz, and he was feeling fine. A storm had just blown through, leaving the streets wet and muddy and the air crisp with that particular tang of having just been cleansed. The clouds broke away and a three-quarters moon glared down at the city like a sleepy eye. Dan kicked his boots against the plank risers to knock loose the clumps of wet dirt slopped onto them, cleared his throat, spat, and then knocked twice.

Inside the house was darker than out, and Dan could barely see the shape standing behind the door looking out at him. Somebody further inside lit a candle which burned with an odd red flame, and the door opened wider revealing a true giant of a man whose scornful stare would have made most men think twice about doing the business they came to do. But Dan craned back his neck, looked right up at the giant and said; "I'm here to see Ling."

The giant pulled the door full open and cleared space for Dan to enter. Another man stood waiting in the foyer, a Chinese man dressed in delicate green clothing that resembled a robe. Dan knew Sun Chou from business they had conducted together in the past, the exact nature of which remained a well-guarded secret.

"O'Barry. I thought it would not be long before we saw you here." Chou spoke better English than most of the Chinese (and most Americans for that matter) in this part of town, and his accent was mild, at least when it suited him.

"Been a while, ain't it?" Dan nodded toward the giant. "Where'd you dig up this little tyke?"

"Mr. Fairchild is from out of town. He's quite capable in most ways, but a little slow and utterly mute. Still, he is quite good at his job."

Dan noticed the way Fairchild's muscles made his clothes look a size too small, and he didn't need to ask what that job was. Chou led the way through the corridor to a back staircase. Two low candles in wall sconces afforded some dim illumination, and a pungent haze of opium smoke drifting from behind a closed door marked a room wherein men answered a stronger call than any Ling could exercise. Upstairs Chou set the strange red candle in a sconce beside the frame of another door. Dan could barely contain himself, so when his guide reached out and grabbed his hand away from the doorknob, nothing more than Dan's preoccupation with entering Ling's room kept him from beating his old acquaintance like a useless horse.

"You pay now," Chou said.

"I pay when our business is done," Dan said. "Then we can

negotiate a fee based on the quality of the service."

What went through Chou's mind at that moment must remain forever a point of speculation, but it just may be that he weighed Dan's reputation for trouble against his good business sense and decided he'd rather risk dealing with Dan after the man had relieved some of his tension. He let go Dan's arm, and Dan entered the dark room.

Across the space he discerned a canopy bed placed upon a low platform, and behind the filmy veil of its curtains, reclined a curvaceous silhouette. Incense burned and filled the entire room with a tenacious haze that dizzied Dan, but it failed to mask the poppy stink that meant Ling was most likely kept drugged by her employer. The figure on the bed writhed behind the curtain, becoming more distinct in the flicker of candles placed on small stands near the wall beyond. Something whispered in Dan's ear, and his blood warmed. He felt the heat of his face flushing and the quickening beat of his heart. Again something whispered, but in the strange atmosphere Dan couldn't be sure it wasn't the sound of the wind or the house creaking. For one moment he knew a completely alien sense of self-doubt.

It was only a moment.

This was Black Danny O'Barry, fugitive, prospector, brawler, legend, both wealthy and brazen, and no slip of a whore was going to unseat his ironclad assurance. Dan swept the curtain away with bluster and bravado and gazed upon his purchase.

Now accounts of Ling's appearance taken from those lucky enough to have enjoyed her company vary in the details. Her patrons spoke of her flawless, dusky skin; her jet-black, silken hair; eyes deep enough to calm the most tempestuous soul; the lush fullness of her lips; the gentle infinite curves of her body. Every man who knew her described her a different way, but every one of them spoke with a sense of awe and respect truly rare among the rough and brawny prospectors who tumbled down out of the mountains like hungry, caged animals let loose in the larder. The one thing they all agreed on? Ling's beauty could stop a man in his tracks.

So with all that in mind, it's safe to say the young lady of the night left Dan suitably impressed.

One might also guess that Chou's confidence in Ling's charms to completely enthrall her customers might explain the foolishness he got himself up to that night. Eager to take his money's worth, Dan set to his congress with Ling with a determination. The fact that Chou made it as far as he did is perhaps the greatest testament to Ling's remarkable skills and Dan's unquestioned pleasure in their exhibition. The very idea of that rough-hewn, black-hearted beast tumbling and rolling alongside Ling's delicate beauty amounts to enough to make most men shudder, but apparently it didn't give Chou even a moment of pause. He pushed open the disguised, well-oiled panel in the wainscoting and crept out onto the floor, inching his way toward the pile of clothes Dan left behind, just as if Dan was any average customer whose purse was there for the taking. Many a guest of Ling's left her bed a sight poorer than they rightly should have, not that one of them would own up to the fact. They all more or less found their time with Ling well worth the price, and those who became repeat customers knew not to carry more than the going price next time.

But Dan, despite his fortune, didn't have it in his nature to be so liberal with his funds, and all those nights of light sleeping gave him an uncanny sensitivity to certain sounds.

The second he heard Chou scuffing along the floor, he was up on his feet, naked as the day he was born, Ling forgotten and practically dumped head over heels off the far side of the bed. Chou mustered all the surprise he could as Dan's iron grip closed around his throat and a thirsty Bowie knife licked at the skin behind his ear. He struggled, then thought better of it and belted out words the meaning of which became obvious when the door snapped open and Mr. Fairchild entered, a shotgun tucked neatly across his arm.

It became abundantly clear to Dan where things were heading, and it took him half a heartbeat to choose his course of action. Chou became the recipient of about six inches of steel delivered quickly to his brain behind his ear. The moment of shock that stayed Mr. Fairchild's trigger finger afforded Dan the time to twist Chou's body around for cover, and when the brute finally did take his shot, only one barrel fired. Apparently the other hadn't been loaded, and Chou's body handily stopped the spray of shot flying across the room. All in all Dan's particular streak of luck held up long enough to keep him breathing. All he had to do to stay that way was defeat the hulking Mr. Fairchild barehanded.

The giant thought about reloading his gun, but Dan left him no time as he threw himself across the room, doing himself some credit by actually staggering his target as he tackled him. Unfortunately, no three men with ropes could have easily taken down Mr. Fairchild, and even Dan's unbridled temper and expert brawling techniques seemed cold comfort as the giant rained blow after blow down on Dan's bare body. Dan's first instinct to go for his Colt abandoned somewhere in the rumpled mound of clothing might have worked if the giant hadn't moved so as to be between Dan and his weapon. Besides which that brought him closer to Ling and he worried what might happen if she tangled him up and held him back while he tried to fight. But as it always had when it felt as if the hour could become no more desperate, Dan's unearthly luck dealt him an uncommon hand.

Mr. Fairchild moved faster than his bulk would indicate, and he managed to get Dan up into a powerful bear hug, lifting him from the ground and squeezing the breath out of him. Dan strained and shook and cursed and pounded with every shred of strength he possessed. He even craned his neck up and clamped down tight on Mr. Fairchild's nose with his teeth, but other than opening up a gush of blood, the bite only resulted in an even angrier opponent. But a calm settled over Dan when he felt the stubs of twin Derringers holstered at the giant's back. Dan had left Mr. Fairchild no opportunity to reach around and draw them, and so there they waited, ready salvation for Dan, who yanked them loose, placed one against each of the giant's temples, clenched shut his eyes and fired. The subsequent smoke choked Dan, but he found the sudden loosening of his chest and rush of air back to his lungs wholly satisfactory. Mr. Fairchild toppled backward, padding Dan's fall in the final burst of luck due him that night.

Dan breathed a sigh of relief at his good fortune to have survived the encounter, for even the meanest of men can appreciate the hard-won extension of his breathing days. So imagine his surprise when he looked up only to see Ling sitting on the bed with his very own Colt freshly retrieved from his discarded holster and now cocked and aimed squarely between his eyes.

At least that's where Dan claimed it was pointed. There are some who suggest it was actually aimed a fair bit lower.

Ling still drifted in the grip of the opium fed to her by Chou. Her eyes remained foggy and glazed and she most probably snatched up Dan's gun out of some instinctive response to the violence taking place around her and her own instinct to defend herself. Dan reckoned all this, but it didn't make him any more predisposed to take a bullet than if Ling had come at him in a blind fury. So he tried talking, and said sweet things and kind words to let Ling know he harbored no intention of harming her. He asked for his gun. He asked her to put it down on the bed. He tried everything he could think of to make Ling let go of the weapon so they could both walk out of there alive. And had Ling understood a thing Dan said, chances are she would've listened to him and acted accordingly. As it was she wouldn't have been able to run for water if you told her she was on fire.

Her first shot jerked her hands wild and the slug missed Dan by a good three feet, but it was enough to get him jumping. He leaped furiously at Ling, meaning to disarm her and pin her down, and that was when, for maybe the second or third time in his life - and ask five people about those other times and you'll get five different stories - Dan's luck betrayed him. He caught his feet in the bundle of clothes he'd left on the floor, stumbled and fell forward to the bed, the force of his movement carrying him over much faster and harder than he'd intended. He hit Ling and as the two of them tumbled backwards roughly, Dan heard two sounds in quick order—a stray gunshot and a snap that chilled his blood. Ling fell against the headboard with all the force needed to snap her neck.

It can honestly be said that Dan felt a qualm of sadness at the end of the scuffle. Cold as he was, he was still human, and it's hard for any man to feel nothing when he kills the woman with whom he has just been intimate, even if by accident. Dan did what he could to lay her out peacefully on the bed, then dressed himself and readied to leave. Before he went he spent a solid fifteen minutes kicking Chou's head unrecognizable and cussing him a blue streak.

The way Dan saw it, Ling's death was all Chou's fault for keeping her drugged so that Dan couldn't communicate with her when he needed to. Which is not to say that he'd seen anything wrong with that when he was a paying customer.

The whole episode left Dan somewhat disturbed, and he took himself to the nearest saloon for a shot of whiskey to settle his nerves. By the next morning the bodies of Chou and Mr. Fairchild had been discovered, most likely by one of the sleepers in the den below in search of additional opium. The news made its way around town in short order, the most interesting bit being the report of Ling's disappearance. From the state of the room, the constable surmised her murder, but her body could not be located. That week found more than a few men favoring the local saloonkeepers as they drowned their sorrows in the bottle. Eventually the incident came back to Dan, and he didn't bother to deny it or confirm it. The fact that he had single-handedly killed Mr. Fairchild enhanced his status as a brawler, but his refusal to explain what had happened to Ling led people to believe he'd killed her out of sheer spite. The assumption confirmed the opinions of those who labeled Dan a mean-spirited son of a bitch whose heart most closely resembled a chunk of a coal.

Such commotions were not uncommon, then, and Dan trusted that the whole event would soon cease to be an issue as people lost interest and got on with things as they always had in the past. No one stepped forward to take Dan to task, and seeing as how no witnesses offered testimony to compel the law to keep after the case, that's exactly what happened.

Or that's what would've happened if it hadn't been for the murder of Tom, a Chinese man with a knack for handling horses which he did for Sun Chou in return for opium. Now a dead opium eater was about as common in San Francisco as manure in a stable, and under normal circumstances, Tom's death would not have merited much attention. But the nature of his demise was so utterly gruesome that it could not easily be overlooked, seeing as how it chilled to the bone anyone who heard its account.

They found him in the stable where he worked and slept, suspended upside down from ropes by one ankle, his body white as salt and desiccated. The doctor guessed several hours had passed since Tom died. All along his arms and legs glistened tracks of tiny puncture wounds, which looked as if snakes had been lined up in rows to bite him and his blood drained neatly and carefully away from its rightful location. Piled on the floor below the body, just beyond arm's reach waited the opium that would've released him from his torture even as he died, cruelly taunting him with salvation he could never obtain. Even worse, Tom's head rested beside a pile of hay, tilted a bit askew, its dead eyes looking up at its body. The most unnerving detail about the entire scene emerged only when the doctor thought to elicit opinions as to how such mayhem could have been carried out while leaving but six or seven small spatters of blood on the stable floor.

No one considered the greater implications of Tom's murder or connected it in any way to Black Danny O'Barry until word spread of the second murder. And a third quickly followed.

Tom's death took place nearly a week after Dan's fateful visit to Ling's, and every other night since then, a similar killing occurred in the small hours. Each was tortured, exsanguinated and viciously dismembered. The particulars differed—the setting, the treatment of the victim—but one thing quickly became apparent. They all had connections to Sun Chou.

In a matter of three weeks, nearly none of Chou's business associates remained alive, though a clever few had fled town, and hardly a soul in the city still knew the man by more than reputation. The constable took to the case night and day, but made about as much headway as he would have spitting into the wind. The streets stood empty after dark, and business on the waterfront fell into a true slump. The only shred of evidence he turned up were reports of a strange, green phosphorescence seen in the night in the vicinity of the murders, lending an eerie flavor to the entire episode. Some speculated Chou's enemies meant to take over his trades. Others claimed a madman ran loose. A few even went so far as to appoint demonic forces as the culprit and warn others that the end days as described in the Good Book were nigh.

Dan kept his wits and whiskey at hand.

He realized there was a good chance that the killer meant to add him to the list of victims, as he had often enjoyed the services of Chou, with whom he had also taken part in certain unpublicized entrepreneurial ventures, linking them closer than anyone suspected. Only Dan knew the full extent of his involvement, and it was enough to make him cautious. Had anyone else known Dan's exact situation, they would have marveled at the fact that he didn't run out of town on the fastest horse he could find.

To Dan's way of thinking, this new wrinkle was no different from the risky life he'd become accustomed to living. And so he maintained his normal routine, sleeping all day, drinking at night at Chesmire's, and generally catering to whatever fancy popped into his whiskey-damped brain. It got to be that some people began whispering Dan's name as the killer, so unaffected did he seem to be. But that notion proved short-lived.

It was during this time that a preacher told Dan that the Devil had come to San Francisco to collect his own, and that given the life Dan had led, one couldn't expect to go on forever before evil birthed into the world sought reunion with its parentage. Dan needed to repent while he was still walking under his own will, save his life and avoid visiting that land of fire and brimstone that waited for him. Dan carefully explained that since he'd never had any truck with God, he couldn't reckon as how he could rightly associate with his counterpart, the Devil, and that even if he did, well that was just fine with him as it seemed the Devil was a sight more agreeable to Dan's nature than the man upstairs. And with that, Dan suggested the priest take his message out to "the heathen Chinese," who apparently needed a great deal more "saving" than he did.

The significance of that encounter has since been disputed. On the one hand, it may have been nothing but coincidence that brought an overzealous young preacher down among the waterfront sinners to try his hand at saving the soul universally agreed upon as the most damned on all the West Coast. On the other hand, it may have been the last touch of Dan's luck trying to do right by its possessor. And if that's the case it's safe to say Dan was mostly responsible for his own fate for not having learned after all those years of hard living just when to let his own natural good fortune steer him right. For the priest was not that far from the mark when he described Dan's situation, though he got the specifics wrong due to his being a man of the cloth and only able to see the world in terms of God and the Devil. Had Dan known then that the hate with his name on its lips wasn't that of an ordinary robber and that its thirst was not for his gold, he might've done things differently.

That same night the killer came.

Exactly how the particulars of Black Danny O'Barry's doom are known remains somewhat controversial. One of Dan's neighbors went to his grave swearing Dan had told him the whole terrifying tale with the last breaths from his dying lips. A theory favored by most thinking men is that the people behind the string of killings that gripped the city that autumn spread the story themselves in the interest of sending a message to those who might otherwise attribute the deaths to undeserving parties. If it had the added effect of further enlarging Dan's already larger than life persona, then so be it. Those who remembered Dan would surely remember his ending. But the truth is something altogether different, for on the night Dan died he confided in me some small information regarding his preparations for his expected encounter, and just a few days later I received a highly unusual visitor at Chesmire's. While the version of events I have pieced together does seem wholly fantastic, I must point out that it also possesses the singular virtue of explaining all the known facts of the incident.

Dan went the night of his fateful encounter to see a man named Leung, who was a Chinese merchant. Dan and Leung spent almost an hour in consultation, and immediately afterward Dan purchased four large sacks of salt at the general store, the record of which exists on paper in the shopkeeper's books and is one of the few facts about that night which can be verified. That done, Dan took his place at the bar in Chesmire's where throughout the night he made cryptic remarks about the "damn superstitious Chinese." It was only after hours of drink and with closing time drawing near that he let slip any real clue as to his actions, and that at the time was utterly meaningless to me. Dan, as he stumbled toward the door, mumbled two words, "*Chiang Shih.*"

The next morning came the report of Dan's death, his body found in his quarters, which showed the signs of a struggle so terrific that even the walls and ceiling had been torn from their frame. Unlike the other victims, though, Dan's body remained intact, though mostly drained of blood, and the first real evidence of the killer appeared - a set of women's clothing, Chinese in design, lay sprawled on the floor beside Dan, inexplicably buried under mounds of salt from four broken sacks which seemed to have fallen upon it as if pressed by a great weight. Of Dan's gold, there was no sign.

Officially, that's where the tale of Black Danny O'Barry ends. The murders ceased and the green mist was never again reported in the city. The constable made a show of scratching his head by way of investigation, and the episode quickly removed itself to the realm of legend.

But a few nights after Dan's passing an elderly Chinese man entered Chesmire's, approached me at the bar and ordered a whiskey, from which he did not drink the entire time he stayed. He was a withered man with a dull gleam to his eyes. A great sadness hung over him and he glanced around the room in random succession, often staring at the door, his attitude one of searching, as if he hoped something he'd lost would reveal itself to him. It was rare enough for Chinese to patronize Chesmire's and even rarer for one so old and unusual to put in an appearance, and I found my curiosity roused. It was still early evening, and business was quiet, so as I cleaned glasses behind the bar I attempted conversation. The old man spoke enough English to respond, and in not too long a time, had rendered a story that left me pale and trembling.

He said his name was Chan, and his journey here from China had taken several months. He had arrived in fact only a few weeks ago, coming in search of his daughter. In China he was head of a noble family, and due to some actions the old man had taken, they had fallen target to a band of outlaws who sought vengeance by kidnapping the old man's only daughter. Before anything could be done the outlaws spirited her away on a ship bound for San Francisco, where they were sure they could profit from selling the girl into prostitution and be certain her family never again saw her. But they underestimated the old man's tenacity. He pursued them and sought out his child in the alien surroundings of the city, but when he finally found her, he was too late - she had perished in her captivity. The old man craved vengeance, but being Chinese and alone in America, he could not openly hunt his enemies.

His daughter's name was Ling.

He took her body from where it rested in Sun Chou's parlor house, and kept it from burial in the rooms he had rented in the Chinese district, for the Chinese believe that the dead too long unburied become restless and angry. In this way Ling's father stirred up what he called Ling's *p'ai*, a powerful spirit force within her, and she was transformed, for the irritated spirit woke her from death, and motivated by anger, gave movement to her lifeless body, resurrecting the girl as chiang shih.

The words, which I had first heard from Dan's lips, turned my blood cold.

What waited for Dan in his rooms when he came home that last night was something not entirely living and not entirely human, something savage and unholy with nothing more than its thirst for Dan's blood to guide it. Imagine what must have gone through Dan's mind as he lit his oil lamp and watched the shadows peel back to reveal Ling watching him with hungry eyes. Might he not have felt a pang of relief that he had not killed her after all? He probably wondered about her appearance - how her beautiful skin had become pale and papery and her lush black hair had turned stark white. Maybe he wondered why her embrace felt so cold.

Ling quickly made her intentions clear by pulling Dan violently to the floor, and all wonder fled Dan's mind as he fought back. Her strength, by then, would have been much greater than that of any living girl her size, which Dan likely found troubling. It must have unnerved him, as well, that Ling uttered not a sound during their scuffle, not even a gasp for breath. She fixated her attention on his neck, her wet lips spreading as she craned her dark mouth toward his flesh. For his part Dan took great annoyance in the idea that she had been able to sneak into his rooms ahead of him and, had he not been so drunk, he imagined Ling would've been bleeding and ruined by gunfire before she'd come within four feet of him. That spark of irritation gave Dan the necessary edge to brace himself on the frame of his bed, flip around and put himself on top of Ling, whose fingers now closed coldly around his throat. He lashed out three rapid blows to her face and broke loose to draw his Colt.

He fired four times as Ling rose from the floor, each bullet ripping through her body like paper, but she barely noticed them. Dan fired twice more, emptying his gun, but still the bullets did nothing.

Ling, still silent, her black eyes laughing, changed. A light, greenish and thick, burned around her like a cold flame, its glow expanding to fill the room. Her skin drew tight around her figure and her hands grew in size, her fingers extending into bony needles whose nails protruded like the talons of a bird of prey. But the one element of Ling's new aspect (and truthfully, at this point, Dan no longer rightly considered the thing before him to be Ling) that delivered the purest note of fear to Dan's heart was her mouth, which widened and drew open to reveal sharp, serrated teeth of mottled bone. It must have seemed then that the Devil had indeed come to collect his own.

The two creatures of the night grappled, Dan failing before Ling's growing strength. She lifted him three inches off the floor, forcing him up against the wall toward which Dan struggled and wriggled to direct them. Their bodies pressed against one another in a mockery of their first meeting. Dan slipped loose his knife and stabbed wildly at Ling's torso, but the blade failed to harm her. It left him no choice. He twisted one arm loose and lifted it up behind him where he could pry at the wall and ceiling with his knife. Ling closed on Dan's neck and the pricking of her teeth against his throat spurred him into a fury. He thrashed and flailed, the knife gouging and chipping the wood behind him, but unable to find home - the crack Dan sought between two boards. Ling's teeth settled into him and he felt his blood begin to drain away. Still he could not find his target with the blade. His head grew heavy and sluggishness began to overcome him.

And then the knife slid easily into place; Dan twisted his arm and pulled, and the trap he'd laid was sprung.

The wall cracked away behind a great weight, a portion of the ceiling followed, and a moment later, both Ling and Dan were buried on the floor beneath a layer of debris which consisted mostly of splintered wood, salt pouring from four large punctured sacks, and an incredible amount of gold that had been placed so as to weight the whole mess down when it fell. Dan could hardly breathe for the crushing pressure of the gold on his back, but he smiled as he watched the salt pour over Ling's body, sending up small wisps of smoke as it corroded her dead flesh away, for salt holds great power over the chiang shih. Ling writhed, but the pain and the weight of Dan's fortune held her down. But even Dan's forethought was not enough to shake Ling's single-minded determination, and she never let loose her grip on Dan's throat.

Black Danny O'Barry had time for one dry laugh before his world went dark.

The salt, while effective, was not fast enough to save his hide.

Ultimately it left nothing of Ling but her clothes, but in a contest of moments, Dan gave up before she did. Her father, who had been watching and following her closely the whole time, broke down in tears at the sight of his daughter's body turned to ash and sent on its way to final peace, sated and avenged. He meant to remove her clothes from the room, but before he could do so, Dan's neighbors grew curious in the silence following the melee. They had listened intently from their own quarters, as they often did when Dan took on an intruder, but not one of them dared to investigate. They sure didn't mind taking off with Dan's gold after the fact, though.

For obvious reasons the truth of this story must remain unsubstantiated. Not even Chan might be consulted, for when I closed the bar that night the old Chinese man still occupied his seat, his drink still stood untouched, and as I went to rouse him, he simply fell sideways, dead, most likely of grief.

But y'know, sometimes the scariest things ain't them as ya don't know or understand, but them as ya know all too well. I can tell yer a fella as likes to ride the open range, responsible only fer himself and to himself. Yessir, I'd allow as you're a true saddle tramp, jus' like my own self.

Folks like us jus' cain't be saddled to any person, or tied down to a particular place. The wide open range is our home, the coyotes and jackrabbits our family.

What scares men like us, eh? Is it Injins, 'r outlaws, 'r them there tornadies? Nossir, ain't none of them, is it?

Look deep, pard; down there where ya stash away them things as riles yer guts and gives ya the shivers on the hottest days.

Yep, we're responsible fer our own selves, fer our own actions - and fer the consequences of them actions......

BACKLASH
BY
ELIZABETH FACKLER

The house loomed isolated on a brown knob in the middle of the grassland prairie, an imposing structure with turrets at the two front corners. Seth ambled his sorrel into the barren yard, seeing nothing growing at all, just the house hewn of gray rocks with all its windows shuttered and a scattering of dust blanketing the steps to the door. A fountain squatted in the dirt, leering faces of gargoyle lizards poking over the edge of the empty granite bowl.

Nudged with misgiving, he twisted in the saddle to look at the riders behind him: Zouri, the girl he'd rescued from outlaws, and Rosalinda, a woman he'd brought along for reasons he couldn't now remember. Though both were pale and raven-haired, their opposition across a spectrum of virtue would be obvious to even an unjaded observer.

Zouri leapt from her horse with a cry of joy as her mother disturbed the dust hurrying down the steps to welcome her home. Feeling better about himself than he had in a long time, Seth leaned to catch the dragging reins of the buckskin Zouri had abandoned. When he looked up again, she and her mother were walking toward him arm-in-arm, their faces beaming. Beyond them, Seth saw the dark silhouette of a young man blocking the door.

Mrs. Carothers was blond and pink-cheeked, her body thick beneath a prim blue dress and starched white apron. With her arm around the slender waist of her wan daughter, she smiled up at him and said, "I bless the day you rode in and asked for water, Mr. Strummar, never suspecting it was you who was bringing and not taking. Allow me to offer at least supper and a night's lodging for all you've done."

"All right," he said, resisting his itch to move on.

"I'll ready the guestrooms."

He winked at Rosalinda, sharing her amusement at the notion of separate rooms. When he looked back, the Carothers women were halfway to the house, still entwined in their embrace.

Rosalinda said, "They love you for what you've done."

"They're grateful is all," Seth said, shifting his focus to the son. "Simon ain't, though."

She watched him welcome his sister with a hug. "Where's the old man?"

"Dead. Thrown from his horse while looking for her."

She laughed. "No wonder you weren't worried about him."

"I'm worried about the kid."

"You don't mean it," she scoffed.

"Yeah, I do," he said, swinging down as Simon came near.

"It seems I'm in your debt," the kid sniped.

"No debt owed," Seth said, offering his hand.

Reluctantly Simon accepted the handshake. "I understand you're our guest."

"Only if I get an invitation from you."

"How can I deny it? You not only rescued my sister from a band of cutthroats, you brought her home in such high spirits it's as if no harm was done. It would be ungracious of me to deny you food and shelter, wouldn't it?"

"Reckon," Seth said.

Simon looked at Rosalinda. "I know this woman. She's a harlot in Comanche Junction."

"She's traveling with me now," Seth said.

Simon snorted. "Do you expect me to allow her in the presence of my mother?"

"Your mother invited us."

"She also invited you to supper when she was alone."

"Yeah, she did. And Zouri's home because of it."

"Miss Carothers to you," Simon said snidely.

Seth sighed. "Give my regrets to your mother."

He swung onto his sorrel and, with Rosalinda following on the puny pinto, led Marley's buckskin toward the vast expanse of prairie. But they had barely made it to the edge of the yard when Zouri's voice turned them around.

"Please, Seth!" she called from the door. Hurrying down the steps and across the barren yard, she threw a bewildered look at her brother.

Out of breath beside Seth's horse, she looked up with pleading eyes. "Whatever Simon said, I'm sure he didn't mean it. My mother and I want so much for you to stay."

Seth shook his head. "I better not."

She whirled on her brother. "What have you done! I owe Seth my life *and* my sanity, if that means anything to you!"

"It means the world to me, Zouri," he answered painfully.

"So you send him away when it's nearly dark and he hasn't had supper! Is that how we show our gratitude? Papa will be ashamed of you, Simon. I am too!"

Seth watched Simon come a few steps closer.

His eyes burning with embarrassment, the kid said, "Please accept our invitation to stay the night."

Seth would have let him off the hook and ridden on, but Zouri asked again.

"Please," she said, her heart in every letter.

He looked at Rosalinda. "You want to stay?"

"I'd love to," she said.

He met Simon's eyes.

"Go on in," the kid said. "I'll put your horses up."

"I'll give you a hand." Seth swung down and lifted Rosalinda from the sidesaddle, untied her satchel and handed it to her, then stood beside Simon as they watched the women walk toward the house.

Finally Simon said, "Zouri seems to be all right."

"Are you?"

"I don't know. Part of me hates your guts."

Seth laughed. "I'll be leaving in the morning."

Simon nodded and led the two horses Seth had taken from the outlaws toward the stable. When Seth fell in step leading his sorrel, Simon asked, "Is Marley still alive?"

"No."

"How'd you manage that?"

"I outdrew him."

"You make it sound simple."

"Wasn't complicated."

A humble hired hand came out of the stable to take the horses. Seth lifted his saddlebags off, then looked at the corral holding a pair of white mares, blooded brood stock well-fed, their ears pricked with curiosity.

Following Simon into the kitchen, he was hit with smells he remembered from childhood. They brought back painful memories arousing a strong thirst, but Simon walked on through and Seth didn't feel he could ask the women for whiskey. Rosalinda wasn't there either, only Zouri and her mother making supper.

He stood awkwardly holding his saddlebags, receiving more radiant smiles than he thought he deserved. "Is there a place I could wash up?" he asked.

"I'll take you," Zouri said.

He followed her along the hall the opposite way from the library and its stash of whiskey. Together they climbed a narrow, angular staircase that switchbacked on its ascent.

Zouri stopped at the top and said, "Second door on your left. Rosalinda's in the next room down."

"Thanks," he said, moving away. Then he turned, thinking to catch her, but she was still watching him. "Any chance I could borrow a shirt? I've been living in this one a few days now."

She smiled. "I'll bring you one of my father's."

"Thanks," he said again, knowing they hadn't yet told her the old man was dead. Hoping they'd wait till he was gone so he could remember her smiling, Seth went into the room she'd said was his. He hesitated on the threshold, taking in the plush red carpet and dark maroon canopy on the massive bed, then walked to the window and looked down on the barren patch of yard decorated only with an empty fountain.

One of the lizard gargoyles seemed to stare straight at him, tempting him to draw his gun and shoot the monster's head off. Instead he turned around and saw Zouri standing in the door holding a folded white shirt.

"Who built the fountain?" he asked.

She left the shirt on the bed and joined him at the window. "My father's first wife, Simon's mother."

He hadn't known Simon was only her half-brother, and he guessed they both resembled their father with their dark hair and pale complexions, since the Mrs. Carothers he knew was blond.

Zouri felt his scrutiny and looked up. "I feel so close to you, Seth," she whispered.

"You're standing close enough to touch," he teased.

"That isn't what I meant."

He nodded. "It'll pass."

"I wish it wouldn't."

Gratitude was understandable, but her declaration triggered a warning in Seth's mind that she wasn't dealing from a full deck. "It ain't proper for you to be in here, you know that?"

"It's just..." She looked at the bed, then back at him, her eyes hungry. When he said nothing, she smiled again and walked out, quietly closing the door.

He laid his gun belt on the bed beside the shirt, fragrant with lemon soap like his mother had used.

When he was dressed again, he walked next door to Rosalinda's room. Finding her under the covers, he sat down beside her.

"I had too much sun." She smiled apologetically. "Riding all day, I'm not used to being outside."

He could see she was flushed, so he reached across and touched her cheek. "You've got a fever."

"Just a sunburn," she said.

He pulled the blankets away, opened her wrapper and lay his palm against the curve of her breast. "You ain't sunburned there, Linda. You've caught something."

"I feel fine. Just tired. Will you apologize to Mrs. Carothers for me?"

"You come down sick and I'll have to leave you behind."

"I'm not sick," she said stubbornly.

He smiled. "Best thing I know for a fever is warmed whiskey. I'll fetch you some."

She shivered and pulled the covers under her chin.

He walked downstairs, thinking it wasn't good to bring sickness into a house. And a woman in her profession was exposed to nearly every disease in the country, so it could be anything.

Relieved to find Mrs. Carothers alone in the kitchen, he said, "I think my friend's caught an ague or something. You got any medicine for fever?"

Her face creased with concern. "Best remedy is a toddy with plenty of lemon. I'll make her one."

"Hope I haven't brought sickness here."

"You've brought my daughter home, Mr. Strummar. I'm very grateful to you."

"Whatever Rosalinda's got, we'll be leaving first thing tomorrow."

"Not if she's ill. I won't hear of it." She moved to a cupboard and took out a full bottle of whiskey, then to the pantry for a tin of lemon extract, poured generous amounts into a mug, and filled it from a steaming kettle off the stove. "I'll go check on her," she said, carrying the toddy out of the room.

Seth remembered where she kept her glasses and got himself one, filled it with whiskey and drank half of it down, then took the more respectable amount over to the window.

Zouri came in. "Where's Mother?"

"She went to check on Linda. She ain't feeling well."

"I'm sorry. Won't she be down for supper then?"

He shook his head. She saw the bottle and put it away. When she opened the oven to peer inside, the room was engulfed with the fragrance of sauerbraten, a dish his mother had often made. He looked out the window again, working at the whiskey.

"That shirt fits you well," Zouri said from behind him.

He turned around. "Smells good, too."

She laughed, coming close. "Yes. I notice a difference."

He set his empty glass down and moved away from her to open the door. "Think I'll check on my horse," he said, walking out.

Unlike the last time, the stable was filled now with horses, all quality stock except the pinto he'd brought. Like the woman, he thought, wondering what had possessed him to bring her along. He found his sorrel well-tended, so had no excuse to prolong his absence from the house.

Walking back, he wondered again where the hands slept and why

Mrs. Carothers didn't have any help. When he went into the kitchen, she was taking a crusted casserole from the oven. She set it by the platter of sauerbraten and said, "I was just going to come call you."

"How's Linda?"

"I'm afraid you'll have to accept our hospitality for a few days at least."

"What's the matter with her?"

"These fevers are mysterious, they come and go. I dealt with many when the children were small."

"She ain't a child," he answered gruffly.

"No," she said, puzzled at his tone. "It's nothing for you to worry about, Mr. Strummar."

"Call me Seth," he said.

She smiled. "Only if you'll call me Marion."

"Don't think Simon would like that."

"He's my son, not my husband."

"Man of the house now, though."

She shrugged. "We haven't told Zouri."

"I could tell."

"She thinks the world of you, Seth. So do I."

"You're misguided. Simon's got a better cut of me than you do."

She shook her head. "Noah would have liked you. He and I rarely disagreed about people. Except in Simon's case. We often disagreed about him." She picked up the sauerbraten and carried it out of the kitchen.

Seth followed her across the hall to the dining room. It was long and ornate, the shutters closed. He wondered why all the front windows were blocked, at least those on the ground floor, then remembered when he'd first ridden into the yard the top ones had been too. His room had been opened, apparently just for him.

"Is it the fountain you're shutting out?"

She looked up from positioning the platter on the table. "What do you mean?"

"All the windows on this side of the house are shuttered."

"Noah preferred it that way."

"Why?"

"His first wife jumped to her death from one of the turrets." She dried her hands on her apron, though they weren't wet. "He couldn't bear the view after that."

"Sorry," Seth said. "I had no right to ask."

"Wasn't any grief of mine, except as it affected him. She was Simon's mother."

"Why'd she jump?"

"The loneliness, I suppose. Noah wouldn't talk about it, except to answer the same question you just asked, which I put to him when he first brought me here. We never spoke of it again."

Seth nodded.

"I suspect Simon inherited his mother's melancholy. The woman was obviously unhinged; look at the house she designed. It's hideous to my eye. And the fountain... Just seeing that every day could drive anyone crazy, don't you think?"

"Yeah, I do."

"I'll get the potatoes and call the children," she said.

Left alone, he was sorry he'd stayed. He didn't like the shuttered windows aborting his view, and the story about the first wife was gloomy. Now Rosalinda was sick and he felt a dread of being trapped in this house by a woman he'd bedded twice and liked, that was all.

It was hearing her beneath Marley that had pricked his need to reassert possession. If he'd used Zouri that night instead of being careful of her feelings, he wouldn't have been listening so intently to what was happening in the other room, and she wouldn't now be looking at him with stars in her eyes. He told himself that maybe instead of trying to reform, he should go whole hog and turn into someone like Marley: unequivocally evil.

When Simon came in and glared at him from the head of the table, Seth said, "Relax. We don't have to like each other."

The women came in laughing. Their light-hearted gaiety was so discordant with Simon's hostility it clashed in Seth's mind as a warning to get out. If not for Rosalinda he would have left right then, but he decided one night couldn't hurt anything.

"Please, Seth," Marion said as she held the chair opposite Simon.

Telling himself it was only one meal, Seth sat down and smiled at the kid's scowl.

After supper, Seth asked Marion for another toddy. Though they didn't speak as she made it, he eyed the bottle until she suggested he take it with him in case the invalid awoke in the middle of the night.

Seth smiled at her polite lie. Thinking how easily he could slide into living with such an accommodating woman, he toyed with the idea of seducing Marion. Her body would be commodious on cold winter nights. And as Simon's step-father, he might bring the kid around to some degree of partnership. Zouri was the kink in that scheme. She wouldn't accept Seth choosing Marion over her, and he knew her well-being was paramount to the family. Suspecting he could marry the girl and enjoy her mother on the side, Seth laughed at himself for even contemplating such a wicked arrangement. But when he met Marion's eyes while accepting the whiskey, he discovered the notion wasn't new to her.

Entering Rosalinda's room as if it were his, he stood by the bed watching her sleep in the light of the lamp she'd left burning. She looked older than he remembered, as if the fever were withering her beauty from within.

By habit he crossed to the window, always wary for the approach of trouble, but his view was blocked. He slid the pane open, unlatched the shutters and pushed them flat against the wall, then leaned out to inhale the evening chill. The gargoyle below gleamed as if from its own light.

He shuddered at its ugliness, and again felt tempted to pull his pistol and shoot the lizard's head to kingdom come. Instead he looked at the turrets on opposite ends of the house. They were octagonal, built of rough-hewn red stone, their parapets boarded up. Something moved in the fountain. He looked back at the gargoyle, but it was immobile, set in stone.

He remembered Rosalinda's illness and slid the window closed. The room was stuffy as a tomb, which bothered him as much as the gargoyle, but he wanted her well. Knowing the tension in his spine meant he was hours from sleep, he sipped at the whiskey while staring through the pane of glass at the lizard below. Its luminous face seemed as ominous as the presence of the house looming around him, but when he finally slept, it was a senseless death undisturbed by dreams.

In the morning he left Rosalinda asleep and walked downstairs to find Marion alone in the kitchen. Feeling magnanimous with his affection, he leaned to kiss her cheek. "Can you look in on Linda for me?"

"Surely," she answered, pleased with his kiss.

"I'll go check on my horse."

He was washing his hands at the basin outside when Marion came to the door.

"Your friend is very ill," she said.

"What's wrong with her?"

Marion shook her head. "Rest is the best medicine."

He wondered if she was chastising him for having slept with Rosalinda, guessing she'd seen that his bed was untouched. "I'll tend her," he said. "You should stay away from her."

She smiled. "There are things no man has the touch for."

He was thinking she meant to give Rosalinda a bath, and he almost laughed that she thought he hadn't seen her naked. "Like what?" he teased.

"She should have an enema."

Then he did laugh. "You're right. I ain't never done that."

"I don't think she'd like you to either, but it'll draw the poisons out and help her recover."

"How long before she can travel?" he asked unhappily.

"We should know by tomorrow."

Seth was glad they weren't eating in the dining room again. The kitchen windows let sunshine flood the room with at least a semblance of cheer. Halfway through breakfast, Zouri offered to show him the ranch. Before he could answer, she invited her brother to go along, too.

"I wouldn't let you go alone," Simon told her, "but we need to talk first."

Seth knew the subject of that talk and didn't think she'd be going anywhere after. His relief was dampened by the prospect of a long day with the grief of mourning torn open around him.

He went back to Rosalinda's room, working on the whiskey and wishing he hadn't stayed. He'd rather be in a town where he could wait out her illness in the masculine company of saloons, a scenario altogether more to his liking.

When someone knocked, he opened the door to Marion with a tray of vile-looking accouterments. Repressing a shudder, he held the door wide and let her pass. She set the tray down and said, softly so as not to wake Rosalinda, "We told Zouri about her father."

"How'd she take it?"

"She didn't cry as I expected, simply asked Simon to walk her up to the grave. They're there now."

He kept quiet, picturing the two of them in the family cemetery sharing their grief.

"Seth," Marion petitioned, "I'm worried about her. It must have been horrible in the hands of those outlaws, yet she acts as if nothing happened."

"Maybe she just put it behind her, like an accident that's better off forgotten."

"But she was violated, wasn't she?"

He didn't answer.

"Tell me the truth," Marion pleaded.

"What does she say happened?"

"Only that they kept her tied till you came and saved her."

"If that's what she remembers, why make it otherwise?"

"I wouldn't, but I want to know for myself."

"Why?"

"When she does remember, I'll know what's true and what isn't. I'll be able to help her then."

"All right," he conceded. "They all had her, seven men, taking pleasure from her pain."

Marion closed her eyes and tears fell across her cheeks. She didn't wipe them away but stood in silence a moment, then looked at him again. "She said you gave her a drink of water, that it was the first she'd had since they'd taken her." Her smile was melancholy. "You came here asking for water."

He waited for her point.

"Simon is jealous," she said. "Do you understand that?"

"Reckon."

"He loves Zouri and wanted to help her. You and I took that away from him, rightfully I believe. Do you think he could have freed her from Marley?"

"No."

"Please forgive him, Seth. It's his own sense of failure that makes him so hard on you." She looked at Rosalinda, still asleep, then back at him. "Do you understand what I'm asking?"

"You're hoping I won't let him rile me."

"Yes."

"I'd already made up my mind to that."

"Simon will break your resolve. He has with any man who's ever stood up to him. Always before, that meant they collected their wages and rode on. I don't want you to leave. Neither does Zouri. And with Rosalinda ill you can't, at least for a few days. I'm hoping, Seth, you can do for him what Noah couldn't: teach him the fine art of wielding humiliation with finesse."

"Whoa." Seth laughed. "My lessons in humiliation don't help anyone much."

"Perhaps, then, if you can find a way to help Simon, you will also help yourself, and we will have given you something in return for all you've given us."

"You don't know what you're asking. There's nothing gentle about the way I control men."

"Try imagining he's your younger brother."

"If Simon was my kid brother, I'd have authority over him. But he ain't, and I don't have any place to stand."

"He wouldn't be jealous if he didn't admire what you've achieved."

"That's a damn shaky structure."

"It's a place to stand."

Seth felt pushed beyond forbearance. "You women sure know how to pin a man to the wall."

"We're dependent on the strength of our men, and demand that they do us justice."

"I ain't one of your men."

She smiled. "There's a story in the Bible about a prisoner who asked Someone for water. And when the water was given, he followed the Giver the rest of his life."

Seth turned away and saw Rosalinda watching, her eyes bright with the illness he'd brought to this house. "I'll do my best," he muttered, walking out.

As he often did when pushed, Seth went to check on his horse. He was running his hands down the sorrel's legs, taking comfort in the animal's familiarity, when Simon came and stood at the end of the stall.

"Zouri doesn't feel like riding after all," he said, his voice noncommittal, "and asked that I show you the ranch."

"So?" Seth prompted.

"So I'm asking if you want to go," Simon said, his voice at least not hostile.

"Reckon," Seth answered. "Would be a long day just sitting around here."

He saddled his sorrel, then led it into the yard and stood holding his reins as he waited.

Simon finally came out riding Marley's buckskin. "Thought I'd see what it's worth."

Seth considered the horse his but decided not to press the point. "It's a little rough," he said, swinging onto his sorrel.

"Belonged to a rough man, didn't it?"

"As rough as they come."

"Not too much for you, though, was he?"

The kid's tone was just shy of a flat-out challenge, but in deference to Marion, Seth answered him civilly. "No man's too rough to kill. I meant he wasn't good company."

"You think about things like that?"

"I don't like to spend all my time fighting," he replied, hoping the kid could take a hint.

Simon dug in his spurs so the horse tore out of the yard. Seth followed at a lope, and gradually the kid reined back to fall in step. They rode for an hour on the rutted road, the grasslands stretching flat in all directions, before cutting across country to climb into the hills.

The day was cool and the breeze sharp under a gray sky as they followed a winding trail to the highest promontory. Simon spurred ahead to gain the crest, then waited, his leg crooked around the horn and his mouth wearing a cocky grin as he watched Seth's ambling approach.

Seth reined up and admired the view: the grass bowing in waves from the wind, the house a dark splotch in the distance.

"Everything you see is mine," Simon crowed.

"Your father built quite an empire," Seth agreed. "I heard a lot of stories, but I never met him. What was he like?"

"In some ways, he was a lot like you."

Seth flinched, remembering the point of the stories had been to extol the cruelty of Noah Carothers.

"Not in looks," Simon said. "He'd been scalped and the top of his head never grew back. But he had a way of taking what he wanted."

Seth nodded. "Your mother asked me to help you."

"Help me do what?"

"Control your anger."

Simon snorted. "She thinks a man can live like it says in the Bible and the world'll reward him for it, but you don't hold a ranch this size by being a good neighbor. When my father first came here, the Comanches thought this land was theirs. He killed as many as he could. Then squatters moved in, and he didn't treat them gentle either. A few years back a Mexican tried to run sheep on this grass. I can show you his grave and the bones of his flock, hundreds of animals my father's men left to rot. Dad would've killed Reb Marley like you did, no questions asked, only Marley hadn't moved against us so Dad wasn't in any hurry. But he had plans to ride in there with twenty men and massacre those outlaws. If he'd done it a little sooner, Zouri wouldn't have been ruined."

"Your mother told me she doesn't remember what happened."

"So what? It still happened."

"Does it matter, if no one knows?"

"I know. So do you."

"What do I have to do with it? I'll be gone soon."

"You had her."

Seth met the kid's eyes. "What makes you think so?"

"Are you saying you didn't?"

"What does she say?"

"That no one's had her and she's still a virgin."

"Why don't you believe it?"

Simon looked away, and Seth caught on. "She wasn't a virgin when Reb took her, was she."

"How would I know?" Simon retorted. "I hadn't seen her for two years."

"Which makes her thirteen and you sixteen, old enough to want it." He was thinking that might explain why she'd been sent to a school so far from home, leaving her open to being waylaid by bandits.

Simon wouldn't look at him.

Gently Seth said, "It's not the first time it's happened, you know."

Simon's eyes were hot. "I know you had her!"

"So what am I dealing with here - an outraged brother or a jealous lover?"

The kid reached for his gun, barely getting a grip before Seth's was in his hand.

Simon glared at him, not giving an inch. Finally the kid asked,

"What do you want?"

"Your gun. Pull it out slow and hand it over butt first."

The kid hesitated, then complied. Seth holstered his own, emptied Simon's, and gave it back. Simon slid it into his holster, still glaring.

Seth laughed at the kid's cockiness. "How many times you think we can come that close?"

"I think we're gonna find out."

"Why?"

"'Cause you had my sister!"

"I brought her home. Ain't that worth something?"

"You brought a whore, too. You're saying they're the same."

"Maybe I brought Rosalinda to help me stay away from Zouri."

"She told me this morning she's hoping you'll marry her."

Seth grunted in surprise. "That ain't gonna happen."

"Are you saying a man in your position would pass up owning half of what Noah Carothers spent his life building?"

"I'd pass up sharing it with you!"

Simon blanched. Jerking the buckskin around, he kicked it into a gallop downhill.

Seth dawdled his way back, stopping to let his horse graze while his thoughts tumbled like the clouds. Buzzards circled high, curious if he was dead enough to be supper, though none came within range of his gun to find out.

It was dusk when he rode into the yard and stabled his horse. He walked reluctantly toward the house, seeing through the kitchen windows Marion working at the stove. She turned and smiled as he went in.

"How's Rosalinda?" he asked.

"The same," she answered, replacing her smile with a frown of concern.

"Where's Simon?"

"In the library." Her brow furrowed deeper. "I was worried when he came back alone."

"I wanted some time to myself."

She nodded. "Supper's nearly ready. Are you hungry?"

"I'll eat with Rosalinda. Think you could fix me a tray?"

"Surely," she said, dropping her gaze with hurt.

But she would deny him nothing, he knew that now. He walked

down the hall and knocked on the library door. When Simon answered, Seth pushed it open and stopped on the threshold.

The kid was at the desk, a pen poised over a paper in front of him. "I was hoping to finish before supper."

Seth stepped in and closed the door. "This won't take long. Will you have a drink with me?"

Simon walked over to the sideboard and poured them both shots of whiskey, then handed Seth one in the middle of the room.

"*Salud*," Seth said, drinking his down.

Simon sipped politely, his eyes wary.

"I spoke out of line today," Seth said. "I don't know anything about your family and it's not my intention to butt in."

The kid's eyes softened with what looked like relief.

"I've lived my life in the gutter," Seth said. "Haven't seen much love outside a bed. I decided maybe I'd miscalled your feelings for your sister, and I came to appologize."

Simon just stared at him.

Seth shrugged. "I'll be leaving in the morning. If Rosalinda can travel, I'll take her with me. Otherwise I'll give her money to catch up when she's able. Sorry to leave her on your hands, if that's how it happens."

Still, Simon was silent.

Seth set his glass down and started for the door.

"Wait," Simon said.

Seth turned back.

"My whole life," the kid said in a puzzled tone, "I never heard my father apologize to anyone."

Seth nodded. "Ain't an easy thing to do."

"He was always saying if something's easy it isn't worth doing. That's a hard rule to live by, though. I never did please him much."

"He's gone, Simon. You're the man here now."

"No one else thinks so."

"Prove 'em wrong."

"You make it sound simple. I guess for you it would be, but my mother says I'm not mentally strong enough to take Noah's place."

"She's your stepmother," Seth said, "and at your mercy."

Simon nodded, though he didn't look convinced.

Seth walked out, deciding Noah Carothers had done his son a

disservice by making him dependent on leadership. As he climbed the stairs, the house hovered like a silent gloomy presence around him. Finding Rosalinda awake, he sat on her bed, thinking she looked even worse than before. "How're you feeling?"

"Marion gave me an enema," she protested weakly.

He grinned. "Kinda sorry I missed it." He touched her cheek. It was still hot. "I'm leaving tomorrow. I'll give you money so you can meet me in Santa Fe."

"Don't leave me here, Seth. I hate this house."

"You're the one wanted to stay in the first place."

"I thought it'd be fun, not that I'd get sick and have her pumping medicine up my ass."

Someone knocked on the door. He stood up and opened it to Zouri with a tray of covered dishes. He took the tray and didn't ask her in, but as soon as he moved away to put the supper down, she was in the room.

"Hello, Rosalinda. How are you feeling?"

"Better," she whispered. "I think I can travel tomorrow."

Zouri frowned. "That isn't what Mother told me."

"I'll walk you out," Seth said. Holding her elbow, he steered her to the top of the stairs. "I'll be leaving early tomorrow, so I'll say goodbye now."

"But Rosalinda isn't well enough to travel."

"Then I'll let her join me later."

She moved closer. "Come to my room tonight."

"I'm gonna forget you said that, Zouri. If you're lucky, you will too."

"I want to feel you inside me," she pleaded.

Astounded, he asked, "Weren't seven outlaws enough?"

She lurched back as if he'd slapped her, then lost it, her eyes wild as she crumpled to the floor, shrieking.

He knelt and shook her shoulders. "Stop it, Zouri!"

Simon came racing up the stairs. He gave Seth an incredulous look, then lifted his sister in his arms and carried her down the hall, wailing and fighting against him.

Marion crested the stairs. "What happened?"

He shook his head, at a loss for words.

"What did you say to her?"

"Just that I'm leaving," he answered, not liking her tone.

"You shouldn't have told her."

"How was I supposed to know that? She seemed fine to me."

Marion sighed. "She learned just today of her father's death. She's reacting to that, and I suspect everything that's happened came back to her. It's not your fault, Seth."

"Damn straight," he muttered, but she was already hurrying down the hall to her daughter.

He stood in the long dark passage as he listened to Zouri's sobbing through the open door of her room. Slowly he walked toward it, then stood on the threshold looking in at the two people hovering over the hysterical girl on the bed. Simon saw him and came out and closed the door.

"What happened?" the kid asked, his voice tight.

"I told her I'm leaving," Seth repeated.

"You must've said more'n that," Simon accused.

Seth was tired of this family. "She invited me to her bed and I turned her down."

"Did you call her a slut for asking?"

He realized he had. "I thought she could handle it."

The kid folded his arms against the wall and hid his face in their darkness.

Seth felt for him. "She'll get over it, Simon. You're lucky she didn't have this reaction from the start."

"You're right, as usual," he said, not moving.

Seth went into Rosalinda's room and locked the door.

"What happened?" she asked in a voice like an onionskin.

"You won't believe it," he mumbled, pouring himself a drink he downed fast.

"I'd like to know, though," she said.

He carried another drink to the window and stared out at the gargoyle. While he told her, the lizard's eyes gleamed as if with malicious intent.

When he'd finished, Rosalinda whispered, "That wasn't a very sensitive remark, Seth."

He wheeled around to face her. "What was I supposed to say? See you at midnight, sweetheart?"

"A gentle refusal would have been enough."

"I ain't no choirboy."

She smiled. "Why don't we leave now?"

"'Cause you're goddamned sick. If you hadn't said you wanted to stay, I wouldn't be here."

"You won't leave me behind, will you?"

"No, they might kill you and eat you for breakfast."

She didn't laugh, so he walked over and sat down beside her. She reached up and smoothed a strand of hair behind his ear. Annoyed, he caught her hand, feeling the heat of her fever.

"My mother used to tuck my hair back like that," he said. "If Marion hadn't reminded me of her, I never would've stayed for that first supper."

"Marion reminded you of your mother?"

He nodded.

"And you rescued Zouri because of it?"

"Pretty stupid, huh?"

"I think it's sweet."

He touched her cheek. "You're hotter'n hell. You really think you can travel in the morning?"

"If you give me a horse I don't have to fight."

"I'll take the pinto. Leave 'em Marley's buckskin for luck."

"Com'ere," she said, holding up her arms as she slid deeper into the bed.

"Let me take my boots off," he grumbled. "Don't want to tear their fancy covers with my spurs."

She laughed, sounding like water whispering over a dam. "I'm going to love loving you, Seth."

"Yeah?" He stood up and unbuckled his gun belt. "It's a helluva beginning we've had to our romance."

"It can only get better."

"Don't believe it. We ain't outta here yet."

Soon after making love, she fell asleep again. Wide awake with pent-up energy, he rose to get another drink, but the bottle was empty. He couldn't remember having finished it and didn't like his awareness slipping that much. When he looked out the window, the gargoyle stared back as if biding its time.

He closed the drapes and got dressed, intending to fetch another bottle, but when he saw the light from Zouri's open door, he walked down to look in on her. Marion was awake in a chair by the bed, the girl a slight silhouette under the covers.

"How is she?" he asked.

"As you can see," Marion answered softly.

"Took a while, I reckon."

"And a strong dose of laudanum." After a moment she asked, "Is there something you wanted, Seth?"

"Ran out of whiskey."

She rose as if in obedience to his command. "Stay with Zouri, will you, please?" She brushed past him, leaving a heavy lilac scent as she disappeared in the dark of the stairs.

He moved to the window and looked out at the two white mares, standing so still they seemed like statutes in the moonlight. When he turned around, Zouri was watching him.

"How're you feeling?" he asked.

"Groggy."

"Your mother gave you some opium."

She smiled. "I used to love it when I was a child. It gave me wonderful dreams."

He watched Marion come out below and cross the yard to the outhouse.

Zouri asked, "What happened to me?"

He turned around. "Don't you remember?"

"I dreamt I fell, tumbling over and over, all the way down the stairs, only they were miles long and I just kept falling. Then..." She stopped, watching him.

"What?"

"You caught me and held me close."

He looked away.

"You undressed me," she said. "Your hands were so gentle and your kisses so warm. You made love to me, and it was like we were falling together, and that made it all right because I knew when we finally stopped it wouldn't hurt."

He sighed, not looking at her.

"You told me you're leaving, didn't you? There at the top of the stairs, and I became hysterical, didn't I?"

"Yes," he said, meeting her eyes.

"Poor Seth." She smiled. "We've been quite a chore."

"It's over now," he said, watching Marion walk back across the yard. He figured it would take her two minutes to go to the library and come upstairs. Just to make conversation, he asked, "Why do you keep those white horses in the corral all the time?"

"They belonged to Simon's mother," Zouri said.

He turned to her in surprise. "They're not that old."

She laughed. "I didn't mean they're the actual horses she used to ride. They're daughters of those horses. We keep them for breeding with a white stallion."

"Where's the stud?"

"He died."

Seth felt a shiver down his spine as he met her eyes, so dark and huge, dilated with laudanum.

"They only bear daughters," she said. "Isn't that odd?"

He shrugged.

"Stallions are rare, aren't they? White stallions with long flowing manes and glistening muscles. Their nostrils are so pink, and their gender is a soft dun color, like new thistles on wheat."

He wondered what was keeping Marion.

"When I was a girl," Zouri said, "Daddy would hold me on his lap and we'd gallop over the prairie for hours. The stallion's mane would sting my face, but when Daddy asked why I was crying, if he was hurting me, I'd say it was because the horse was so beautiful."

Seth wished Marion would hurry.

"He'd give me opium," Zouri said with a wistful smile. "Not laudanum as Mother does, but a purple gum we'd smoke in the gazebo. Then he'd take me riding, and it was like drifting through the sky miles and miles above the prairie."

She stopped and held his gaze across the distance between them. "It felt like that when you and I were making love as we tumbled through the air. I'd like for it to happen again."

"That was just a dream, Zouri."

"Didn't you make love to me once?"

"No."

"I remember it, Seth, and I remember my father laughing and

saying I should thank my lucky stars."

"That was Marley."

"What?"

"It was Marley who said that."

She shook her head, bewildered.

He moved toward the door.

"Don't leave me!" she cried in panic.

He turned back and said gently, "Take it easy, Zouri."

"You're angry, aren't you?"

"I just don't think we should be alone together."

"Why not?"

Thinking she sounded like a spoiled child, which he guessed she was, spoiled in a particularly vicious way, he smiled and said, "'Cause you always cry."

"That's not fair! I learned to be pretty when I cried because you said it pleased you!"

He saw the laudanum and moved to the bed, lifted the bottle and sat down beside her. "I think you need some more."

She sat up eagerly. "Yes."

He filled the spoon with the thick white liquid, pulled her close with his arm around her waist, and slid the spoon between her lips. She swallowed, then leaned against his chest.

"Don't leave until I'm asleep."

"All right."

She looked up at him, her eyes losing focus as the drug hit her bloodstream. "Kiss me, Seth. Won't you, please?"

He shook his head. "I've been drinking. Opium and whiskey don't mix."

"Don't you want to ride with me?" she whispered, so close her breath was warm on his mouth.

He laid her down and pulled the blankets to her shoulders, then stood up and saw Marion standing on the threshold. "I gave her some more laudanum," he said. "She was crying again."

Marion smiled. "I forgot your whiskey. I'll go back."

"No! I'll get it myself."

He pushed past her and kept moving down the dark hall and stairwell to the heart of the house. A blade of light sliced beneath the closed library door. He pushed it open and caught a whiff of lilac in the room.

What had Marion been doing here if not fetching his whiskey? Simon was deeply asleep with his head on the desk, and Seth wondered if she hadn't been conniving with the gargoyles to drown the kid's dreams.

Chiding himself for such thoughts, he knelt in front of the sideboard and opened the door to reveal a row of full bottles, all catching light in their amber depths of promised solace. He was touching one when Simon lurched awake.

Over his shoulder, Seth saw the hammer rise on the kid's gun. Instinctively he whirled and drew his own, pulling the trigger in the same instant he heard the click that told him Simon's was still empty.

The explosion echoed through the house as if it were ricocheting off the walls of the turrets, then he realized what he was hearing were feet on the stairs. Through the smoke he saw enough blood to know his remorse was useless. Numb, he watched Marion come in and hurry across to kneel by the kid. She felt for a pulse in his throat, then looked up at Seth.

"You'll have to stay now," she said. "You can't leave us without a man in the house."

He moved back till he hit the wall and slid to the floor, his gun still in his hand as he hid his face in the dark of his arms, as trapped as if his feet were set in stone.

*Y*ep; consequences, obligations, and duty. All of them there are some might frightening critters. Prob'ly more so than any of them other things I've been yarnin' about, eh, pard?

Yessir, duty can take a body down some mighty weird trails, and there's some as jus' ain't got the snuff fer it. But then there's them others who do what needs doin', no matter what this strange ol' world throws at 'em. Ain't sayin' they ain't scared doin' it, but they signed on to do a thing, and by damn it's their duty to see it through - if only so's they can keep on a'lookin' at themselves in the mirror.

You heard tell a Canadian Mountie always gets his man, ain't ya? Well, I'm here to tell ya son, they get whatever-all it is they go after. Whatever-all it is...

THE
NORTH-WEST
MONSTER POLICE
BY
CLAY & SUSAN GRIFFITH

It was the shank of another black winter evening in Bloody Hole when Black Jacques Schramme entered the saloon. His appearance was announced by a hammer blow of frigid wind and snow that scattered playing cards and well-thumbed newspapers. The startled prospectors looked up from their watery drinks and unsatisfying diversions.

Bloody Hole was a small, dilapidated Yukon settlement of hastily hammered shacks and patched tents thrown up in the wake of streaming hordes of men searching for gold. Nearby Borrowers Creek was now under two feet of snow and another foot of ice. The town's wretched population of disappointed remnants consisted of twenty ragged, raw-boned men who spent their time sitting under dim oil lamps and gathering around the crackling stove in the town saloon. They drank and talked about gold. They drank and talked about whiskey. They didn't talk about women. Most of them had been wandering the gold fields, trapped on the edges of civilization for too long to have a clear memory of decent female company.

Black Jacques Schramme would give them something to talk about; those that survived anyway.

Schramme towered over six feet tall with long black hair and a full beard caked in ice. His skin was burned dark by the sun and snow, and his eyes were pinpricks of sinister light. Swaddled in a thick bearskin coat and sporting a heavy fur hat, he looked like a grizzly that had wandered in from the forest for a drink. He shook snow off his shoulders and pulled off heavy fur mittens. On his left hand, he wore a tight leather glove.

"Whiskey," he said with a hint of Old French. He leaned back on the bar and eyed the men in the room. Schramme reeked of wildness, of a type of incivility that even these rough men, isolated from polite society as they were, had only heard about in tales of voyageurs. Schramme clearly intended to do whatever he wished in this saloon and anyone who questioned him should be prepared to risk his life. He slammed his whiskey glass down and the bartender promptly refilled it.

"Well, what a sorry lot." The bear of a man spat on the floor. "But you'll have to do." He threw back another whisky and wiped his sleeve across his frozen, matted beard. "Every empire has to start somewhere."

From outside came the sound of howling.

Constable Alexander Steele of the Northwest Mounted Police heard eerie howling in the wind that thundered across the frozen, forested countryside. His sled team reacted violently to the sound. Some dogs pulled in tangent directions, desperate to escape. Some simply stopped in their tracks, with their tails between their legs, and whimpered. Only Sargon, the lead dog, kept his head. He turned ferociously and tried to nip his followers to restore order.

"Hold, Sargon!" Steele shouted and the lead dog instantly stopped and looked expectantly at his master.

Steele was tall and thin, with calming eyes. He was wrapped in a heavy greatcoat lined in caribou fleece and fur hat with the earflaps loose. Steele judged the howling to be less than a mile away. Bloody Hole, he thought.

He removed his Winchester rifle, snowshoes, and a package wrapped in leather from the wooden sled, then overturned it. He unleashed Sargon and let him stand. He half-dragged the frightened dogs behind the makeshift windbreak of the sled. With downcast eyes the dogs circled and settled nervously in a pile, their fur tufted by the hard wind. Without a word, Steele started off through the blizzard. Sargon hopped dutifully behind him.

Soon, he squatted behind a rise and peered at the lonely town of

Bloody Hole. He couldn't make out details through the blowing snow. The only lights came from what he assumed was the town saloon. In the street in front of the saloon was a sledge with its team settled on the ground around it. The three pitch black dogs were gigantic, well over five feet tall at the shoulder, and frightening to see in stark relief against the white snow.

"*Loup garou.*" Steele let out a quiet breath. He had heard tales of these creatures and he knew Schramme often used their services. The beasts' senses were preternaturally acute. Steele would have to stay downwind and deal with their master first.

But Black Jacques Schramme would not be easy prey. He was a vicious man. Steele had been on Schramme's trail since he massacred a family in Regina three months before, disappearing into the night with the family's teenage son. Steele had been the only constable on the frontier available to pursue Schramme and bring him back. More murders followed the Regina outrage, sometimes for robbery, sometimes for pleasure. Along the way, two more young men disappeared after Schramme had attacked their homes and families. He easily could have skirted these isolated frontier homes on his way north, but instead sought out brutality. Steele felt sure that down in the street of Bloody Hole he had discovered the savage fate of those three unfortunate young men.

It was another of Schramme's crimes that truly chilled Steele's heart, and it was the reason he was the sole constable available to hunt down Schramme. The monster had committed a horrific assault on a NWMP customs house near Fort Chipewyan. Schramme's pitiless enmity toward the North-West Mounted extended back beyond the memory of even inveterate officers like Steele's beloved mentor, Inspector Thomas Collingwood. It was said, although many refused to believe it, that Schramme had been a leader of the Red River rebellion. Even in those wild days, though, the stories of his crimes had been circulating for fifty years.

Steele thought about the horrible murder of Inspector Collingwood that Schramme and his *loup garou* slaves had committed several weeks ago near Fort Chipewyan. He recaptured the sickening vision of his mentor's decapitated body lying frozen on the floor of the customs house, a cup of tea turned to ice sitting untouched on a nearby table. Steele thought back to the words of his mentor, given him at his first muster barely a year earlier: "We represent civilization," Inspector Collingwood said. "That is our sacred duty. The uniform is a powerful symbol of that duty." Then the Inspector had brushed a fleck, imaginary or real, off Steele's tunic. "Duty first, my boy. It's what separates us from the monsters."

Sargon nudged Steele as he inched through the snow next to his master. The dog caught a scent of the werewolves and started growling. Steele shushed him sharply and Sargon quietly shrank back. The constable rolled over and, with his back resting against the icy ground, he rechecked the silver loads in his rifle and service revolver. Then he untied the leather bundle he brought from the sled and rolled it out to reveal his red serge tunic.

"I said drink it!" Schramme threw the miner against the bar.

The frightened man stared at a glass of whiskey. Normally he wouldn't refuse a free drink, but after Schramme had dragged him from his table, the frightening stranger had brought a vial from under his bear coat and poured a clear liquid out of it into the whiskey.

The prospector looked up at the powerful Schramme and stammered, "Thank you for the offer. But I believe it might be Sunday, and the Almighty frowns on excessive imbibement."

Then another man stood up slowly. "Mormon" Jim Barkley wasn't a Mormon, but he was a large man, nearly as big as Schramme, and he had a more confident face than anyone else in the saloon. In fact, prior to Schramme's appearance, Mormon Jim had been the town threat. The room seemed relieved and emboldened by the fact that he now rose to put this stranger in his place.

Mormon Jim cracked his knuckles and stared at Schramme. "Mister, I think you best stop. Cabbage Tom is Presbyterian."

Cabbage Tom, the terrified prospector who stared at the whiskey glass on the bar, nodded vigorously. Schramme glanced at Mormon Jim, then he walked silently to the door of the saloon. The room let out a collective sigh of relief. One prospector near Mormon Jim slapped him on the arm. Schramme opened the door and walked outside, leaving the door wide open. The little saloon filled again with icy wind and blowing snow.

"Cabbage," Mormon Jim shouted over the wind, "close the door, how about it."

Cabbage Tom tore his eyes off the whiskey glass, noticing for the first time that Schramme was gone. He took a step toward the door, then let out a startled yelp. Schramme came back through the door, followed by a gigantic, black wolf. The room froze in shock. Schramme closed the door behind him. Then he casually pointed at Mormon Jim and snapped his fingers.

The huge wolf crossed the saloon in one bound and knocked the big prospector to the ground. Mormon Jim started to scream, but his throat was gone. The werewolf jerked its head up and Mormon Jim's head sailed across the room. Blood spurted like a geyser, coating the miner who had just given Mormon Jim a congratulatory arm slap.

Schramme shoved Cabbage Tom back to the bar. "Now drink."

Cabbage Tom couldn't stop watching the wolf as it noisily snapped through the dead man's rib cage and buried its snout in Mormon Jim's steaming organs. Tom dutifully swallowed the liquor.

"Welcome to my army." Schramme smiled down at Cabbage Tom. He pulled off the leather glove to reveal a left hand covered with tattoos and scarification. He placed the palm of his left hand on Tom's forehead. Schramme began to chant. The werewolf looked up from its twitching meal and began to howl, blood dripping off the matted fur of its snout.

Cabbage Tom began to howl too. It was a strange, painful sound from deep in his gut. He doubled over while Schramme raised his tattooed hand and continued chanting. Tom fell to the floor and continued to scream and howl. The horrified prospectors all watched Cabbage Tom writhe and twist his palsied limbs as he slowly transformed into a gigantic, black wolf. The fresh beast lay completely still except for its heaving chest, like a newborn. Its harsh breathing filled the otherwise silent saloon.

Schramme knelt and fingered open the new wolf's eyelids, studying its pupils. Satisfied, he pounded the beast's shoulder with rough, good-natured bonhomie. He chuckled as he stood and pulled several more of the vials of clear liquid out of his coat and placed them on the bar.

"Set 'em up," he said to the stupefied bartender. "Please pull drinks for all my new courtiers."

"Put up your hands, Mr. Schramme, and step away from the werewolf."

Constable Steele had come through a door from a back room and stood at the end of the bar with his service revolver at waist level pointed straight at Schramme. Even Schramme was speechless at the sudden appearance of this straight-backed, clear-eyed, clean-shaven policeman walking out of a blizzard in a small town at least two days from anywhere, looking none the worse for it, wearing his red dress parade uniform as he might on any sweet summer evening in Regina.

Steele heard the growling of the werewolf that was feeding off

Mormon Jim. But he didn't avert his rigid gaze or unwavering pistol from Schramme. "Let's have no nonsense. I'm loaded with silver."

Schramme's brow wrinkled with surprise. He held up his hand and grunted at the wolf. It continued its deep, throaty rumble, but was no longer primed to attack.

Steele said loudly, "Jacques Schramme, I place you under arrest in the name of His Royal Majesty, King Edward the seventh, and by the laws of the Dominion of Canada. Kindly place whatever weapons you may be carrying on your person onto the bar."

"Are you insane?" Schramme shook his head, eyebrows raised. He leaned on the bar and grinned, showing his brown, broken teeth. "I don't know how you showed up here in this way, but if you are loaded with silver, then you know who I am. And you must know what more I have outside. Do you think you can kill them all? And me?"

"I have no intention of killing anyone. Rather, you will accompany me back to Regina where you will stand trial for multiple murders, including that of Inspector Lawrence Collingwood of the North-West Mounted. And, for your sake, I sincerely hope you have the ability to transform these wolves back to men."

Schramme adopted a contrite air. "Very well, Constable. You have copped me fair and square. But I am afraid I cannot change these men back." He picked up a whiskey bottle and placed a booted foot on the prone form of the werewolf that used to be Cabbage Tom. Its eyelids were just starting to flutter as if coming out of a deep sleep. "Although you are clearly capable of shouldering more than your share of poor weather, you won't subject a prisoner to these conditions. Even me." He took a deep drought of whiskey and wiped his mouth. "So, we can't do anything but wait here for a break. You may be new to these parts, so I can tell you it may be a day; maybe a week. I wonder how long you can hold that pistol on me. Because the first time a distraction causes you to glance away or when your heavy eyes start to droop in all-consuming sleep, I think I'll kill you."

One of the prospectors shouted, "Kill him now, Constable! He killed Mormon Jim and turned Cabbage Tom into a big dog! He was going to turn all of us into dogs! And that ain't right!"

Schramme announced, "Mormon Jim threatened me and the unfortunate Cabbage Tom I needed to show you what I can do. But I promise you all, this Constable is sadly unhinged if he thinks he can stop me. This is my country; and his kind have no place in it. Those of you who join me will share power. I need brave men too, not just . . . these." He nudged the werewolf at his feet. "Whoever kills this Mountie can be a baron or earl in my new empire."

Several of the miners exchanged glances of interest.

Steele said, "I strongly caution you gentlemen against believing him. Promises of ease and wealth are the tools of a despot. He will betray and discard you as it suits his whims."

Schramme laughed. "You cannot lecture men such as these about the vagaries of life. They understand the uncertainties of the pursuit of wealth and power. Or else why would they be here? They would be haberdashers in *Monréale*. No, they know about life. They expect no promises. After all, what has his government given you?" Several of the prospectors nodded.

Steele answered, "The government promises nothing except to maintain the laws by which we all live. It is what separates us from the fanged chaos Mr. Schramme represents. I would remind you gentlemen that in the last two months, this man has murdered at least ten people - innocent men, women, and children. There is no count of the people he has massacred in his lifetime. I am here to insure he doesn't kill any more."

Schramme drank more whiskey and slammed the bottle down. Then he stretched his arms wide with pedantic fervor. "I have killed in my time, it's true. But you see, I am over one hundred and fifty years old." Men gasped. "Yes, one hundred and fifty. I was born before the British came. This power and more I took from ancient Indian medicine men, Cree and Blackfoot and tribes of the eastern woodlands that no longer exist. But unlike those savages I understand the ways of our modern world. That is why I am here to conquer the gold fields. For that will give me the financing to build an empire." He swept his arm across the saloon's company. "And none of you need die. Ever. I have the power to preserve all life. If you don't believe me, let's ask a recent traveling companion of mine."

Schramme made a motion toward his coat. Steele tensed his gun arm. Schramme held out his hands, palms out, and smiled. Then he slowly pulled open his heavy fur coat. Hanging from his wide leather belt by a cord was a canvas bag containing something about the size of a cabbage. There was a dark stain on the bottom of the bag. He set the bag on the bar and untied the twine that closed it. The bag fell open.

Steele unwittingly exclaimed, "Good God."

Sitting on top of the bar was the head of Inspector Lawrence

Collingwood. Its eyes were open and its mouth moving.

Lost in the horrible sight, Steele began to lower his pistol, but caught an expectant glint in Schramme's eye and brought the weapon back up. He felt as if the wind had been knocked out of him and he couldn't suppress a shudder.

Schramme laid his left hand on the graying brown hair of the disembodied head and whispered several words to it. Then he said aloud, "Inspector Collingwood, don't you have a fond greeting for your brother in red?"

Collingwood's mouth churned wordlessly for a few seconds followed by a croaking sound and then a sibilantly pathetic, "Please."

Several men in the room audibly gasped. Steele pointed his revolver at Collingwood's head.

"Oh, he absolutely will not die unless I release him," Schramme warned. "But he can still feel pain; so if you wish to inflict more on him, feel free."

Steele took a second to steady his voice and said to the terrified prospectors, "I hope you can see that this man is a monster. His empire is an abomination."

Collingwood's voice slithered out again, "Steele, please . . ."

Steele's mouth tightened into a slit. Schramme chortled.

Collingwood's eyes rolled. "Save yourself."

"Duty first, sir." Steele mechanically brushed the front of his tunic. And he glanced at the tortured face of his old friend.

The werewolf on the floor by the bar, the former Cabbage Tom, suddenly scrambled to its feet and lunged at Steele. The Constable lowered the pistol and fired. It screamed; it front legs splayed and it collapsed on the floor. Instantly, Schramme whistled and the more experienced werewolf exploded out from between tables.

Steele swiveled his arm and fired twice. The beast hurtled through the blue cloud of gun smoke and slammed into Steele, knocking him to the wooden plank floor. In the melee, miners scrambled under tables while Schramme walked to the front door.

Steele was pinned under dead weight. He struggled to free his gun arm from beneath the still-quivering corpse of the werewolf. The werewolf that had been Cabbage Tom kept scrambling forward despite its wound, trailing blood behind it. It snapped at the constable. Steele twisted his foot and caught the bite against the hard sole of his boot. The werewolf gnawed and Steele knew that it wouldn't be long before it tore through the leather of his boot.

He kicked the biting snout of the werewolf with his other foot. At the same time he managed to drag his right arm out from under the warm dead wolf body. Cabbage Tom tore away a portion of the boot sole, revealing Steele's wool sock. The Constable brought his pistol up and down over the dead wolf and shot poor Tom in the forehead.

Steele managed to push himself from under the dead werewolf just as two more were at the front door. They struggled to be first through the door, giving Steele time to fire his last two bullets as he regained his feet. He grazed the lead wolf in the shoulder, but the second shot popped into the door frame.

Steele raced through the half open back door, dropped the revolver, and grabbed the Winchester that he had placed just inside the room. He slammed the door shut behind him and heard the heavy thud of the wolves crashing into the door followed immediately by the sound of splintering wood.

Steele crashed out the window, fell in the snow, and rolled. He came up on one knee and leveled the rifle back at the saloon. He fired at snarling, dark hulks that crowded the window.

One werewolf dropped dead across the window and tumbled heavily back into the room. As Steele levered another shell into the chamber, he briefly saw the red eyes of the second wolf glaring at him. Then it turned and disappeared back into the saloon.

Steele edged quickly through the alley. He tightened the chin strap on his hat to keep it from blowing off because appearance was half the battle. He felt chilling wetness on his foot where Cabbage Tom had bitten off part of the sole of his boot. With his rifle trained carefully on the open front door of the saloon, he stepped out into the snow-blown street.

"Jacques Schramme!" he called out over the wind. "I call on you to surrender yourself in the name of the law."

He saw Schramme inside the warm, yellow light of the saloon. The big man walked to the door and stood in plain view. The last werewolf prowled behind him, snarling and snapping.

"Here I am, Constable," Schramme shouted. "Surely you want to kill me now."

Steele eyed the villain. It would be a simple thing to kill him; just because he had conspired to live more than a century didn't mean he couldn't die. He deserved it for what he'd done to Collingwood, for the families he'd killed in the south, and for the four men whom he'd transformed into monsters. Steele felt the heft of the rifle in his hand.

Duty first. It's what separates us from the monsters.

Steele responded evenly, "You will face a jury for your crimes."

Schramme gave an exaggerated, theatrical shrug. *"C'est la vie.* Your laws do not apply in my empire. So shoot me or freeze to death. But do one of them soon."

Steele stood impassively in the roaring snowstorm, ready to fire only if Schramme made a move toward transforming any more of the prospectors in the saloon. He didn't move a muscle even though he began to lose feeling in his feet from the cold.

Schramme watched the immobile Constable for a moment with a smile. Then as the minutes passed, the smile faded. After a few more minutes, Schramme began to snarl. Finally Schramme spat and turned back inside.

Steele watched him stalk to the bar and seize the head of Inspector Collingwood by the hair. He returned to the door and threw the head out. It landed in the snow and rolled to Steele's feet.

"Here!" Schramme screamed. "Have some company while you wait!"

Steele kept his Winchester trained on the door with one arm as he knelt and turned his friend's face up. Collingwood's mouth was working grotesquely.

"Hand," Collingwood rasped.

"Sir?"

"Hand," was all he said then his eyes shut as if in exhaustion.

Steele stood and brought the rifle up smartly to his shoulder. "Very well, Schramme." He sited down the barrel. "Have it your way."

Schramme was surprised and momentarily confused. But then he saw Steele take the rifle down and look at it. It had misfired. Schramme stepped out onto the wood board porch and pointed his left hand at Steele, snapping his fingers. The last werewolf bolted at the Constable.

"Weapon!" Steele shouted as the werewolf struck him in a brutish collision. It's jaws clamped around the Winchester he thrust up for protection.

From the darkness beside the saloon, Sargon loped into sight and bounded up onto the porch, clamping his jaws around Schramme's extended left hand. He had been waiting patiently since Steele placed him downwind of the werewolves. "Weapon" was his trigger to seize a target by the nearest exposed arm or hand and not let go until released. The dog bit deeply into the unprotected hand, shaking his head vigorously.

"No! No!" Schramme screamed, trying to pull his hand away from the dog's mouth, but that only tore more of the tattoo markings and scarification.

Steele's face was bathed in the steaming breath and hot spittle of the werewolf. The creature tensed its shoulders and shook him like a terrier shakes a rat. He saw the werewolf's teeth punching holes in the rifle's metal fittings. Another few seconds and it would snap the Winchester into two pieces and Steele's throat would be vulnerable.

But then the creature suddenly stopped shaking him and released its grip on the gnarled rifle. Its bulk still loomed over Steele, but it apparently forgot about him. Its nostrils flared and it looked back at the saloon door. Then it raised its head and released a terrifying howl.

"Back!" Steele shouted. Sargon released Schramme and stood. Steele scrambled out from under the werewolf as it slowly turned its monstrous body toward Schramme. "Go!" Steele commanded and Sargon began to back away, his fur bristling, switching its eyes between Schramme and the werewolf.

Schramme fell back against the door jamb. He cradled his bloody left hand. Then he saw the werewolf striding purposefully through the snow in his direction. He held up his hand to ward it off, but it was useless. The magical configuration of tattoos and scarification had been permanently destroyed by the Constable's dog. His power was gone.

And the werewolf felt it.

Schramme started to turn and run, but the werewolf was on him. He was brought down instantly, slammed against the saloon floor. The creature latched onto the back of his head and bit down. Schramme quivered and lay still. The werewolf lapped at his blood.

Steele hastily examined the Winchester. He had feigned a misfire to lure the werewolf's attack, leaving Schramme vulnerable to Sargon. Now he tried to work the lever, but it was stuck fast. He was defenseless. When he stood up, the werewolf quickly responded, whirling to face him. It lowered its head and snarled. Its red eyes glowed and blood dripped from its snout. Steele moved one foot slightly and the wolf charged.

The black blur was suddenly intersected by a smaller streak of gray. Sargon struck the large wolf and knocked it off its feet. The dog had the advantage of position, snapping viciously at the werewolf's shoulder, trying to avoid the gnashing teeth of the beast.

Steele ran past the tooth-filled battle into the saloon. He vaulted over the blood-drenched corpse of Schramme and scrambled past overturned tables and chairs. In the back room, he recovered his abandoned revolver, snapped open the cylinder, and shook out the spent shells. He dug into his belt ammunition pouch for more silver bullets and ran back to the door. Only taking the time to slip in three shells, he clicked shut the cylinder and raised the pistol.

Sargon was down. The werewolf had the dog by the back of the neck and was shaking him. Steele stepped closer and, as he did, took careful aim along the barrel. He fired two shots into the broad, black back of the werewolf. It released Sargon, who flopped into the snow like an old rug. The wolf reared on its hind legs, snarling and howling. It looked at Steele.

Steele sighted the werewolf between the eyes. When he fired, it was gone. He grabbed instantly for his ammo pouch. Then he saw the beast racing away from him, running like a wounded animal, but still making incredible speed into the roaring blizzard and dark forest.

Steele walked to the limp body of Sargon, lying in the red snow. He knelt beside the dog and placed his hand on the animal's chest. Sargon's breathing was shallow. The dog opened its eyes, raising its head and whining in pain at the effort.

"I'm sorry," Steele said softly. "Duty, boy. Duty."

Steele looked out the window of the new customs house. It was dark outside. Snow was falling again and the full moon would be rising soon, awakening the hidden landscape in brilliant luminous life. Steele could hear the comforting sound of the coming moon already ringing off the luscious snow.

After the Schramme affair, Steele's superiors had dictated that it was imperative to place the steadying and civilizing hand of the government on Bloody Hole. And they commanded that Steele should man the new post. It was left to Steele to decide how best to exert the mandate of progress over the lawless frontier.

"I'll be back in a minute," he said and went out the front door.

He trudged through the deafening snow to a stout fir tree behind the cabin. Sargon was bound to the tree with an enormous chain that seemed completely unnecessary for a dog his size. The dog wagged his tail cheerfully as Steele checked the strength of the chain for the tenth time that day.

"This should hold you better than the last one." He scratched Sargon behind the ears. "We can't have you nearly escaping like last month; my control is not that strong."

He left the dog and returned to the cabin.

"The fire is fading," a voice greeted him as he entered.

Steele stomped snow off his boots and nodded to the head of Inspector Collingwood, which rested on a cushioned footstool near the crackling hearth. After Schramme's death, his magic began to fade. Steele made an exhaustive study of cryptic notes he found among Schramme's goods and managed to preserve the fading health of his old friend's head and allowed Collingwood to retain his gruesome semblance of life. Collingwood's ability to speak had improved, in a way that Steele could not understand since he had no lungs. The head had unnerved Steele at first, but in the intervening weeks he had become quite used to it and thought no more of it than attending to a beloved, invalided relative. In addition, Steele felt bolstered by the traditions of the service represented by the presence of his old commanding officer; and he felt the continuity was significant in creating an aura of governmental authority in the region.

He placed another log on the fire and held his chilled hands in front of the flame for a luxurious moment. He flexed the fingers of his left hand. The scarification had left a numbness in the knuckles, which grew worse in the cold.

"Will the thaw begin soon?" Collingwood asked.

"Another month, I think. I'll cast bones later this week. That should give us a better notion."

"Good."

Steele nodded. "We'll have a lot of men passing through. But I expect we can keep them in order."

"Duty," Collingwood croaked.

"Duty. Quite right." Steele heard Sargon howling outside, beginning to change with the full moon. Steele stood and straightened his well-pressed red serge tunic. He smiled at the head of his commanding officer. "It is what separates us from the monsters."

Strange what some men'll do if they's pushed to it, eh? You'd be surprised what a feller kin get used to in these parts, especially if there ain't no choice in it. And all in the name of justice.

And there's all brands of justice, don'cha see? There's the kind that the law brings with it, but sometimes that there sort of justice don't bring a body no satisfaction. Then there's another sort, which don't have much to do with the laws of men, but will surefire get the job done fer ya.

But ya gotta move real careful-like if yer after that sort of justice, 'cause ya jus' might find you've got yerself a mountain lion by the tail - or somethin' a whole heap bigger...

ALL AROUND THE MULBERRY BUSH

BY C.J. HENDERSON

Now, there's some people what say it's all a myth, just a tall tale some yokel spun one night when there was more liquor than coffee in his cup, and more fools than sensible folk gathered 'round the fire. Lord knows you might be inclined to think that's the truth in this case, 'cause this is a hell of a tale and I'll tell you right now even I can't hardly believe it.

Of course, you know how that works - a story catches on, gets told and retold a mess an'a half a times, and suddenly it's woven into the fabric of American folklore. Some'll say it's an out-and-out lie, and some others'll hoot at 'em and get all belligerent and start citin' ancestor worship and religious freedom and a few more fancy whozits, but I believe we can forego such things. What I think might be best is if'n I just tell you what I was told and then you judge the facts for yourself.

That all being said, why don't you sit back and let me tell you the story of Gao Chi Lin. Now ol' Gao, he was one of the unnamed many who helped put together the railroads back in the 1860s. He wasn't working any ordinary track push, though, nosiree. He was part of the Homeric drive to link the mighty Union Pacific and Central Pacific railroads, the move that would finally stretch an unbroken transport line thousands of miles, from one end of America to the other.

Not that Gao cared much about moving cattle or indoor plumbing parts or anything else from here to there. His was not what you might call an executive position. No, Gao was one of the Chinese workers who struggled to lay all that track, a blistering, backbreaking, merciless job for any human being. Not that ol' Gao had been given much choice in the matter.

You see, the railroads sent representatives to all sorts of places lookin' for workers. Those what went to China found a whole lot of people without a whole lot of money. What seemed like slave wages back in America came across like a princess' dowry in the Middle Kingdom. So, a lot of Chinese signed on to lay track not quite knowin' what they were gettin' themselves into. They found out, though. Oh Lord, they surely did.

Track got laid from dawn till dusk. It got laid in the freezin' rain and the broilin' sun. It got laid during every moment there was light, and sometimes that meant working under lanterns and next to bonfires. Of course, workin' at a frantic pace under less than ideal conditions can lead to accidents. And there were certainly accidents a'plenty gettin' the railroads built. Men died in all manner of ways. They died in land-clearing explosions. They died from insect and reptile bites. They died from falls and they died from the chills and the runs and plenty of 'em just up and died from exhaustion.

Gao Chi Lin, being a most practical sort, decided early on that he didn't especially want to die. Not in a strange land far from home where the food was bad and the people were ugly, anyway. Laying track, he decided, was no job for a skilled poet. So, Gao, he prayed. He prayed to go home.

Now at first his prayers were pretty elaborate things. They involved him making fools of the railroad bosses and freeing all his fellow workers. They were colorful dreams, with lots of sword fights and wicked Western women who would try to tempt Gao and all manner of pitfalls that he would prevail over with ease. As you might expect, he and all his fellows (excepting, of course, for some of the more boisterous Irish workers, like Kevin Peter Norton, but then that's another tale, ain't it) would all end up with sacks of gold and ivory and jade teapots and the like, and everyone would acknowledge that they owed all their good fortune to Gao.

They were fine hopes backed by bags of sincere and righteous praying, but they didn't change anything. Every night Gao would pray with reverence and dream with hope, and every morning the line boss would hand him a pick or a shovel and the misery would begin all over again.

After a while, both Gao's prayers and his dreams got remarkably simpler. It really didn't take all that long before he wasn't interested in vanquishing foes or proving moral superiority or gatherin' bags of wealth. All he was prayin' for at that time was to get back to China. And he wasn't at all fussy about how he got there, either. Gao didn't care if'n he was swept up on a cloud and flown home, or swallowed by a giant fish, or anything. He just prayed to go home each and every night with a fervent desire before he went to sleep.

But, every morning he was jarred awake by the line boss's less than soothing voice. As he rubbed the sleep from his eyes someone would shove a pry bar in his hands and Gao would see that he was still in America, which for him was just another name for the Hell the Irish and Mexican workers jabbered about constantly.

After not much longer, Gao gave up praying for wealth and happiness. He even resigned himself to never seeing China again. At that point his prayers were all aimed at just gatherin' in some relief. You know what I mean - for the sun to beat less brutally, for his pick to not seem so horribly heavy by the end of the day, for just a bit more food at dinner.

Of course, as you might be able to guess, his condition did not change to any degree sufficient for him to even pretend to recognize the hand of divine intervention. After a few more months his devotions became irregular and his heart hardened. As hope ran out so did his sense of charity and after a while his prayers became demands with the chance to shuffle off this mortal coil the chief concern of his heavenly insistence. But once again there was no relief. Every night Gao's last thoughts were of never waking, and every morning he heard the gods' laughter crawling through the desert heat. And finally, one day, well, it just all got the best of him.

It'd been a horrible day, even by the standards of railroad work. The Mexicans had finished clearing the debris from the day before's blasting, which meant a full day of uphill track work for the Chinese crew. The supply train was a week behind because of a washout down the line, which meant the crew was down to hardtack and cold beans. There was no wood to cook with, no water to drink outside of a man's ration of three sips a day, and no reason for anyone workin' track in the 118° heat to think that life was ever goin' to be anything more than one slab of misery after another, each one heavier, hotter and smellin' worse than the one before it.

On that day, Gao fell over from heat exhaustion four times. Each time he lay where he fell, the sand and rocks burnin' his skin, waitin' for a boss to slap him in the back of the head with a pick handle or nudge his kidneys with an over-sized boot. On that night, Gao consolidated all his previous dreams and hopes and desires into one burnin', fervent prayer for vengeance.

And that, my friend, is when things got interesting.

It was 'round about three in the morning that Gao woke up. There was a scuffling noise comin' from the direction of the altar he'd put together for himself unlike anything he had heard before. Oh, there'd been nights when other workers had crawled over, greedy to filch the scraps of food or the pennies he'd put out as a sacrifice, but this was different. This wasn't any kind of human noise he'd ever heard before.

Turnin' as slow as he could, Gao peered through the desert night, the silver illumination of a large full moon revealin' the most unbelievable sight to him. There at his makeshift tabernacle stood a humanoid figure that froze his heart and made the wind twirl his hair. It didn't stand more than five feet tall, though the size it'd chosen to appear in wasn't really all that important. It was merely a convenient height for walking the world of man.

Even with its back turned to Gao, the poet knew what he was looking at. The thing stood studyin' Gao's altar, strokin' a small but animated cloud that moved before it in the air like some cumulus spaniel. It had a body short of leg and long of arm, decked out in a wardrobe of the finest Chinese silk - resplendent robes covered in delicate designs, stitched with thread made from the purest gold and silver - a body with knuckles hairier than many a man's pate, topped by a head with a simian face and eyes that saw men's souls as just so many leaves, pretty things that fell and dried and danced at the merest whim of the breeze. Falling to his knees, his face pressed into the ground, Gao gasped in fear...

"Shiu Yin Hong!"

And the great and terrible Monkey King turned to study his petitioner. Of course, Gao had not prayed directly to the volatile entity that stood before him. Now, it's true enough that the heat and pain and never-ending hate churnin' within him had probably made him a bit crazy by some standards, but certainly not enough to unleash Shiu Yin Hong on an unsuspecting world.

The problem with the Monkey King was his unpredictability. He was a powerful enough being - there was no doubtin' that. He could grow to the size of a mountain or shrink down to a height compatible with jugglin' electrons. He could jump a hundred miles, fight an entire army, drink a river; the number of cosmic parlor tricks in his arsenal were practically without number. He could confound men or gods with equal ease and had been punished by the lords of the Heavens as often as he'd been rewarded by them. But no matter how often he was punished for annoyin' others of the celestial company of players, he really couldn't help himself. Creating mischief was his main goal in life, and he just didn't care who he annoyed or how badly he did so in his constant quest for personal amusement.

Appearing directly in front of Gao's prostrate form - the Monkey King couldn't be bothered to walk a few paces when ripping a hole in the fabric of space and sliding through it was just as easy - Shiu Yin Hong gave the poet his audience. Pulling Gao up from the ground, he asked the nature of the poet's petition. After so many months of fruitless prayer, Gao was more than happy to unburden himself.

He told the Monkey King of the conditions of his being plucked from China. He spoke of the loss of face and family, of the cruel sea voyage, and the miserable conditions he'd experienced working on the railroad. He went on with some eloquence about the horrible heat of the day and the desert's nighttime frost. He painted vivid pictures of sandstorms and flash rains, bison stampedes and prairie fires. And with his poet's flair he described in aching detail the terrible labors he and his fellows were forced to perform. He spoke of backbreaking duties, of dragging ponderous oak ties and lengths of rail, of endless hours of sledging spikes and lugging barrels of the same. And he told of the cripplings and maimings, of the shattered limbs and ruined eyes, of teeth and fingers and legs lost, of blood and sickness and the endless parade of casual death that he had witnessed.

Now, up until that point Shiu Yin listened with a kind of reserved indifference. Considerin' the amount of human tragedy he'd caused in his time, Gao's story hadn't up to that point really managed to touch him in any way. He kept listening, however, because Gao was an animated and interestin' storyteller and being somewhat of a god, well it wasn't like he had any kind of schedule to keep. On top of that, cleverly Gao hadn't relayed the elements of his tale in an order of importance as they related to him. Being an at least adequate poet, he knew to tell his story as things would concern his audience. Thus, after telling of the fate of his best friend in the work force - a pleasant middle-aged man from Xian who had ended his days when a rail car's chains had burst, splitting the worker with a shower of steel lengths - Gao suddenly, innocently, asked the Monkey King of his last meal before he left Heaven.

Well, Shiu Yin Hong painted a wonderful picture. He told of a platter of sliced meats and tripe followed by heavily sauced scallops, scallions and carrots, served in a basket made of delicate strips of french-fried yam. He mentioned chickens braised, steamed and flash-fried in sesame oil, beef on sticks and in gravies, fish in oil and parsley and fried rolls filled with all manner of meat and vegetables. There had been a course of battered shrimp lain on a bed of broccoli topped with candied walnuts and a plate of yellow bean sprouts chopped with beef and coated in pepper. There was shark fin soup and ginger candy and lotus paste buns and many other deserts that made the Monkey King smack its lips in greedy memory as Gao did his best not to drool as his mouth filled with saliva.

When Shiu Yin had finished relating the requested menu, he inquired as to why ol' Gao had asked. The poet told him. He told him what he and the other railroad workers had been fed since their arrival in America. He spoke of hard tack and salt pork and stale, dry crackers, of navy beans served in a watery tomato sauce and greasy, lard meats, thin and stringy and riddled with maggots. He spoke of paste-lumpy porridge and cactus sage and boiled snakes. And then, suddenly, Gao dared peek at Shiu Yin Hong's face, and he saw that the Monkey King was weeping. Globs of water and salt the size of grapes springing from the creature's eyes, he spoke in a voice layered with outrage.

"You shall be avenged."

And that was when everything finally got set into motion.

Stepping up onto the faithful mound of cloud that'd been swirling around his legs, the Monkey King flew upward into the sky and began studyin' the area. He looked over the track route as it was obviously planned, and the territory toward which it was headed. You see, Shiu Yin didn't plan on just slaughterin' the work bosses or anything simple like that. No, the revenge he planned to extract for Gao had to be in kind. Those who had orchestrated the terrible indignities visited upon his petitioner could not simply be killed or tortured, they had to be made to feel that a cold and indifferent universe had abandoned them, just as Gao had felt it. And for that, he needed to strike them in their most vulnerable spot, the place where they thought themselves strongest, but were actually weakest.

Their pocketbooks.

You see, the Monkey King knew a thing or two about tyrants. Oh, he'd dealt with more than a few of them in his time. He knew just swoopin' in on them and killing their families or tearing their heads off really wouldn't balance out any scales in any kind of cosmic sense. No, they'd taken a lot from ol' Gao, and they'd done it slowly with an almost childlike indifference. So, that was the way they had to be paid back. And, after studyin' the lay of the land for a while, Shiu Yin saw just how to do it.

You see, the line had just reached Selby Pass, the spot where it was gonna push the railroad on through the mountains. Dynamite and picks and mules and men had been workin' in the area for months, clearing away a monumentally impressive amount of rock. That crew was now some miles ahead, workin' on leveling off the next disruption an indignant nature had thrown in the path of the almighty rail line. But, back at the building base it was time to slap track on through the passage and move on. With a chuckle, the Monkey King put his cloud into a dive and landed himself right in the middle of the pass. Then, jumpin' down to the ground, he burrowed under the desert floor with a speed unbelievable, headed for a destination so insane that if Gao'd known what he was up to the poet might literally have died.

Far below the sand and sage above, Shiu Yin Hong made his way steadily downward. You see, what all good Chinese know, but others might not, is that inside the Earth resides a powerful and ancient force known as the Eternal Dragon. This critter is an easily irritated and somewhat irrational beast, one given to moods both radiant and terrible at the least provocation. Dig a well with just the right dimensions and it might cause gentle daily rain throughout the growing season. Build a house at a bad angle and you could bring a tornado down on your roof.

The Chinese have a whole kind of religion built up around keeping the dragon happy called Feng Shui. But Shiu Yin had no need of it that day. If'n there was anything he was plannin', it didn't have nothin' to do with keep that dragon happy.

Finding his way to the great sleeping beast, the Monkey King worked himself down around to its face, or more precisely, its muzzle. Then, positionin' himself before the creature's left nostril, he reached down into the lower recesses of his left lung for any faint aroma of that last glorious meal he'd consumed before he'd left Heaven. Sucking the tender fragrances upward, he breathed them gently into the gaping cavern before him. Hints of shredded ginger and lobster meat intertwined with a mix of peaches and peppers. Whiffs of coconut and apple, succulent beef, tender pork and crispy chicken all tickled the great dragon's nose, causing the creature to shudder in gentle delight.

The Monkey King stifled his urge to laugh. Powerful as he was, still he was not a being to challenge such a fearsome entity. Instead, he worked his way to the base of his right lung, pullin' up every last vestige of culinary memory it contained, releasin' the tantalizing aromas into the dragon's right nostril. Oyster sauce and lotus root, pineapple melon cake, hard sausages graced with onions and mushrooms, and a score of other, more wonderful smells tingled the sleeping titan's memories of such luxuries. Great, city-swampin' pools of saliva began to form within the dragon's cheeks. As the happy dreamer shuddered with delight, the Monkey King scrutinized his target. The normally guarded monster had relaxed into a comfortable, accepting position. A wicked grin cracking one side of Shiu Yin's simian face, he said,

"Why, I do believe you're ready."

And so, turning his back on the Eternal Dragon, the most fearsome force in all existence, the Monkey King dropped his embroidered silk drawers, bent over, and with a thunderin' "blat" released a staggering burst of rancid gas directly into the great beast's face. Shiu Yin disappeared into the surrounding darkness in an instant, only a split-second before the dragon awoke with a frightening start. Banana-scented it might have been, but the Monkey King's fart was a wet and horrible wake-up call, and the dragon was not amused. Its roar tore open the sky, pullin' down rain, hail and a barrage of toads that were just as surprised as those upon whom they fell. The spines on the dragon's back tore through the air as it rolled in disgusted surprise, bringing down the mountains on both sides of the pass as well as cracking open the Earth in every direction.

The Eternal Dragon was awake for only a moment, but the damage was done. For some seven miles back the way the railroad had come, the line had been shattered like matchsticks. Ties and rails lay in shards, bent and broken about each other like so much china after a drunken kitchen fight. The Monkey King delighted at creating such a splendid amount of chaos. Back at Gao's side, he put his arm around the poet, spreading his hairy hand across the horizon to point out all he had accomplished.

Of course, having fulfilled Gao's request, that put him in the situation of having to *keep* filling that request. Taking on the responsibility once meant he'd taken it on for good. In other words, if the train came back to Selby Pass, the Monkey King would be obliged to respond if Gao wanted to see it torn up again. But, Shiu Yin didn't really care much, since it'd been such fun to do so - especially by tweaking the Eternal Dragon to do so.

Now, in truth, Shiu Yin had the power to cause that amount of damage all on his own, but that just wasn't his way. Making the Dragon do his bidding not only cleared him of any cosmic responsibility - in his mind, anyway - but to him it was just more fun to create that amount of mischief and not get caught.

Even Gao went along with his way of thinkin'. Sure, all that damage just meant harder conditions and more work than ever, but at that point the poet simply didn't care anymore. He'd grown too used to the thought of spending his life clearin' rock, breathin' dust and wearin' heat like a bonnet. But for the first time since he'd arrived in America, ol' Gao was finally smiling. As he saw it, things hadn't changed for him, but they had for the rail bosses. He still got the same amount of food and water and sleep and all, but those men who owned the railroad were no longer enjoyin' the same life. No, they had lost something. They had lost money and they had lost face. And it pleased Gao no end to think on it.

That day while everyone else groaned and gnashed their teeth, Gao worked with a renewed spirit. He swung his pick with extra vigor, even leading his countrymen in song at one point. Over the next few weeks, work practically flew by for Gao as all the incredible damage the Eternal Dragon had caused was repaired. He worked with a fevered look in his eye, pushin' those around him to work harder and faster. By the time they reached Selby Pass once more, he was practically in a lather. Of course, that might have been because he knew what was comin'.

And, that night, well, it surely came. Long after dark the Monkey King returned, asking his poet if he felt the railroad owners still needed to be punished. Gao answered in the positive and ol' Shiu Yin was gone in a flash, back to the snout of the Eternal Dragon. Again came the delicate hints of crystalline sugar candies, leechee nuts and roasted pork buns, of buttered jellyfish, sesame chicken and curried spinach. Again the dragon's unconscious desires lowered its defenses to sniff the air for more of the delicious hints. And again the Monkey King let rip a green and purple cloud of curdling fumes so noxious the dragon opened both eyes simply to allow its tears to wash away the blinding poison.

Once more the Eternal Dragon rolled and tore and stamped, snorting in extreme and calculated displeasure. When it was through, lightning shattered the night sky in response, splattering against the plains below, illuminating the terrible damage. The dazzling light showed that some twenty-three miles of track had been destroyed, sliced and broken in so many different ways that for the rail bosses trying to explain what had happened, no words were adequate.

Gao, of course, was simply gleeful. Some might have called him crazed, but terminology was a looser thing back then, so I don't guess we'll ever actually know for certain. But, what we do know is that the bosses got everyone movin', just like they did the time before, and the whole stretch was replaced, and when Selby Pass was reached once more, well, of course, didn't Gao summon the Monkey King and didn't they do it all over again.

And like they say, the third time's the charm. The Monkey King's epic third teasing of the dragon left an entire stretch of forty-five miles of track bent and worthless, and didn't that inspire the president of the railroad to send word that he would be comin' out - personally, mind you - to see this Selby Pass for himself. What's more, didn't he plan on bringin' every other bigwig in the company with him.

Well, ol' Gao was tickled silly at that point. For the entire time it took to get the line back up to Selby Pass, it seemed he couldn't have been more content than if'n he'd been crowned the emperor of China himself. Ironically, the amazing dedication and seeming loyalty he'd shown in his single-minded devotion to rebuilding the railroad after every earthquake had brought him favorable attention in the rail bosses' eyes. Slowly, he started to be given less and less physical labor to do. Recognizin' that there was something to his manner beyond that of the average coolie, the bosses made Gao somethin' of a boss himself. In fact, after the third quake, why Gao didn't touch a pry bar or a sledge except to pass it out to another worker. He was a boss himself, with more food, less work, and a much better place to sleep. Incredibly, he found himself givin' orders to some five hundred other Chinese, and being well paid to do so.

Some say it's just the American way. Whatever, when the crews had dragged their weary way back to Selby pass for the fourth time, and the special train carryin' all the railroad brass pulled up in the early morning, Gao was no longer in much of a mind to see any more retribution casually thrown around. In a way, he realized, his prayers had been answered. He was eatin' better, sleepin' longer, and workin' a lot less hard. He was management, for gosh sakes. And maybe, just maybe, he thought, it was time for him to take a look at the big picture.

Besides, he was being given a special honor. He was going to be presented to the president of the railroad as the most outstanding worker the line had ever seen. Word had reached to the coast about the coolie who worked harder than any two white men. What those sendin' the messages couldn't have known, of course, was that Gao's positive attitude in gettin' the line back to Selby Pass didn't quite have as much to do with promoting the glory of the Union Pacific Rail Company as they might have thought. Still, he'd done the work and was going to get his due.

So that's why it was, when the president's private train pulled into the work camp, Gao was clean and shaved and proper for presentin' to a captain of industry. Gao and his foreman advanced on the sitting train, waitin' for the rear door of the president's car to open. It did after a moment, and Gao and the foreman were waved inside. And wasn't there a whole world of surprise waitin' within for the poet. You see, all Gao knew of trains were the cattle cars he'd ridden in and the flat beds that brought in the work supplies. He'd never seen a Pullman car, let alone one designed by a man with unlimited resources for his own unconditional comfort. To say that the poet was startled would be the most grievous of understatements.

A cut crystal chandelier hung from the ceiling. Exotic potted plants were set in delicate planters on the walls, walls made of the richest mahogany, inlaid with gold. A vase of ostrich feathers sat on the president's desk, only one of a hundred casual, expensive touches that stood about no matter which way one looked. Gao's eyes sought to take it all in, but his time to be amazed was cut short as the president, a stout and balding man, advanced from behind his desk to meet his hardest working employee.

At the man's side came a dog of some type, a round thing that waddled on fat legs, leavin' splotches of drool on the polished floor wherever it went. Gao's first reaction was to be amused by the pathetic thing. But then, his poet's mind went causin' trouble for him. In a moment of clarity he realized that somewhere along the line, that glazed-eyed sack of flab and hair had somehow pleased the railroad owner - just as he had.

It was a startlin' thought - a dreamy, self-deluded lap dog - that was what he'd become. Suddenly Gao remembered, he'd expected his repeated destructions to cripple the railroad, to bring the bosses to their knees, desperate and beggin' for relief. Looking around the richly appointed car, he saw not the slightest hint of poverty. Staring at the beefy railroad president lumbering toward him, he noted no signs of despair. Not in the man's freshly pressed suit, fat, flush face, or in the well-manicured hand extended to shake his own.

Nothing had been crippled, Gao realized bitterly, except his own resolve. And then, as his hand traveled upward automatically to shake that of the president, Gao's gaze drifted past the man's face out the window of the car. His fingers mere inches from the railroad owner's, the poet saw the other workers outside in the desert heat, struggling with their labors, and in a flash of shame, well, ol' Gao could do only one thing.

"Shiu Yin Hong!"

The president of the railroad took a step back, not knowin' exactly what the Chinaman before him was shoutin', but understandin' the man's tone well enough to realize it wasn't some sort of greetin'.

Outside the car, the rail workers all looked upward as the sky opened and a dazzling streak threw itself down to the Earth and into the again-reached Selby Pass. It was, of course, the Monkey King, who went straight off to work teasing up and ultimately annoying the by-this-point quite aggravated Eternal Dragon. But this time, things went a bit different. Oh sure, Shiu Yin got things rollin' with the scent of treats, and of course, he turned his britches into knee warmers and gave the dragon a face full of monkey steam, but he'd forgotten one thing. The three times before he'd used the cover of darkness to hide his escape.

But now it was morning.

Well, didn't that change everything. The Eternal Dragon opened its eyes, just about as mad as anything in all of creation has ever been. It started to roar, instinctively believin' that it'd been got once more. But then it went quiet, shocked silent by the sight of the Monkey King standin' there before it. At the same moment Shiu Yin realized his mistake, the dragon realized that it had been the Monkey King tormentin' it all along. Well, that really knocked over the stew pot, if you know what I mean. The Eternal Dragon shook its body with a force that moved several states and then it roared in a pain not felt by the universe since the galaxies first were born.

Fire exploded from the dragon's muzzle with brutal force in tidal amounts. The Monkey King threw itself out of time, but the dragon followed, bellowin' and rippin' apart the fabric of space with a ferocity that made mother tigers protectin' their young seem like one of Grandma Tilly's tea society garden parties. The two chased after one another motivated by fear and hate, crushin' some fourteen parallel dimensions and wreakin' considerable havoc in the one they started in just by their leavin'.

Even though their battle only took place within our own plane of existence for what they call a nanosecond - which I'm told is a powerfully brief spell o'time - still the land above was scorched to atoms. Mountains fell and new ones arose. The desert collapsed in on itself, sand and cactus and coyotes thrown high into the clouds only to come crashing down again in a brutal tangle.

Well, afterwards things did change a mite. To the best of my knowledge, the Monkey King has never been seen in America since that day. As for Gao, well, sadly he disappeared in the melee along with a whole lot of other folks - good and bad, rich and poor. You see, after that last confrontation, there was no more Selby Pass for anyone to worry about. The railroad had to get itself some new owners and those what took over had to find a whole new route so's they could join up with the Central Pacific.

You see, the dragon did more that time than just wreck a couple dozen miles of track. That time, it tore open a hole that was more than a mile deep. When the smoke cleared it was found that the crater it left was some twenty miles across and, I believe, over three hundred miles long. And that was a fact of nature that was only goin' to be dealt with by a detour.

So, the Union Pacific went around and eventually met the Central Pacific at Promontory, Utah, on May 10th, 1869. They had their ceremony with their golden and silver and iron spikes, tryin' to forget all that happened, but their nerves were bad an' it showed. Governor Stanford of the Central Pacific was so frightened of disturbing the ground he missed with his first sledge swing and hit the rail instead. That's okay, though, because the very same thing happened to Vice-President T.C. Durant of the Union Pacific when he tried.

But, eventually the last spike got drove in and the railroad was finished. And all the survivin' parties involved went about their business, most never again tellin' what they'd seen in the desert because no one ever believed them. But anyway, that's the story of how a Chinese poet created the Grand Canyon and I swear it's the absolute God's truth.

At least, that's how I heard it.

WEIRD TRAILS

Yessir, *a feller can really round himself up a passle of trouble when he has truck with them there god-like bein's, on account of, one way or t'other, trouble will surely come of it.*

So can you imagine what kind of trouble these here god-like fellas can git into all on their lonesome? See, bein' such powerful folk, their problems are natchally bigger 'n yers 'r mine, and solvin' 'em ain't no easier fer them as it is fer you an' me.

Here's one I heard direct from a Novato shamman that'll shed a little light on my meanin'...

BATTLE ON THE BRIDGE OF THE GODS

BY

JESSICA AMANDA SALMONSON

The giantess Loowit had lived to great old age. She could hardly believe it, but after thousands of years, she had become a terrible looking crone. Her cheeks sagged; her chin sagged too. Her hair that once was a splendid midnight waterfall had become white and wild like a tormented frothing river. Underneath her tired old eyes were large red cups full of melancholy, which at times spilled forth to wet the earth in sundry sorrows. Her hands, that once were so delicate and slender, were like the claws of eagles, with long sharp dark nails.

Even so, in her heart, she had never aged. When she went to the river with a bucket, she betimes chanced to see her own reflection. She was startled by her appearance, her crinkled complexion, her eagle's nest of wild white hair.

Where, she wondered, was the beautiful maiden she once had been? She was still present, inside an old woman.

Loowit was a very great shaman in the days when humanity was newly made. All people were giants then and often mingled with gods. Loowit was the inventor of a fire-making device. For a long time she kept this device a secret, hidden as it was in her cavernous home in the heart of a certain mountain today called Mount Saint Helens. This mountain's hollow was well lit on account of her ingenious invention. The mountain was like a tipi to Loowit, with the smoke of her miraculous fire rising through the smoke-hole at the top.

Then as now, the means and methods of certain arts were protected as secrets among artisans. Those who did not know the secrets of an art imagined such things were done solely by magic. Having told no one of her invention, various valley peoples and peoples near the sea believed Loowit manufactured fire by a supernatural method. Such peoples came to the door of Loowit's cavern and paid homage to her. She would then deposit a single coal inside a clamshell that each visitor brought along for the purpose. By this means, these individuals were able to deliver fire to their various villages.

But if in a village the fire went out, they knew not how to make another. In the winter, travel was difficult, and they might not be able to reach Loowit's mountain. They must therefore live in misery until the journey could be made. Then again, since Loowit was an ascetic, she was not always available with a new coal, for she was deep in the labyrinth of her cavern, lost in meditations. Thereby many made the terrible journey only to find their efforts fruitless, since Loowit did not invariably come forth proffering the burning coals. No one expected Loowit to be at the instant beck and call of people foolish enough to let their fires die. Therefore none complained to her about how often they went without fire.

Yet when Loowit went into the world in the guise of an elderly beggar, she saw that people suffered cold misery during many a winter. Rain, wind, flood, or some error of neglect, was apt to douse a fire, after which there befell terrible woe. People lived in blind fear of the night, wherein ghosts cried out with the voices of owls. So, too, having no fire to cook their venison and salmon, they ate raw flesh, their white teeth gnawing.

Loowit became heartsick to see the peoples wet and cold. She said to herself, "If I show them my ingenious device, each will be able to make a fire without need of my services. Their lot will be improved. But once I have revealed my secret, what will I be but an old woman of no importance to anyone?"

Even so, her heart could not deny the world. Children had frozen to death, and Loowit could not allow such tragedies to continue. She went to her cavern and prayed to Tyhee Saghalie, Chief of the Gods. He heard her in his heavenly place and came striding down the Milky Way from the north and trod along the Cascade peaks. As he was visible from a long way off, two of his earthly sons saw him, and they arose from their places to join their father. These sons were called Pahtoe and Wyeast, who dwelt in the mountains later known as Adams and Hood. The Great Chief together with his powerful sons sat in counsel with Loowit, who was indeed a marvelous shaman to speak with such gods as these.

She showed Tyhee Saghalie her invention, which was a drill that made fire when it was whirled with correct dexterity. For his own needs, Tyhee Saghalie always made fire with great explosions of lightning. This was not entirely practical for just anyone, so he was very impressed by Loowit's cleverness.

Loowit said, "Tyhee Saghalie, I am too old to travel about the nations of all the peoples of the valleys and the shores in order to teach this great secret. So I am giving my drill to you. As you can see, it is easily duplicated. Will you and your sons deliver my gift to the peoples, so that they may easily achieve their needs whenever fire is required?"

"I and my sons will do as you have asked," said Tyhee Saghalie. He held the drill in his hand, and parted it by a miraculous means, so that there were two drills. He gave one to his right-hand son, and the other to his left-hand son, instructing them, "Tell the peoples this is the gift of the mountain witch Loowit." And the two princes sat in awe of the soul of Loowit, which was a very great and giving soul.

Then to the old Shaman woman, Tyhee Saghalie said, "But what of your own future? Do you think I did not see you had horded your invention? Do you think I knew not why you kept the secret for so long? Now that you have given away the only thing you possessed, you will have nothing."

"Will I not have the affection of the people?"

"You will have the affection of the people," said Tyhee Saghalie, "and in honor of your selflessness, potlatches will be held each year, and the richest of every tribe will give their wealth to others. Never will such selflessness go unrewarded by Tyhee Saghalie. To you, Loowit, I will grant whatever is the one thing you have most in your life desired. What is there you would have from me?"

"I am forlorn of my youth," said Loowit, "and would live in happiness to be once more that which in my heart I have always remained."

Therefore the Chief of the Gods restored Loowit to her former maidenliness. And because she was a priestess, but no longer sole guardian of fire, he made her, instead, the guardian of the Bridge of Gods. This was the bridge, which in former times joined the Washington Cascades to the

Oregon Cascades, spanning the Columbia River, a river known to Chinook peoples as Wauna.

The bridge over the Wauna was made in days before there were people, when Coyote was digging in the ground as coyotes do even now. Coyote dug through under the mountain range so that the Wauna flowed to the sea, and salmon swam to villages on the upper Wauna. Beneath the bridge there arose a lonesome island, invisible in the darkness, upon which dead fish, broken canoes, rotting bits of lodges and human corpses were strewn as flotsam. There was good magic above the bridge so that mystagogues were able to pass from it onto the Milky Way, and visit the country of Tyhee Saghalie.

"By this bridge," said the Chief of Gods, "I am visited by the giants of the earth. You, Loowit, will be the guide who opens and shuts the spirit-bridge that exists in tandem with this physical span. Those who are giants of body but not of soul must never have the spirit bridge opened to them, but you will advise them on the Road of Mountains. Those who are giants in spirit, whatever their physical proportions, for these you may reveal the spirit-bridge, that I may see them."

Having been greatly honored with a signal duty, Loowit left the cavern of her mountain. She went to live in a small stone house in the middle of the bridge high above the Columbia.

Loowit was thereafter very beautiful. Many people came to the Bridge of Gods to worship her as a Goddess. The sons of all the chiefs in every tribe desired her in marriage, but she rebuffed them in a kindly way. She remained an ascetic and a guide to many, belonging to no one man.

The princes Pahtoe and Wyeast had been impressed by the greatness of her soul even when she had the appearance of a crone. Now, whenever they gazed upon her, they each knew there was no other wife for them. They boasted each in turn that he and he alone would marry her. When they were rebuffed as swiftly as were her common beaus, the two mountainous princes declared to one another their intent to induce her by any means to chose between them.

After they had given to the peoples the gift of fire, in accordance with the directions of their father and Loowit, each returned to the Bridge of the Gods in order to woo the maiden. She said, "I am flattered by your sincere attentions, but must ask that you desist, as I am an ascetic and devoted to the well being of the whole of the world. I cannot be restricted to the needs of a single man or a single house. Simply put, I do not wish to marry, and will remain pure in my duties as a priestess."

The princes said to one another, "If she will not decide between us, we will do battle with one another. Who wins will take Loowit by main force, whether or not she agrees." Having said this, they threw off their white robes, and rushed at one another.

They had many of the powers of their father the Supernal Chief. For this reason, their battle was terrible to see. Their feet gouged new rivers in the land, and heaped up new mountains, changing the direction of the Wauna River and causing whole forests to become submerged. Where the princes fell down wrestling, a vast wilderness was laid waste. They rolled about clinging body to body so that prairies were ironed out. They dashed at another, Wyeast with hurricanes, Pahtoe with fiery bolts of lightning. They were not yet worn out when they began to shove one another back and forth along the Bridge of Gods until that mighty span collapsed into the Wauna River.

Now they sat in the rushing river of the gorge, alarmed by the destruction they had wrought. At the sound of the bridge crashing down, Tyhee Saghalie came striding down the Milky Way and stood atop the Cascades with his arms folded, his eyes flashing with anger. He snatched Wyeast and fixed him in the heart of Mount Hood, from whence he never could escape to cause mischief. He grabbed Pahtoe from the river as well, and fixed him in the heart of Mount Adams.

Loowit sat on the edge of the river, looking at the ruins of the bridge. She said, "Now I am guardian neither of fire nor of the wonderful bridge. Was it my vanity that brought about this ruin? O Tyhee Saghalie, I will retire anew to the furnaces of my cavern, and never go forth among people, lest the beauty you have bestowed upon me inspire further harm."

Taking pity on her, Tyhee Saghalie said, "The Spirit of the Bridge of Gods exists within you, Loowit. Only the material bridge is ruined. I have reduced the size of humanity, so that no two may commit such harm as my sons have committed; but the hearts of people I have not changed. Some have great hearts, some have little. At my command, Loowit, you will unfold the spirit-bridge for those of the earth who are giant of heart. But if my will, and my laws, and my creation are hampered and harmed in future generations, then know that I have bestowed upon you a very grave power of destruction, so that even my spirit-bridge may fall, if ever I command."

Did ya ever find yerself runnin' from trouble, only to find yerself smack in the middle of worse? Yep, I can see that you have. Ain't gonna ask you about it; t'ain't none of my business.

Still, I have to allow as there's some as deserves the troubles they get into, like this one sorry soul who figured to outrun his tribulations, only to find hisself faced with something far worse.....

SALT OF THE EARTH
BY
DON D'AMMASSA

His horse shied away when they reached the ravine, but with half a dozen or more Navajo warriors close behind, Jake wasn't about to let her have her head. He used the spurs to emphasize his opinion and got an angry whinny in reply.

"Sorry, girl, but this is no time to get temperamental on me." The possibility occurred to him that a mountain cat might be upwind but that was a chance he was willing to take.

He noticed the quiet almost right away.

Even the sound of the wind was muffled by the steep, rocky walls on either side. The hoofbeats slowed to a trot and lost their sharp percussion. He was heading due north, right into the face of evil if the Navajo were right, but he had no inclination to turn back. They'd kill him for certain, whether or not they believed Sakaja had joined him willingly. Even now, fleeing for his life, he remembered the way she had moved against his body under the blankets, and twisted in the saddle uncomfortably. Sure, he'd known she was the chief's favorite daughter, but she'd come to him voluntarily and he'd treated her gently until she'd balked after she'd already gotten him thoroughly aroused. And then she'd tried to raise an alarm and he'd only meant to quite her for long enough to get away, but he'd underestimated his own strength and her neck was broken and here he was.

The ground rose steadily and his progress slowed even further. Jake glanced back over his shoulder. The foot of the ravine was still in sight and his pursuers couldn't be far behind. He knew their kind; they could track him for days over bare rock. He couldn't outrun them and he couldn't outlast them but maybe something would work to his advantage.

The grade began to level off as the walls closed in more tightly, forcing him toward a narrow notch. The footing grew even more treacherous and Jake crouched low over his mount's neck, willing her to place each foot with care. He was sweating with more than the day's heat when they finally reached a level spot. He turned for a final look back.

The Navajo were at the foot of the ravine.

There were eight of them, each carrying a bow and full quiver. Hunting arrows, not war arrows. Jake was a despoiler of women, an animal to be chased and killed, not an honorable enemy. Their mounts milled about nervously as if they too sensed something threatening ahead.

Oddly enough, Jake felt no imminent danger. He pulled back on the reins and his mount obediently halted, while he twisted in the saddle and stared at the men sworn to kill him. The tableau held for an uneasy minute, then another. He was within bowshot, but none of the warriors reached for a weapon. They just stared at him, silently, as if waiting for something to happen.

They seemed disinclined to enter the ravine.

Jake knew the Navajo well enough to guess what had happened. He'd wandered into one of their taboo places. Maybe some wise man had died up here and his chindi was still around, looking for a new body to inhabit. Although he wasn't a religious man himself, Jake knew the kind of grip that fear held for the Navajo. He met a preacher once who'd "converted" a band of Navajo, but even though they showed up regular at his church, they still built their hogans facing away from the north and carried their sick outside to die in the sunlight.

Thanking the god he didn't believe in, Jake turned away and urged his horse into the notch.

The ground was level for the next half mile or so, winding through a series of wind-scored mounds. He found a thin, fast moving trickle of water after a bit. The water tasted of alum and made his mouth feel funny, but it was cold. He drank some, then filled his canteen. The horse lapped up a bit, stopping every few seconds to snort and shake her head.

There was no sound of pursuit. No sound at all for the most part. Jake picked up a piece of loose shale and bounced it off a nearby boulder just to break the silence. Even then the crack was muted.

He was about to remount when he noticed the stains on his chaps. "What the hell?" It was a greenish brown residue, almost like mold. When he brushed it off, streaks of color remained behind.

Ten minutes later he lost the horse.

The trail had widened and smoothed out enough that he'd picked up the pace a bit. The mare fought him at first, still balking at something she sensed ahead. Jake was ready to use his rifle if a big cat or other predator attacked, but it was a much more prosaic fate that claimed its victim.

A patch of ground collapsed under a pounding hoof. Jake alertly jumped clear as the horse rolled, avoided being crushed in the fall although he bruised one shoulder badly when he landed. The mare's right foreleg had snapped just above the hoof.

"Sorry, old girl." Jake expended one of his bullets without hesitation, then uncinched the saddle and dragged his gear into the shade of a rocky outcrop.

He had a number of options, none of them good. Reversing course was certain death. Spooked or not, the Navajo would camp where he last saw them for at least several days, long enough to be sure he wasn't coming back that way. He might be able to scale the cliffs to east or west, but there were wide bands of desert in both directions, too wide to cross on foot. North was unknown territory but he suspected these twisted ravines and canyons went on for quite a way. There were mountains beyond, but he estimated they were at least a week's hard riding, and distances out here were difficult enough to judge that it might be twice that. Even if he had a horse, which he didn't.

Jake took the line of least resistance. With his saddlebags over his unbruised shoulder, he started walking north.

The sun was starting to drop below the line of rock to the west when Jake began thinking about camping for the night. He still had almost a full canteen of water; it tasted stale and unpleasant but he'd had worse. There was enough jerky in his bags to last for a day or two if he stopped eating when the pain went away instead of when he was satisfied. He'd been keeping an eye out for game, but hadn't seen a single animal since entering the ravine. No vultures circling hopefully overhead, no snakes sunning themselves on the exposed rock, no vermin scattering at his approach. Not even a tarantula or a scorpion.

Then he saw the coyote.

It had been dead for a long time; the bones were sun-bleached to pure white. Jake wasn't a particularly imaginative man, but he was not unintelligent. He saw right away that there was something wrong. The skeleton was too perfect. Every bone was exactly where it should be. No scavengers had worked at the carcass, searching for the best parts. The animal had died peacefully and laid undisturbed ever since, losing its flesh to the elements.

"Hey feller, I don't suppose you could tell me where to find some fresh water?"

Jake spoke to break the relentless silence, but his voice was hoarse and uncertain. He considered that fact, then tried again, first clearing his throat and spitting.

"The Navajo, they say you talk to them. Call you their brother. You got any brothers might come talk to a desperate man?"

The coyote didn't answer.

There was enough light that Jake could have kept on for another hour or so, but his legs were shaking and the sun had given him a spectacular headache so he decided he could resume rushing toward his death in the morning.

"You ain't the best company a man could have of an evening, but then I ain't in the mood for much conversation anyways."

Just upslope from the coyote, a shallow declivity in the rock face offered a natural shelter. Jake tossed his saddlebags into a corner and began scouring the area for firewood. There were plenty of dead trees around, all stunted and gnarly, but the wood was so rotten that a lot of it crumbled to powder in his hands. By dusk he'd accumulated what he hoped would be enough to last if he didn't light a fire until it was full dark.

The bizarre silence seemed to intensify with the coming of darkness. Jake deliberately stopped thinking about it consciously, but the eerie atmosphere of this place continued to nibble at the corners of his self-possession. He finally started his fire not for the heat or light but simply to listen to the crackling of the flames. They at least seemed perfectly normal.

The rotted wood flared up with unusual brilliance, providing an almost cheerful pool of light that swept down from Jake's bedroll to where the dead coyote lay facing him. Jake's brow furrowed briefly. He'd come up from below when he'd first seen the coyote, and he could have sworn it had been facing back the way he'd come. Might there be two of them?

He uncurled his stiff legs, picked out a relatively solid brand from the fire, and made his way downslope, past the skeletal remains. There was no sign of another; he must have been mistaken.

But that didn't seem right. Jake had lived most of his life in the wilderness; he had a good eye for detail and the wisdom to realize that small mistakes could have fatal consequences. He returned to the coyote, crouched to examine it more closely.

Something moved.

Jake hastily retreated a step, holding the flame defensively in front of him. "What the hell?" When nothing further happened, he advanced again. The skeleton seemed undisturbed but changed somehow. He squinted and lowered his head, trying to figure out just what he was seeing.

The edges of the bones had lost their sharp edges, grown fuzzy. At first Jake thought it was his eyes failing to adjust to the flickering light, but then he saw more clearly that the bones were thickening with unnatural life.

The body cavities were beginning to fill in, but the coyote was still just a sketch of a creature when it stirred and raised its head.

Jake had fought Indians and outlaws, lawmen and angry women, rattlesnakes and wolves and angry steers and wild horses. He wasn't the kind of man who panicked easily. But the sight of that unholy thing suddenly reanimated struck right past his defenses into the primitive fears we all hide within our souls. He broke and ran through the darkness, away from the coyote, away from his fire, off into the night.

For several minutes, the only thought in his mind was to get as far away as possible. Heedless of bruised shins and scraped hands, he scrambled over the rocks, sometimes climbing, sometimes sliding down a crumbling rock face, sometimes running foolishly even when he couldn't see where he was going. This headlong rush ended only when he lost his footing completely and slid down a gravelly slope, finally coming to rest with his breath gone and his panic partially abated.

The night was silent again.

Jake picked himself up and waited for his breathing to return to normal. Now that he was once more a rational creature, he realized that he'd abandoned what remained of his food and water, along with his blanket and rifle, even his gun belt. He climbed carefully to the top of the nearest slope, then scanned the horizon, hoping to spot the reflected glow of his campfire. But either the faint light of the flames had been swallowed up by the bright moonlight or, more likely, the fire had expired during his panicky flight, because Jake couldn't see anything that might guide him back.

"Just as well," he whispered softly. In the daylight, he'd stand a better chance of retracing his path, and with the darkness banished, he'd be more willing to face whatever needed to be faced.

He was crouched in a hollow, trying to doze off, when he heard the horse.

There was no question about the sound; the steady clip-clopping of iron shod hooves on hardened soil and rock. Not a Navajo mount; there was a distinct metallic sound. And the pattern of the feet was wrong, every fourth impact slightly mistimed. Jake felt ambivalent, but was too desperate to let the chance go by.

He pressed hard against a swell of rock, concealing himself in the shadows, waiting as the sound grew rapidly louder. And there, in the distance, a shadow moved, a large one, and a horse emerged from a twist in the rock and began trotting in his direction. The horse had neither saddle nor rider.

Jake was astounded at his luck. Some stray or runaway had shown up at just the right moment. He pushed away from the cold stone, started forward to intercept the horse.

And froze in astonishment.

The arrhythmic pattern was more apparent now, along with its cause. One of the forelegs hung at an odd ankle, although the animal seemed to feel no pain when its weight came to bear. This was the same mount that had reluctantly carried Jake into this place of damnation, trotting smartly through the darkness even though he'd put a bullet through its brain not twelve hours earlier.

This time Jake's panic didn't abate until he'd run square into a protruding finger of rock and knocked himself unconscious.

It was daylight when Jake opened his eyes this time. His mouth tasted sour, his lips and eyes were crusted with salt distilled from his sweat, and his muscles protested when he rolled over and rose to his knees. Blood had dried in a broad band from his forehead to his cheek, and his head throbbed with a pain so intense it made him dizzy.

Moving very carefully, Jake stood up and slowly surveyed his surroundings.

The rock in most directions was unscalable, but there was a clear path leading upslope. Jake's major concern at the moment was water; his throat felt as though he'd been eating sagebrush. High ground would provide a vantage point from which he might be able to spot either running water, or at a minimum vegetation.

Some of the cramps in his muscles faded but many remained unabated as he climbed up into the sunlight. But all pain, even the thirst, was forgotten when Jake reached the lip of a hollow and saw what lay before him.

Jake had seen the craters left by cannon fire and this reminded him a little of that, although the scale was all wrong. The depression below was at least a hundred yards across and much deeper in the center, and the edges had started to crumble with the passage of time. But it was almost perfectly circular and the slope was uniform around the entire perimeter, too regular to be entirely natural. Dead center was a man-sized lump of black stone, the blackest thing he'd ever seen. It almost seemed to suck in the light from all around it.

On the far side, just above the crater rim, a Navajo hogan had been erected under an overhanging rock.

Jake hesitated, but only for a moment. If the hogan was occupied, he might be marching to his death, but if he didn't find water soon, his extinction was even more certain. The shortest route was directly across the crater, but something warned him to go around, a silent voice too solemn to ignore.

He gathered his strength and set out.

Although there was no one in sight, the hogan appeared to be in good repair. Jake approached cautiously at the last, but he'd been exposed to casual view for the entire trip around the circumference of the crater and wariness now served little purpose. He bent low at the entrance, drew a deep breath, and slipped inside.

The first thing he noticed was the skin of water hanging from a peg, and he didn't pay much attention to the rest of the interior until he'd slaked at least the worst part of his thirst. Perhaps because he'd been so long without, the water seemed particularly sweet and fresh, with no trace of the alum taste he'd noticed previously.

A neat pile of blankets had been placed at the opposite end of the hogan, along with some beaded pipes and mats that he recognized as Navajo work. He walked slowly to the opposite end and stared down at them for several minutes, his thought processes still fogged with fatigue.

"Welcome to my home."

Jake spun on his heel and staggered, not having realized how weak he was. Although he was a Navajo, the old man who had just entered the hogan seemed too frail to pose a significant threat. His skin was dry and unhealthy looking and his hands were trembling.   But Jake remained cautious nevertheless.

"Please, make yourself at ease. You have been expected, although I had thought it would be one of the People."   The old man spoke good English, with just a trace of Navajo inflection.

"Who are you?"

"I am...He Who Watches, though my eyes have grown weak and I fear I will watch for little longer. You are injured, I see."

Jake raised a hand to his bloody forehead, dropped it quickly. "It's nothing. What is this place?" He gestured with his hands to indicate he meant more than just the hogan.

"This is where the gods of the sky touched the Earth, the birthplace of the skinwalkers, the playground of the Laughing God."

Jake shrugged impatiently, allowing himself to relax. "I don't suppose you have anything to eat?"

In reply, the Navajo withdrew from the hogan. Jake followed and saw that a freshly killed rabbit had been spitted and was roasting over a small fire. The smell made his stomach rumble.

"Are you alone here?" Jake crouched by the fire, watching driblets of fat drop sizzling into the flames.

"I watch over this land, as did the watcher before me, and the one before him. As will the one who comes after."

That didn't really answer his question, but Jake let it pass. His mind always worked better when his belly was full, and he'd lived among the Navajo long enough to have picked up some of their talent for patience.

They ate the rabbit in companionable silence.

When they were done, the old man impaled the carcass on a stick and carried it to the edge of the crater. Jake followed a few steps behind, watched as the remains of their dinner was thrown down into the declivity. A step or two closer and he saw that it had landed on a bare spot surrounded by dozens of other clusters of bones. All of the skeletons had been picked clean, but he was able to identify rabbits, coyotes, plains deer, even what appeared to be a wolf. He wondered idly if the old man had eaten them all.

He allowed the Navajo to clean the wound on his forehead, wincing slightly as his long hair was extricated from the bloody gash.

"You must rest a while."

Although he felt uneasy about letting his guard down, Jake recognized that his body had been pushed to its limit. After only a very brief protest, he retreated into the hogan to escape the hot sun, and fell asleep almost as soon as he lay down.

It was dusk when he next opened his eyes.

Jake emerged from the hut, half expecting to find his pursuers waiting for him, but the only person in sight was the old man, who stood at the crater rim, spreading white powder in a thin line from left to right.

"What are you doing?"

"Marking the border between the land and the sky. When the darkness comes, the spirits of the sky gods can no longer tell one from the other. But they will not cross the salt."

So saying, he scooped another handful from the pouch hanging at his waist and extended the existing line. Jake watched in puzzled silence as the Navajo completed a circle around the hogan before relenting.

"We will be undisturbed now."

Whatever Jake might have said next was precluded by a rustling from within the crater. His hand instinctively went to his side, but his Colt was somewhere back in the ravine. The sounds grew louder, more insistent, more numerous, and despite a growing conviction that he really didn't want to know the source, he moved cautiously to peer down toward its origin.

The dead creatures, re-fleshed, were stirring, moving with initial uncertainty, then with more assurance as the new forms grew solid and coherent. Jake stepped back, his heart racing, but the old man was at his side.

"They cannot cross the salt. It is of the earth and they are of the sky."

Unconcerned, the Navajo returned to the hogan and, after a while, Jake joined him, though his thoughts strayed to the perimeter constantly and he slept uneasily all that night.

The days that followed sank into a comforting routine. Each morning the two men would leave their haven to hunt for food. There was little to be found nearby, but to the north lay land untouched by the blight. There was game here though not plentiful, and the old man proved to be a fine shot with the bow, although they did better after the ninth day, when Jake found his rifle and his Colt. There were roots and berries in considerable quantity, and wild grain that they ground into paste. But each day, without fail, they traveled to the salt flat near the hogan and brought back enough to redraw the line of demarcation around the hogan.

And each night the dead things in the crater crowded around the edges and looked in.

One afternoon Jake suggested gathering up all the bones and burying them inside the perimeter, but the old man just shook his head.

"It is better to know where the sky things are than where they aren't."

The old man's health continued to deteriorate and he began setting aside pieces of firewood they gathered each day for another purpose.

"When I die, you must burn my body and return my ashes to the earth."

This puzzled Jake greatly because he knew that the Navajo were deeply superstitious about death. Unlike the plains Indians, they invariably disposed of their dead by entombing the bodies in rocky cairns where they were protected from scavengers. He thought to ask, but remembering the animated corpses that spied upon them nightly, he answered his own question.

Even though he'd been expecting it, Jake was devastated by the old man's death. It came quietly, while he was spreading the salt barrier. Jake saw him fall and ran to his side, but the last breath had already passed his lips by then. There was enough wood for the cairn, and Jake was preparing the pyre when an idea occurred to him.

He thought about it some, and then he thought about it some more. When he was done thinking, he wrapped the old man in a blanket and buried him in a shallow grave near the hogan. And that night he was very careful about leaving no gaps in the line of salt.

Jake spent the following morning making several trips back and forth to the salt flat. By the time the sun was directly overhead, he had filled one corner of the hogan with salt. During the afternoon, he collected all of the skeletons from the crater and buried them inside the salt line. He spent an uneasy night despite the double line of salt he'd spread about. There seemed to be something whispering within the crater, although when he concentrated he could hear no sound at all.

Just before dawn he rose and lit the fire. A half dozen creatures stood just outside the salt line, staring at him. As the sun came up, they sank back to the ground and the stuff of their bodies receded. He collected these bones as well and added them to the mass grave.

He spent that day building a travois, using his Bowie knife to cut down two stout young trees, then cannibalized two of his remaining three blankets, sewing them with a thornbush needle to secure them to the frame. Only three new skeletons greeted him in the morning, and he buried these as well, then returned to the ravine where he found the bones of his mare. It took two trips to carry them back to the hogan, and even then he was forced to leave many of the smaller bones behind. Then he rested until dusk, eating what remained of his food.

The sky turned pink as the sun retreated for the evening. Jake began spreading salt, but this time he consciously left a single gap in the line. Satisfied, he wrapped a bandanna around his face and began the unpleasant task of unearthing the old man's body. Even protected by the earth in which it had been interred, his flesh had begun to spoil, an acrid odor which penetrated the bandanna easily. Jake persevered, dragging the body to a point near the gap in the salt line.

"Sorry, old man, but it's needful."

Full darkness fell and the night was as silent as ever. Jake sat by the fire, keeping vigil over the body, waiting for what he knew had to come. Even so, even expecting it, he was almost taken by surprise.

The smell subsided, but Jake thought that might just be that he was getting accustomed to it. There was no sign of movement, not from a distance, though had he been closer he might have seen the falling in of the flesh as parts of it were taken away and replaced by something else, something that masqueraded as earthly life even though its origins were elsewhere. The furious activity of replacement was largely internal, and Jake wouldn't have wanted to see it even if that had been possible.

There was a sigh, like escaping gas, and Jake's head turned suddenly. Sure enough, the fingers of one outstretched hand were beginning to twitch, and there was movement in the torso, although it was nothing like breathing.

Then the old man sat up.

Jake stumbled backward as he rose to his feet, and the Colt was in his hand even though he hadn't given it a thought. The face was still recognizable from time to time, although there was a constant churning movement beneath the surface that altered the contours in an unnervingly fluid fashion. The eyes were open but sightless, the soft parts gone and replaced with something blacker than the night. And when the old man's mouth opened and something vaguely like a tongue writhed and twisted, Jake forgot his plan for the moment and fired six rounds without thinking about it.

Jake was a good shot, and all six shells hit their target, three in the chest, three in the forehead, but for all that, the old man's body didn't even shudder. It was like the bullets passed through or around the counterfeit flesh, punched holes in bone and passed on.

The old man started to get to his feet. There was a sound now, a gurgling as though something was trying to master the mechanism of speech. Jake dropped his Colt and stepped back to the hogan, reached inside for a handful of salt.

The old man was lurching toward him now, one arm reaching out, and from his throat came a hideous moaning that seemed to originate in the depths of space. Jake threw a handful of salt directly into its face.

The flesh began to boil and bubble like a fresh egg dropped into hot fat. The top layer peeled back and sloughed off, exposing the next within. But still the body was moving forward, each step a bit more self confident than the last.

Jake threw double handfuls of salt at the thing, aiming for the exposed arms and legs. Oddly enough, there was no smell, neither the honest putrefaction of earthly flesh, nor any unworldly odor from the invader. Two more handfuls and one leg collapsed. The torso hit the ground heavily but the arms were lifting forward, clawing at the soil, still trying to move toward Jake. He threw more salt, furiously now, and the fearsome advance stopped only inches from the hogan entrance.

Jake wasn't satisfied until he'd completely buried the old man's remains with the last of the salt, and then he built the pyre and set it alight and with the last of the salt he inscribed a tight circle directly around the hogan, in which he slept until well after the sun rose.

The black stone at the center of the crater seemed nothing more than that, although it was honeycombed with pits and holes and tiny tunnels. Parts of it were clearly hollow because it weighed much less than he'd expected, but still enough that it took most of the day and all of his strength to drag it to the rim of the crater.

It was easier from there. Jake's travois held together almost all the way to the cliff above the salt flat, and when it failed, he rolled the black stone the rest of the way, then pushed it over the edge. Night fell while he was burying it there in the middle of the salt flat, but nothing came to watch him with eyes that weren't eyes.

But when he had finished, he still gathered enough salt to draw a circle around the hogan for the night, even though he felt that it was all over, that the unearthly life would never walk in earthly bodies again.

Or would it. An insect landed on the back of his hand and he crushed it, then peered closely. Was it really an insect, or had something else taken its form? Jake rubbed the back of his hand in the remaining salt and lay down, seeking unconsciousness.

The hum of diminutive wings filled the night. Earthly life returning to reclaim the ravine, or something else? Jake couldn't muster the courage to find out.

Sakaja's oldest brother, Wokani, spotted the white man trekking out of the forbidden place. The rest of the hunting party had given up long before, but he'd stubbornly insisted on remaining behind to avenge his sister's - and thence his own - honor. But even he had begun to believe that either the white man had escaped, or more likely that he'd succumbed to whatever curse hung over the forbidden place.

Wokani urged his pony forward to meet the man.

His heart cried out for this man's blood. He had dreamed of his vengeance nightly at first, burning off the white man's testicles, pushing slivers up under the nails of fingers and toes, pressing thorns through the tongue and eyelids. But the anger had simmered and cooled until now he felt only a sense of duty, of balance.

The white man had offended and now he must die. That was the right of it, and there was nothing else to say, no reason for anger or regret.

Jake made no effort to avoid the mounted warrior, stood silently in the open while Wokani circled him once, then dismounted, knife in hand. The warrior peered into Jake's face, saw the white residue of the salt the man had smeared all over his body, saw the tears leaking from irritated eyes, sensed the pain emanating from the numerous cuts and scratches that crisscrossed the white man's body, all liberally caked with salt.

Then he looked into Jake's eyes and saw a pain greater than any he could inflict. Wokani sheathed his knife and left him there, content that justice had been done.

Right scary stuff, eh? Wellsir, din't I tell ya there's some mighty strange goin's on goin' on in this ol' West of our'n? And most of it is mighty nasty, too.

There was this one particular bit of nasty that comes to mind. Some range-roughened cowpoke told this to me once over coffee an' beans up Montana way. It has to do with a fella who was jus' too consarned curious fer his own good.....

SHEEP-EYE

BY

DONALD R. BURLESON

What Jud Willis found, deep in the desertlands of New Mexico, wasn't anything he had gone there to find.

He hadn't intended to stop in the Territory of New Mexico at all, in fact. California was the Promised Land at the far, far end of the trail - California and its beckoning fields of gold, its lofty dreams of wealth and the carefree life.

Naturally, that had been the dream, back in Boston three years ago. That had even been the dream a year ago in Missouri, when he had joined the caravan and hit the trail, once again trading the comforts of a warm bed for the uncertainties of the open country. He had seen the same dream in a thousand faces, and wondered if it glowed with the same avidity in his own.

But those wearying months on the Santa Fe Trail had been enough to dim the glow in any face. Before the horses and mules and wagons had pushed very far into the yellow prairie expanses of western Kansas, where the only trees were gnarled and furtive-looking cottonwoods and the only roof the limitless sky and the only sounds the sounds of the caravan - long before he and his companions had crossed into New Mexico, Jud Willis had come to feel that California was receding to a more distant realm every day, not drawing closer. Even when the terrain changed, and waving fields of prairie grass became infinite seas of sand and pungent sagebrush, and the plains of Kansas became the mountain-ringed valleys and canyonlands of New Mexico Territory, the image of California seemed to fade like a dream that flickers and passes into oblivion when the sleeper wakes. And Jud Willis had awakened to the realization that he was not going to California.

He supposed the change of heart had come sometime back up the trail, not long after the caravan had entered the Territory. Crouching beside the wagons with his traveling companions and making coffee over the fire, he had tried to look into his own mind, tried to examine his motives, his real wishes. What did he really want? He hadn't been sure. Still wasn't sure.

What he *hadn't* wanted was more weeks or months on the trail with a caravan. True, he had grown to like the people he was with, the familiar faces, the familiar voices; but he needed to be on his own. Sometimes when the group had pressed onward, he had wanted to stay longer, or take a different route, or proceed more quickly, or more slowly.

Alone now, he could do things his way. Not that he had any particular plan, but that was part of it; he needed to be free to have no plan.

Watering his horse now at one of the little streams that trickled down cold and clear from the foothills, he surveyed the scene around him. The rocky hills sloped gently down to a sandy plain dotted with mesquite and spiky-headed yucca and spectral armies of cholla cactus stretching away westward to meet the crimson remnants of a setting sun. Somewhere in the distance, a hawk fell across the sky like a meteor. Suddenly Jud felt very alone.

When he had left the caravan at the banks of the Pecos River, many days' ride north of here, the others had tried to talk him into going on with them; but even then the group was splitting up, some heading on to Santa Fe and beyond, some leaving the caravan to make their way northward, seeking the gold fields of Colorado. Jud himself had ridden into Santa Fe to gather supplies, returned to the caravan camp to bid the others goodbye, and saddled back up and followed the river south.

And while the ensuing three weeks in the New Mexico desert hadn't done much to clarify his reasons for leaving the caravan, he had no real regrets at this point. He had done a little prospecting in the streams after he left the river course to ride southwest. Panning for gold, he had found none, which was about what he expected. But this was more than compensated for, he felt, by the splendor of the landscape itself, which seemed a world away from the political turmoil of Santa Fe, and a universe away from the streets of Boston. The land was gold enough. It was a dream world, this sun-dazzled sea of sand and rock and cactus under a dizzying dome of turquoise-colored sky. It was beautiful, but if you didn't keep your wits about you, it could kill you.

Somehow its beauty was laced through with a certain - darker - quality.

As if to underscore these thoughts, a dry burring sound came up from nearby. Some yards away, its mottled colors blending with the colors of the sandy ground, a prairie rattler coiled itself in the shadows at the base of a yucca and sounded its warning. After a while the snake uncoiled and sidled away. Jud really didn't mind these creatures. You just had to keep your eyes and ears open, and give the snake a little room.

No, something was strange, and a little disquieting, about this place, but it wasn't rattlesnakes.

Looking to the west, away from the foothills behind him, he thought the impression had something to do with the low, rocky hill that rose from the land some four or five hundred yards ahead, its craggy form obscure in the red-orange blaze of the sunset. The sight of this hill gave him a creepy sort of feeling, as if there were something about it that he should know, but did not.

He climbed back into the saddle and pointed his horse in the direction of the hill. Maybe the way to dispel this odd feeling was just to ride over and have a look.

Up close, the hill was a dark rock pile jutting sharply from the desert floor, too steep on this side to give access. Jud made his way around to the western end, where a more gradual slope presented itself. There was even a rough, narrow footpath leading up among the rocks, and Jud hitched his horse to a mesquite and began to climb the hill, his shadow long and thin ahead of him on the path.

His impression of strangeness grew rather than diminished now that he was here. The stone surfaces were covered with odd patterns and etchings, sometimes densely crowded together, sometimes isolated. Here a stone bore the figures of primitive hunters, there another stone showed circular patterns like swirled disks; there another stone was covered with zigzag lines. The figures on the stones must have numbered in the hundreds. They were no doubt the work of ancient peoples; even a newcomer like Jud knew that Indian tribes had been on this land for hundreds, maybe thousands of years. He had seen Indian pueblo settlements further north, and occasional little groups of Indians along the way south, interspersed with Mexican ranches and desert farms. This land had been part of Mexico until recently, and part of Spain before that, but it was the Indians who were truly *old* in the land, and these etchings in the rock only served to remind him of that.

The footpath gradually rose among the angular outcroppings of rock, and after half an hour he came to the end of the path, where it ran blind up against a natural wall of stone. He retraced his steps, and by the time he was halfway back it was getting dark, so that the figures on the rocks were immersed in shadow.

Even so, he noticed now, to his right and several yards off the path, a curious figure he hadn't seen on the way up. He stepped across to get a closer look.

The stone in question stood somewhat taller than Jud, and contained one large etching, a full-size stick-figure man that somehow made Jud's flesh crawl to look at it. The arms, legs, and trunk were long, thin, almost willowy, but it was the head that was striking. Like the rest of the body, it was etched in thin outline, a circle enclosing a rudimentary face turned sideways so that only one eye was showing. Or maybe the face was looking frontward, and only *had* one eye.

It was this huge eye that Jud couldn't stop looking at.

It wasn't etched into the stone like the rest. Rather, a natural bump about the size of a fist rose from the general level of the stone face, and the ancient artist had used this protuberance for the eye. The effect was chilling, somehow, as the eye seemed to look at you with a bleary kind of insistence. Jud shuddered and turned away and stepped back toward the main path.

And ran headlong into someone.

He gasped for breath, his heart pounding. "God! Who the devil are you?"

Now that he had a chance to look, he saw that it was two white-haired old men. One was Mexican, one was Indian. While the Indian just stood and watched, the Mexican nodded to him and spoke in a dry, cracked voice.

"*Ese dibujo,*" he said, motioning toward the strange figure on the stone, "*se llama Ojo de Oveja.*"

Jud had picked up a little Spanish along the way, but he couldn't follow this. He shrugged. "I'm afraid I don't..."

"*Ojo de Oveja*," the Mexican repeated, nodding toward the stone figure again. "*Ojo de Oveja.*"

Jud opened his mouth to try to say, again, that he didn't understand, when the old Indian spoke up.

"Sheep-Eye," he said.

Jud blinked at him. "What?"

The Indian looked away, not toward the stone but away into the gathering night, then looked back at him. "Sheep-Eye. The people call Old Sheep-Eye. Always been here. People afraid. Sheep-Eye have great power. Walk on the wind."

"I see," Jud said, though he didn't.

"*Es leyenda que se ha contado desde hace muchos siglos,*" the old Mexican said, but Jud didn't understand. He thought perhaps it was just as well.

"We go," the Indian said. Jud wondered whether he meant all three of them, but the two old men started back down the path and didn't seem to object to his not following them.

"*Buenas noches,*" the Mexican called back to him.

"*Buenas noches,*" Jud replied. That much Spanish, at least, he could manage. In a moment the two men had been swallowed by the night. A waning half moon had risen, but it showed no one but himself.

And the figure on the stone, barely visible from the footpath. Jud glared at the thing. "Sheep-Eye. What nonsense."

But there was something in the blind-looking stare of that great bloated eye that almost made the words stick in his throat.

When he had faltered his way back down the hill to his horse, he went riding off in search of a good spot to bed down for the night. Some distance to the southwest of the rocky hill he passed a little adobe house shrouded in shadow, its battered wooden door closed against the night, its tiny windows lightless. He wondered if anyone lived there. In any case he was going to spend this night the way he now spent all his nights, under the open sky.

Further along, he chose a spot suitably flat and free of snake holes, and made a small fire and spread his bedding on the ground beside it, tethering the horse nearby. A light breeze had sprung up, making spikes of yucca wave eerily in the moonlight like seas of tentacles. Even with the brightness of the moon, the black vault of sky was crusted over with a million stars. One didn't see a sky like this back in Boston. He ate a strip of beef jerky, drank some water from his canteen, rolled himself into his bedding, and slept.

And woke.

What on earth was that?

Some sound, some sound off in the night somewhere beyond the feeble glow of the campfire.

He sat up and listened. The wind had risen a little now, so it was hard to tell...

There it was again, a wispy, windy kind of sound, not like the wind exactly, but like something *with* the wind. He heard the horse whinny once, nervously.

Then the whole impression was gone, and the wind dwindled, barely stirring the fire's dying embers. Silence reigned, broken only by the far-off cry of a coyote. Jud lay back and stared at the star-frosted dome overhead until the light of a new day crept across the heavens.

He breakfasted on dried beef and coffee and repacked his saddlebags and rode off toward the southwest, heading in that direction till midday, seeing nothing but open prairie. But he changed his mind and turned the horse around and rode all the way back to the little adobe house, not knowing why he did so. He reached the house just as the sun was going down.

This time there were signs of life. Behind the house, which was little more than a dilapidated hut of cracked adobe, a Mexican woman was washing clothing in a little stream. Evidently she hadn't heard him ride up. He hitched the horse to a small tree near the front door and stepped around to the right side of the house and called to the woman.

"¿*Señora?* "

The woman was clearly startled, dropping her wash into the stream and fishing it out before turning to face him. "¿*Señor?*"

Now what? he thought. "I... I was passing through and saw your house..."

The woman smiled wanly and shook her head.

"You don't speak..." Jud said. "¿*No habla inglés?*"

The woman placed the wash on a stone and stepped closer, wiping her hands on her dress. She was simply but cleanly attired, and rather pretty, evidently a decade younger than himself, perhaps twenty-five or so. "*No,*" she said, "*no hablo inglés.* "

He stood at a loss, trying to think of something to say, when a sound came from inside the house. It was the thin crying of a baby, clearly audible as the door was open.

The woman started toward the door. "*Mi niña*," she said. When she stepped through the door, she motioned for him to follow, and he did, having to stoop to get through.

The place was only one room, with crude furnishings - a small wooden table, two rickety chairs, and a kind of wicker crib ensconced in a shadowy corner. The glass panes in the windows were so small and so dusty that they admitted very little light, but he could see that the mother bent over the crib, took up the baby in a ragged blanket, rocked it until it was quiet again, and placed it back in the crib. Turning to Jud, she said, "*Tiene usted hombre?*"

Jud made a helpless gesture with his hands. "I'm sorry, I don't..." The woman touched her fingers to her mouth and pointed to him, questioningly. He nodded. "Hungry, you mean. Yes. *Sí*. But I couldn't ask you to..."

However, the woman was out the door. He followed her out and watched as she built a little fire in a sandy pit between the house and the stream. She was soon cooking a kind of vegetable stew in an ancient-looking iron pot. At length they were back inside, seated across the table from each other, having their dinner.

The woman smiled at him from time to time but seemed ill at ease, often glancing at the windows, where the night had fallen and was relieved only by a little oil lamp on the table where they were finishing their meal. Once he felt emboldened to take the woman's hand in his, but she gently pulled the hand away, averting her eyes. Outside, a wind had come up, and she half rose to go and close the door, but Jud got up and closed it for her, sliding the rusty bolt.

Sitting back down, he pointed to her, rummaging in his mind for the right words in Spanish. "*¿Cómo se llama...?*"

"Lucinda," she said. "*¿Usted?*"

"That's a pretty name," Jud offered, hoping that she might somehow understand. "My name is Jud."

She seemed to turn the name over in her mouth. "Chood."

"Right." He had to ask something else now. There should logically have been someone else here. "Where is your..." He fished for the words. "*¿Dónde está su...?*" What was the word for *husband?*

But before either of them could say anything more, a kind of slithering seemed to pass over the outside of the house, moving from the front door to a side window. Lucinda's face was now a mask of fear, and Jud jumped up and ran to the window, having no idea what he was supposed to do.

He had little time to consider the matter, because a kind of face, emerging from the blackness of the night, framed itself in the window, looking in. If it was really a face, it was one Jud had seen before. Drawn like a smoke-ring against the dark, bobbing and undulating, it leaned against the window opening but was too big to break through. Jud could just see a neck and a pair of arms, flailing and jittering. The figure withdrew itself from view almost before Jud could notice that the face had only an appalling hole where its great single eye might have been.

He turned to see the apparition reappear at the opposite window, scrabbling at the frame with its wiry hands and pressing its eyeless visage against the window. Lucinda only buried her face in her hands, wailing.

Now a second voice joined her. The baby was awake again, its thin gurgling little voice swelling into a chorus of crying as the wispy thing outside the house moved around to the front and began scratching and thumping at the door. Lucinda rose from the table and went to see to the baby, looking over her shoulder in terror at the sounds coming from outside the door. But mercifully these sounds ceased, and a kind of rustling whisper ensued, as if something were moving itself across the sand, away from the house. It was only now that Jud noticed that the horse, tethered near the front door, had been neighing and snorting pitiably.

Jud turned to see Lucinda pick the baby up again, wrapping the blanket tight around it. He stepped closer to see if the baby was all right, but Lucinda turned away with it, rocking it in her arms, crooning some lullaby in soft Spanish tones.

Suddenly the whole horror of the situation seized his mind like a vice, and later he would barely remember bolting out of the house, unhitching his horse, and riding away into the night. That much would remain a blur in his mind. What would burn itself more indelibly into his memory was what he saw when he stopped.

Riding at full gallop, he was managing well enough to point the horse away from cactus and mesquite and snake holes, until the moon went momentarily behind a cloud. The sudden darkness was so disturbing to his senses that he pulled the horse up to a halt, and instinctively turned and looked behind him as the moon came back out.

It was there, all right, old Sheep-Eye following him at a distance but coming closer, that unthinkable stick-figure, its limbs like pencil strokes on the night, its eyeless head nodding. Eyeless, because when it had come down off the rock, it had left that part behind, in the stone.

The thing whispered forward a few paces, the spindly legs bowing and straightening and closing the distance without quite touching the ground, the wire-thin arms reaching, reaching. It stopped, turned a blind face more squarely toward him, and sniffed the air. Catching his scent, it came rushing toward him like a vapor.

He rode furiously, desperately, scarcely daring to breathe or to blink his eyes or to think how close the thing might be. He seemed to ride forever. In the end, he outran the pursuer, and all the next day and night he would lie prostrate with exhaustion in a dry arroyo far, far to the west, visited by the great spidery shape only in his nightmares. He now had time for reflection, and his thoughts kept going back to Lucinda. By all rights, he should have felt like a cad for running away and leaving her, but he had had his reasons.

Because what would haunt his dreams even more hideously than the dreadful thing itself was that *other* glimpse he had had of the gaping eyeless face. It had been bad enough, the way he had seen it first. But it was worse, seeing that ghastly contour not in stone, nor in the mad night air, but on the tiny pink face of Lucinda's baby.

WEIRD TRAILS

Now, anybody can spin hisself a tall tale; ain't nothin' a'tall hard about it. Toughest thing, y'see, is to be able to back it up, and ain't that the hard ride!

This here next fella, now he could tell a right fine tale when he'd a mind to, and this here's prob'ly the tallest tale he ever did tell.

But jus' remember what I done told you about backin' it up...

SKINNING THE DEVIL
BY
TIM CURRAN

They were gathered in the cookhouse chewing on buff steaks and sucking down shine when Doc Chambers came in, his beaver coat flapping around him like a sheet on a line. His hair was white as mountain snow and his beard framed a face with more ruts and scars than a strip-mined hillside. He grabbed a table away from the others and helped himself to some coffee. "Gents," he said. "What's it about this time?"

The other cowhands just lounged about, full and fat, muttering amongst themselves. They'd been yarning, as was the custom after a long day of riding fence and gathering strays. They were a hard and weathered lot, but next to Chambers they were all babes suckling their mama's tit and knew it to a man. For Chambers had done things and seen things the rest would only read about in dime novels. Nobody knew how old he was for sure - could've been seventy, could've been a hundred (even Chambers himself couldn't remember) - but they knew he'd been a mountain man and hardrock miner, bounty hunter and railroad man, Indian fighter and army scout. Wasn't too many things he hadn't done. Now he was the line rider for the Bar X outfit and he only came down from the high country once or twice every few months.

"Just spinning a few yarns," Charlie Lee said, filling a tin plate with beans, sowbelly, and biscuits for Chambers. "You know how it goes, Doc."

Chambers nodded. He cleaned his plate with a wooden spoon and said not a word while the others finally forgot about him and started telling tales of famous desperados they'd known, strikes they'd been on, who they'd ridden shotgun for and Injun war parties they'd barely escaped from. But it was all bullshit, and about the time it got deep enough for hip waders Doc Chambers cleared his throat and lit up a hand-rolled.

"Full of tall tales, the lot of you," he said, laughing low in his throat. "And tales is all they are. You're all a bunch of pups and not a one of you is old enough to recall, let alone have experienced, any of these things. So I'm gonna tell you one you never heard before."

That shut them up. The bottle started to pass around and all eyes were on the old timer because they knew he was about to start reminiscing and with the way he told things, it was almost as good as being there.

Chambers blew out a stream of smoke. Firelight flickered in his eyes. "It was back in '92 to the best of my recollection that I lost two of my best friends. Finer men God has yet to put on this rock; Billy Creek and Salt River Tom Mohdesy. And how did that happen, you might ask? Well, let me just say it weren't outlaws or bandits or Apache raiders. What killed them was the sort of thing you boys have never heard of - nor dreamed of - in your wildest nightmares…"

Well, it started (he said) when Salt River Tom came to see me, asked me if I fancied being rich. Course, I told him I fancied it like a man fancies having a pecker he can skip rope with or a half-dozen young wives who can piss fifty-dollar bills. Anyway, Tom told me that his brother and a crew of ten, twelve men had struck a rich lode of silver ore up in the Sierra Madres. But they'd run afoul of bandits and had lost most of their burros. Word had just reached Tom and he wanted me and one or two others to accompany him with a pack train of burros to bring the ore down. We'd get an equal split on everything. Tom chose me because I had a certain reputation as a shootist by that point. I wasn't the fastest, surely, but I always hit my mark. So I volunteered. The third man was Billy Creek, an old army scout like myself. Billy was half Chiricahua Apache and like all his people, he could've tracked a pea through a hailstorm. A tough old hand was Billy, could eat gunpowder and lead and shit bullets.

What Tom had were two men practiced at the art of killing in all its forms. And that was important because the Madres were and are a rough country where men get their throats slit for a slab of bacon or a water hole, let alone money pulled from the ground.

Well, we provisioned up and off we went. It took us three weeks to reach that silver camp, which was well southwest of the *Barranca del Cobre* - the so-called Copper Canyon. And what a hellish three weeks it was. Handling those burros along those mountain passes was no easy bit, I'll tell you. You were never sure if you were handling them or they were handling you. But those animals always seemed to find a footing even in places where a man couldn't. At night you had to picket them or they'd wander off. Sore and dusty and tired after a long day and what you needed was a good, long sleep. But did you get it? Nope. Those goddamn animals strayed and you spent the night beating the bush rounding them back up. It was no easy job, I'll tell you. All that kept me going were two things: my friendship and respect for Salt River Tom and the fact that maybe, just maybe, I was going to be a rich man.

We covered terrain that ranged from high, arid passes where frozen winds from snowy peaks above froze your balls up just as sure as stones in a creek to desert slopes that were blown by dust storms where you couldn't see five feet in front of you. We hacked our way through jungle valleys and trod through swamps and peeled red leeches fat as your thumb from our hides. It was miserable country. Mosquitoes and poisonous snakes and Gila Monsters and spiders bigger than your hand and little red-yellow scorpions that would kill you within half a day if you were stung. At night you could hear the roaring of big mountain cats and the drums of the Tarahumara Indians. We knew them Injuns were everywhere, but you'd never see 'em unless they wanted you to. Now and again we'd come upon a flat basin and there would be a little Indian *ranchito* and their sheds of corn, beans, and squash, dirt farmers was what they were, scratching out an existence in that stony, dead soil. Up on high ridges we saw little white crosses marking their burial grounds. But other than that, they were invisible.

We lost a few of our burros and, as luck would have it, we came into a fertile valley with a little village set at the foot of an old Spanish mission. It was a beautiful place with a crystal clear river running straight through it. It was thick with orange, lemon, and banana trees, bougainvillea, birds singing and lovely dark-eyed Spanish girls. There were sheep grazing on the slopes. We bought burros from a man there, a very sober and uneasy man. He charged us more than he would have the local peasants, us being *gringos* and all, but it was still a steal in comparison to prices north of the border.

As I said, it was a beautiful little place. But for all its natural wonders and riches, it was not a happy place. The locals wouldn't speak much with us. They seemed to be a worried, frightened lot. The women were always crying and crossing themselves. Daily, they made a pilgrimage to the old Spanish mission and you could hear them wailing up there like horny cats. The men, when they weren't working the fields or livestock, would sit up on those red-tiled roofs and scan the mountains. The richer ones had field glasses and the poorer just used their eyes. It was almost like they were expecting something. What? We didn't know and couldn't seem to find out. All we knew came from the storekeeper and he told us something had been carrying off the sheep, some animal, and that, of late, some people were missing.

But it was a local affair and we had business elsewhere, so we pushed on. We arrived at the silver camp about two days later...or what there was of it. It was set in a little craterlike valley with fields of surrounding wildflowers and twenty-foot cactus plants jutting up like bloated fingers. The wind was howling and the sun was blazing above. And even a mile out you could smell something bad about the place. You knew you were riding into the shit and it turned your guts to sauce.

Ruins is what we found. Tents were torn into confetti, shacks were collapsed, equipment scattered in every which direction. We thought bandits right away, but that didn't make no sense. We could see right away that no human force could have wrought such destruction. We found literally dozens and dozens of spent shell casings. But the worst thing was not the desolation, the carnage, the emptiness, but that stink, that smell of decay. Like a ditch full of bad meat. That's how the camp smelled. And there was a goddamned good reason for it.

We found horses that had been literally sheared right in half and gutted. Same went for burros. Same went for men. Most were crushed and disemboweled, squashed flat, their guts hanging out like those of a dog crushed beneath a wagon. Others had been decapitated and still others were limbless, arms and legs plucked off like the wings of flies. We found bodies and parts of them stuck in the top of those cactuses - thirty feet off the ground, some of them. None of it made any sense. Something had caused this, but what?

I wish that smell of putrescence was the worst thing, but it wasn't. There was another odor, too. A high, pungent smell almost like ammonia that went right through you like knife blades. Now and again, you'd catch a strong whiff of it and it was enough to put you on your ass.

Billy Creek just stood there in the middle of that graveyard, shaking his head, narrowing his eyes and staring up at the mountains. He walked through the wreckage, sniffing, sniffing like a hound on a rabbit. And every time he did that, he'd look back up into the mountains.

"What in Christ is with him?" I said to Salt River Tom.

Tom just shook his head, "Who in the hell knows? Goddamned crazy Injun. That's what." But Tom was in a bad way. We could find no trace of his brother. "Goddamn," he kept saying.

Poor Tom. It was bad enough for me - losing a fortune maybe and having to look at this atrocity - but to have kin up at that camp...well, you get the idea.

After about thirty minutes, I went up to Billy Creek and said, "Listen, you're giving me the willies. What gives here? You're acting like you're seeing ghosts out here."

"Maybe I am."

"Don't gimme that shit. What is it?"

But he just shook his head real slowly, made the hairs stand up on the back of my neck. "Something," he said in a low, haunted voice. "Something...something has come down from the mountain...and now, now it has returned..."

And swear to God, I loved that goddamned half-breed, but right then...well, dammit, I was not in the mood for any mystical bullshit. Not whatsoever. Something *had* been at work here, something by all rights big and powerful and pissed-off. Something that apparently ate bullets like a two-dollar hooker ate meat and was no worse for wear because of it. But that something was flesh and blood. I knew that like I knew too many hours in the saddle gave me piles like grapes at harvest time.

Tom was in a bad way. He was near to useless, wandering in circles and mumbling and sobbing and swearing, crazier than a stripper at a revival meeting. So, like it or not, Billy Creek was all I had and here he was, doing the one-eighty on me, his eyes gone dark and liquid like ink in a well. And he had that Ghost Dance-look about him, spookier than a scream in an empty house, just standing there sniffing the wind like a sailor sniffing for kitty, jerking off with the Great Spirit.

He seemed to feel me watching him like a little boy peeking in on his first peep show. He grinned. "Come over here, Doc," he said and the way he sounded, well, it wasn't pleasant. I'll swear upon the one and true Lord Jesus Kee-Rist that his voice didn't sound right at all. Like maybe them ancestral spirit warriors had crawled right up his ass, liked what they found, and decided to stay a spell; were doing his talking for him. "Look at this. Look!"

He was excited, yes. Excited like maybe he found an unopened pack of naked lady cards. But that wasn't it at all. Near the remains of a sluice trough where the ground was muddy and clotted like clay, there was this print had to be well over three feet in length, half that it width. A flat and heavy foot had set down there and sunk in a good three inches, triple toes splayed out in front, something like a claw or spur at the rear. It looked exactly like the track of a bantam rooster...but it was no goddamn chicken and I knew it.

"Thunderbird," is what Billy Creek said, as if he'd suspected it all along.

I just stared at him. "What the hell might that be?"

Salt River Tom wandered by and said, "Goddamn giant devil bird. That's what."

Billy told me that, yes, that's exactly what it was. He explained that these thunderbirds weren't just some Apache tale, but a story that was common to most tribes in the Nations. Even the Sioux up in the plains and the Huron up north believed in such a thing - a giant bird who could make thunder with its beak and create tornados and storm-winds with its wings. It was an evil, ancient creature that woke from its slumber every fifty years or so (and sometimes not for a century). But when it did, it raised holy hell of the purest sort.

I didn't want to believe any of it, but looking around at the destruction and that godawful print, what choice did I have? "You know where we can find this sumbitch?" I said.

Billy smiled and looked up at the mountain peaks. "Yeah, I think so."

We left the burros in that valley to graze and the three of us began our trek up into the high country. We took four burros with us to pack our provisions and just about every gun we could lay our hands on. But I'd seen all that brass laying about; .44s, .38s, you name it. I wasn't too happy with the idea of Winchesters or Remingtons. In the remains of one of the shacks I found something that cheered me considerably - a Sharps 1875. The so-called "Big Fifty" .50 caliber buffalo gun. I'd used one in my days as a buff hunter and I knew there wasn't nothing God or the Devil had created that it couldn't drop. So I took it along. It had such a long range that the Sioux called it the "shoot today, kill tomorrow" gun.

Three more days of riding higher and higher up into that desolate mountainous country, where there was nothing but rocks and scrub and that wind howling all the time. It got under my skin, got to where my flesh was ready to crawl off my bones. Billy Creek led the way on his chestnut and he had gone native on us and painted up his face like an Apache warrior and tied feathers to the barrel of his Winchester. Every night that sonofabitch sang his death song. Salt River Tom, overcome by grief, was no better. He was acting just plain strange. I kept away from the both of them whenever I could because I thought they were both crazier than a bluetick hound humping the business end of a twelve-gauge.

Yeah, it was lonely and godless country. One night we made ourselves a cold camp because Billy said we'd better not draw attention to ourselves. So we were sitting in that blowing darkness chewing jerky and drinking whiskey, and Billy was singing about his upcoming death and Salt River Tom was arguing with his brother who, of course, was not there and me, I'm miserable and scared shitless because this whole thing is just plain bad. And it's not just my companions, either, because I can feel something bad settling around us, something malignant and completely awful. Like being in the shadow thrown by old Satan hisself.

Like I said, we were sitting there and all of a sudden I heard this sound that filled my bladder with chipped party ice. It came from a long ways off - a deep and bellowing roar that rose up and up until it sounded like a dozen women screaming shrilly from the depths of a cave. And then it faded and broke up into a cackling echo that bounced around those barren mesas and empty valleys.

Before I had time to see the shit land or smell its color, there came a rushing cacophonous sound like a tornado plowing over the horizon and it was building and building and I was ready to shit an engraved gold necklace and the three of us were holding onto each other for dear life. The ground shook and trembled, and it seemed the hills were going to come apart. Horses were whinnying and burros complaining; but suddenly you couldn't hear a goddamn thing because it was right on top of us, that roaring and thundering sound. A huge black shadow fell over us, and then it was gone…but so were two of the burros.

After that, we were true believers.

Two more days of hard riding and climbing, and Salt River Tom had pretty much lost his mind and taken to pissing and shitting himself and singing old campaign songs. In a little arroyo scooped from that blasted red earth, Billy halted us. The arroyo was sprayed with something white and festering and stinking. It was like that ammonia smell again, only a lot worse; decaying, rotting.

"What the hell is that stuff?" I asked Billy, but he didn't answer and he didn't have to.

Because I knew. Like a bolt from the blue or a spur in the ass, I *knew*.

It was bird shit.

About ten gallons of the stuff and all tangled with clumps of hair and fur and half-digested things and bones, some of which were human and all scathed and cut with ruts and furrows in 'em like old driftwood. And it stunk so bad my eyes watered and vomit crawled up my throat like a bullsnake out of a mouse hole. Jesus H. Christ.

The next day, we found the thing's valley. A windy bowl of blasted rock dusted by fingers of snow with an atmosphere like a violated tomb. We'd arrived, all right.

How did we know?

Billy Creek knew. I saw it on his face and I felt it in my belly. That whole valley was full of this rancid, stagnant stink that was ugly and thick as coal dust in a Kentucky mine. Even Salt River Tom knew. He wandered around in circles and sang hymns and crossed himself. Me and Billy went down, but not Tom. We followed that smell and pretty soon we were looking down into this immense gully you could've lost a wagon train in. We started down and that entire chasm was filled with bones - human bones, horse, cattle, burro, sheep, dogs, you name it. Some of them were so old they'd gone yellow and shattered into powder when you touched them. Others were fresh with bloodstains and pitted with ragged teeth marks a half-inch deep. Looked like somebody had used an axe on 'em. But it wasn't just bones, but weathered pieces of saddle, gnawed boots, rusted gunbelts, even the feathered lance of a Membreno Apache chieftain. And the smell was worse - a stench of rot and worms and buried things. Everywhere more of that white, snotty bird shit stinking just as acrid and nauseating as a death pit sprinkled down with quicklime.

We began climbing over that heap of bones. Because on the other side of it there was a gigantic cave mouth an easy twelve feet in height and three times that in length. So we clawed and scrambled over that mass grave of skulls like rats in a crypt, over crushed rib cages and snapped femurs, and they were all green with mildew and frozen tight with blankets of black ice. And then we slipped up into that cave mouth. It was just as murky as old sin. But we had an oil lamp with us.

"You sure this a good idea?" I said to Billy.

"The thunderbird is a night hunter, Doc," he told me. "He won't come out till near sunset. We're safe until then."

The floor of the cave angled upward and we had to climb that rise that was slimed with thunderbird shit and litter from its meals and we kept going, panting and grunting and just about scared witless. All you could hear was water dripping somewhere, and maybe it wasn't water at all. We made it up that rise and it leveled out for maybe eight, ten feet and you could see the drag marks and spoor of something immense that had rooted there. And then the floor was gone; it dropped right into the darkness. We were looking into a huge shaft that reached straight down into the earth. I threw a stone down there and never heard it hit. Carefully, Billy lowered the lamp and that cloying darkness just swallowed the light sure and easy. A warm and rancid breeze blew up from the depths. It was a hot and black stink that just about withered you inside.

"If we had us a rope…" Billy started to say and let it go.

We looked at each other and we both felt it down deep, that nameless horror that settled into us like ice in a cistern and we got the hell out of there fast like two cats with burning tails. When we got back to our horses, Salt River Tom was gone. We followed the hoof prints of his horse for an hour, but with that twisting expanse of bluffs and craggy valleys and canons, we just couldn't catch sight of him. And the sun was sinking low and the shadows were starting to crawl up thick as snakes in a pit, so we went back.

After we hobbled our horses in a sheltered arroyo, we took our two remaining burros and picketed them near the gully on clear open ground where that bastard bird would see them and where we could get clean shots at it.

Then we waited.

And waited.

Maybe twenty minutes before the sun sank beneath the hills behind us, we heard that howling, roaring sound and knew the bird was waking up and stretching. We were hiding behind a row of flat table boulders. I can honestly tell you I've never felt fear like that in my life, before or since. And I've been in some spots. I would've gladly rutted with a pissed-off she-griz rather than face what I was about to face. It was like somebody had opened a floodgate in me and every terror from childhood on came rushing through me, filling me up like blood in a bucket.

When it finally came out of the gully, it was bigger than I thought. It slinked out like a bat, folding its wings and crab-crawling up through those bones, making these hollow shrieking sounds that filled me with cold jelly, and then with a single thrust of those short pillar-like legs it was in the air. Those immense wings were spread and flapping; and they created tempest winds, and dust and dirt were flying and it was like being in a sandstorm. The thing went up quickly and glided right over us with a rushing, booming sound. Then it swung back and came right down on the burros. Before they could do so much as whine, those huge clawed feet slit them into so much meat. The thing landed amongst them and started feeding.

The whole time my jaw was sprung so wide bees could have built a hive in my mouth.

In that fading light, I finally really, truly saw it.

Standing on those gigantic hind feet that were splayed out like the claws of a storybook dragon, it stood upright eighteen, twenty feet. A hideous thing from some antediluvian nightmare. It stank of old blood and rotting meat. Its wingspan had to be near-on a hundred feet and held in place by a network of arm bones bigger 'round than drainpipes and ending in these clawed fingers that had to be two, three feet in length and just as sharp as straight razors. Its skin was leathery and pebbled like the belly of a sand lizard.

Billy Creek started making a funny sound in his throat.

But I wasn't paying much attention.

I was watching those gigantic wings and how they were membranous and drawn taut as wet leather, slimed with something sticky and the color of dirty green swamp algae. That body was thick and rippling with muscles, bigger than a draught horse and had a whipping, jagged tail. It's skull was shaped like an anvil and looked about the size of a birch bark canoe, that fanged beak ripping out fifty pound chunks of meat with each stab into the burros.

As I was about to pump a bullet into that horror, Billy Creek suddenly jumped up and let out a war cry, and it was so goddamn loud I thought somebody shoved a hot branding fork up his ass. He charged down through that stony soil and right at that demon bird. Its beak darted out like the head of a snapping turtle and gave a full, thundering roar that nearly put old Billy on his heathen ass.

But Billy charged right in, firing rounds from his Winchester. But he might as well have been throwing salt. The rounds hurt it, stung it maybe, and it didn't like it. You could see that. But they were hardly lethal. Before Billy could get within ten feet, it snapped forward with that beak and cut him in half just as sure as he was a paper doll snipped by scissors.

I let out a scream myself and locked down a round into the Sharps. That devil bird looked up at me with flat, remorseless eyes just as green as emeralds and bigger than baseballs. I knew what I didn't want was for it to get airborne, so I put a round through its wing. The fifty punched in a nice hole and wind whistled through it. I ejected the spent shell, opened the breech and inserted a new one and quick as you please put another window in its wing. It was crippled and pissed off.

I figured it was no good without its wings, but I figured wrong.

Making a deafening screech like the roar of a freight train in a tunnel it came right at me, flapping its wings and sprinting. You see, it wasn't so much running as leaping and hopping and, dear Christ, by the time I realized that, it had gained ground. Serious ground. It was wailing and snapping that beak and kicking up dust devils and bathing me with a stink like a half dozen bull bison rotting in the summer sun.

I chambered another round and shot it straight in the chest.

It spun around, pissing blood and meat, and came right on. I put another in its belly and third in its left eye. With a horrible scream it rose up flapping those wings, and they sounded like the shrouds of a big four-master snapping in a high wind, and then it crashed down, dead. I can't say its blood was red exactly, it was too dark. Just running and stinking and greasy black like shit from a dead man's bowels. Its body trembled for a time and then it died proper, the jaws falling open.

And that's how I killed the thunderbird.

Oh, and if you're wondering, no, I never did see poor old Salt River Tom again. He must've succumbed to the elements and his bones are still out there.

There was silence for a time after that.

Nobody in the cookhouse said a damn thing. But they were relieved it was over with. They'd been on the edges of their seats and now they finally relaxed, finally breathed. They looked at each other and didn't know what to say.

Charlie Lee, the oldest of the lot but still a tit-weaned pup to Doc Chambers said, "Quite a story, Doc. Gotta be bullshit, though. Ain't never was a bird like that, being half dragon and half bird and what not…entertaining, though."

Doc just laughed at that. "Bullshit, you say?"

"No offense, Doc, but…"

But Doc was still laughing. "Young pups to a man." He reached over and turned up the oil lamp so everything around him was bright and clear. His face danced with shadow. He kicked his feet up onto the table. He wore high-topped boots that came nearly to his knees. Everybody looked at them and looked hard. They were made of a dull green, quartz-colored leather. Like snakeskin they were scaled, but the individual scales were bigger than dollar pieces. They were shiny, oily-looking. To a man, they'd never seen reptile hide like that. "Yes sir," Doc Chambers said, sipping his coffee, "I skinned that bastard and had a fellow down in Tucson tool me the finest pair of boots I ever did own. And that's the truth, boys."

Ever hear that sayin' that there's two sides to every story? Well this here next one's somethin' like that, only both sides of it 'r tall ones!

All sorts of folk pass through this land on their way to paradise or perdition. Lots of foreigners from places like China, Africa, 'r even Australia. Thing is, most of 'em leave somethin' behind when they pass through; junk, most of it, but I'd allow as here 'n there something turns up as is stranger than the land it came from, and a fer piece too dangerous fer anyone to be messin' around with.

Take these two gents who ended up both gettin' exactly what they wished for - mostly.

A TREATISE ON CORPOREALITY OR JINN AND TONIC, WITH A WHISKEY CHASER

BY

MARK MCLAUGHLIN AND MICHAEL KAUFMANN

I weren't always an all-American hero. Hard as that is for me to remember at times, it keeps me humble to recall that 'tweren't that long ago I was a varmint. There was a time when I'd have just as soon looked at you as killed you. They called me Wild Bill Whiskey. Them was the days of my drinkin'. 'Tain't a short story, so set a spell and listen. Don't worry if you nod off, I'll just notch your ear with a well-aimed .44 to wake you up.

Well sir, 'tweren't but a few years back that I couldn't rightly call myself a man, let alone a hero to the pioneerin' folk crossin' the mighty Miss'ippi on their way to greener pastures. No, I reckon I barely had fuzz on my lip then, 'stead of the pearly white handlebar you see today. This here scar from my eye to my ear, that weren't there, neither. No sir, not back then. Back then myself weren't all I was full of. I generally had four or five slugs in me, and only one of 'em was lead. The rest was liquor.

Oh, I fancied myself a man, but I wasn't no 'count, not then. I know it's hard to believe, seein' me now, but bear with me and I'll show you how it all came about.

It was the spring of '54, it was, or was it '55? That was the year of the drought, and... No, it was '54. '54 or I'll drink my age in fifths. Uh, that is, that's what I *would* have said, back in '54, before Prescott showed up. Yessir, I remember it like it was yesterday. Or the day before.

Me and Deke and Cooter was playin' five-stud, jokers wild, at Old Man Ying's saloon. We was all scrapin' the bottom of the barrel in them days, so we played for shots instead of dollars. I reckon I'd won myself a good pint when in walked Twelve-Step Prescott, sure as the sunrise and brimmin' with a zest for life...

Allow me to introduce myself. My name is Cuthbert Prescott; I'm known by friends, however, as Twelve-Step, as I was born on the twelfth day of the twelfth month, and was placed on the twelfth step of the orphanage. The top step was the thirteenth, and to be left there would have been unlucky.

I was only twenty when I first met Bill W. He liked to call himself Wild Bill Whiskey, and when I met him he was rumored to have killed two men for not addressing him as such. My guess is that Bill started the rumors. He was always pulling capers like that to win friends or influence people. In fact, I'd have just as soon never laid eyes on the man, but fate cursed me with a singular gift: rescuing drunken sots and helping them become respectable sots.

I'd been practicing medicine, such as it was, at a sanitarium in the foothills of Oklahoma. A man (I'll call him Tom W.) was brought under my care by a concerned physician - to use the term loosely - who wanted Tom W. to sober up. I'd seen worse cases, but not many. Tom went through a rough spell, fell off the wagon a time or two, then went straight. Two months later he caught the pox and died. But before he did, he told me in heartfelt tones of his son, Bill, who was following his father's footsteps around the sour mash. Tom W.'s clear love for his son, his renewed concern for his son's health and sobriety, inspired me to search out his prodigal and bring him kicking and screaming into the life of temperance.

That, and the bag of ore Tom W. pressed into my palm with a threat that if I didn't cure his son, his cousin Calamity Darla would hunt me down and gut me like a fish.

I found Bill W. in the town of Westerly, in a squalid rat hole where one could buy foul concoctions that somehow passed for liquor. I hesitated at the door, deciding whether or not the bag of gold was worth this, and whether Tom W. really did have a cousin who would be checking up on me. Just as I was turning to leave, some burly hulk of a cowboy propelled me through the door with scarcely a notice, sending me skidding across the floorboards on my chin and sending my brand-new bowler flying. I lay there on the floor considering my plight. My vest was ruined, my trousers ripped, and my life had scarcely looked more bleak. No amount of threats or gold could possibly be worth living in this sty of a town for even a day, let alone the months it would take to bring Bill W. to his senses.

Bill W., as it happened, was indeed in the saloon where I'd been told he would be, playing some inane drinking game and fully making an ass of himself. From the look of him, I wasn't sure that he'd ever gone a day without drinking, although his father had assured me Bill hadn't touched liquor until he was eight. Beer before that, sure, but no liquor. Tom W. was nothing if not a dedicated father.

Bill stared at me with a curious mixture of fear, self-loathing, and honest puzzlement. He opened his mouth to say something. To my disgust, his greeting was preceded by a belch that made my eyes water...

Yessir, Prescott was a dandy, no doubt of that. He burst through the door of the saloon as bright as Easter, with his English clothes and a funny hat and a smile as big as Montana. That boy had a purpose that day, sure as shootin', and he shot right over to me. He had a mission and he aimed to see it through.

I saw he was a gentlemanly sort, with all the class of a preacher man or an undertaker. So when he picked himself up off the floor, I stood and touched my hat to him. "Sir, my name's Bill Whiskey but my friends call me *Wild* Bill on account of my capacity as a malt liquor connoisseur. I'd be obliged if you'd join me in a friendly game of five-stud."

Well, his eyes just sparkled at that, being noticed by a heroic cowboy feller such as myself, and he pulled up a chair and put his hat on his lap, all proper and dandy and that. His hair was slicked back with saddle soap, and polished to a fine black sheen. His hands was all soft and white like the ladies Old Man Ying kept upstairs. Not that I knew firsthand, mind you, but the other, less-scrupled fellers talked. My heart, mind you, still belonged to Big Old Vonda, as it had back when she was my wet-nurse.

But that's all by-the-by. Prescott, he looked up at me with those big brown eyes of his with all the admiration in the world. I couldn't have been that much older than him, but I reckon a born leader such as me just naturally invokes awe in them highbred highbrows...

I decided I had to go through with it despite myself, and despite Bill's self as well. By the looks of things, he was on a course to reach complete liver failure by age thirty-two, and I couldn't in good conscience let him drink himself to death without at least trying to help.

So I righted the chair that one of Bill's cronies had tipped over when he passed out, and sat down beside Bill. Looking at the man, I could barely contain my revulsion. His eyes were bloodshot and haggard, his face was drawn and sallow. The one bright spot in that whole mess of a countenance was his nose, which would have made even reindeer laugh and call him names...

Well sir, I took Prescott under my wing, and together we rode the trail on McClaren's ranch.

Prescott, he was always talkin' about drinkin' and not drinkin' and whatnot, and how I couldn't expect to quit cold turkey but had to take it one step at a time. I weren't ever real sure what Prescott was talkin' about, but if I noticed him lookin' at me I'd nod real polite like, and he'd be content with that.

I s'pose he just needed someone to talk to...

When Bill sobered up the next morning, I told him of his father's dying wish. Bill nodded at me over his eye-opener and said I was welcome to ride up to the ranch with him to talk more about it. I think he expected I couldn't ride.

I explained to him the benefits of Temperance and the effects that the poison he drank had on his body. He nodded every once in a while so I knew he was hearing my message of sobriety, though I was distressed to catch him sneaking a swig from his boot flask now and again when he thought I wasn't looking. It would take more than a few eloquent words to convert this ruffian.

As I considered Wild Bill's sorry plight, my eye fell upon his tattered bootstraps. Pulling himself up out of his mean state - as though by those very bootstraps - would be no small feat. Yes, the first step would be to get Bill to admit he even had a problem. Perhaps he was under the mistaken impression that a cowboy's life had to be lived in a booze-addled morass of dizzy wantonness...

Well, sir, me and Twelve-Step got along swimmingly from the start. Me bein' the rough-and-tumble cowpoke that I were and him bein' the nancy-boy that he were gave us plenty to talk about. And talk he did, like to give my ears calluses. But then one evenin' my life changed as never before.

We was sittin' in Old Man Ying's saloon, as was our habit of a Thursday evenin' after a hard day's work. I was workin' on my fourth or fifth shot, and Prescott was yakkin' away over his sarsaparilla. A dandy, he was. Never touched liquor. I still don't know why.

He was goin' on about how there was a Higher Power, and I didn't have to think of Him as God if I didn't like the way I thought about God, but I had to see that there was something higher than me. I looked up at the ceiling to see what he was carryin' on about, and durned if I didn't lay eyes on it. There, stashed up in the rafters of Old Man Ying's place, was a nice fancy bottle labeled *Jinn*. I ain't no school marm, but I could see somebody'd spelled their booze wrong. But no matter, it would still do the job just fine.

I set up with a start, seeing my Higher Power more clearly. All these years of drinking whiskey, and turns out I'd have had better luck with gin.

Well, sir, I says, "I got it!" and jumped up on the table to get the bottle. The table was a bit tipsy, and I like to fell off a time or two, but Prescott finally held the table steady and I reached up to grab my prize. The label had a lot of fancy writin' on it in French or Sanskrit or whatnot. Now I ask you, what sort of fool needs instructions for drinkin'?

Many of my conversations with Bill W. took place in that rough saloon, so determined was I to rescue the man from himself. I felt sure that with persistence, my rhetoric would serve as tonic for his sickly soul.

We were discussing the finer points of spirituality one evening, and I was explaining to him the logic of believing in a Higher Power to help him get sober. He leaned back in his chair and squinted his eyes upward, and I imagined he was actually trying to see into the heavens.

Imagine my happy surprise when his eyes went wide and he yelled out, "I've got it!"

He attempted to crawl up on the table, but his intoxication made this no small task. After falling off a time or two, I steadied his legs while he stood up on tiptoe - reaching, I finally saw, for a bottle hidden in the rafters. He grabbed the dusty old thing triumphantly and my heart sank as I realized he only had found a free drink.

But then something else caught his attention, and he squinted through a knothole in the ceiling. He grinned lasciviously, and it dawned on me that he was spying on Old Man Ying's secondary source of income upstairs. I tugged on his pant leg to get him down, but then his face turned slowly into a mask of rage. He yelled something incomprehensible and fell off the table, winding up in a tangle of chairs and limbs and broken glass...

Well, sir, I had just grabbed the bottle of gin when I heard some strange sounds from above. At first I thought I was gettin' a message from that Higher Power, but then I spied a knothole in the floorboards and peered through. Old Man Ying was selling more than liquor upstairs, so I figured I'd watch the show for a while.

Simply put, I finally recognized the lady in the room upstairs as none other than Big Old Vonda, beloved nurse from my childhood. Bigger than ever, and older than ever, she was nonetheless my Big Old Vonda, and I weren't a-goin' to stand for her bein' debased that way.

I wanted to run up them stairs and put a .44 caliber stop to the evil I saw above me. But I must've forgot I was teeterin' on a table, and I woke up in a pile of broken wood and glass, with a low-flyin' cloud floatin' out the door and Twelve-Step standin' over me...

I would not have believed this had I not seen it with my own eyes, but when that bottle broke, there was a puff of smoke and then a huge, misty form arose before me. It had the face of a man, with deep-set eyes and a cruel sneer. He sported a thick black Vandyke and golden hoops through his earlobes. A white turban covered his hair. I then saw, on the floor, the label from Bill W.'s broken bottle.

The label said *Jinni,* though I had to squint to see the second 'I', since it was half-obscured by dust. And that word conjured up images from my childhood reading of the "Arabian Nights." A jinni was a powerful spirit in Moslem legend, of great size and supernatural powers.

The Jinni looked down first at Bill, then at me. Seeing that Bill was unconscious, he laughed maliciously and fixed his gaze on me.

"Hear me, mortal," he thundered. "Because the man who freed me from my prison is unable to now call on my powers, I am released from his bondage. And soon, I shall finally possess the very thing all humans take for granted!"

With that, he flew out the door. Stunned, I revived Bill W., my mind spinning at what had just transpired...

Well, sir, I woke up with a splitting headache and more'n a few cuts and bruises. I aimed to ease the pain with that bottle of fancy gin, so I was right peeved when I saw it was broken. Then Twelve-Step started jabbering about the bottle being empty except for some blustery thundercloud with a bee in his turban.

"Empty?" I says.

"'Ceptin' for the jinni," Twelve-Step says. "And he left without givin' you your three wishes."

"That, sir, cannot be tolerated," I says, and dusted off my duds and checked my six-gun. "Besides, that critter's a cheat and a scoundrel. 'Tweren't a drop of gin in that bottle!"

Bill had looked better, I was sure, but I couldn't say exactly when. When he fell off the table, he grazed a nail sticking out of a chair, splitting his skin from his eye to his ear. He insisted on only a rudimentary cleaning and bandaging of the wound. I think he wanted a scar to improve his image.

I explained what had happened, and although he seemed at first dubious, he soon forgot all about whatever had startled and angered him so much before he fell. His new mission was to track down the jinni and collect his three wishes.

To make sure he did nothing rash, I accompanied him.

Well, sir, it's no easy job to track a jinni. No tracks in the dust and that. We headed up to McClaren's ranch, just to get some supplies for the hunt and tell Mister McClaren we'd be taking some time off.

The ranch were abuzz when we got there. It seemed a half-dozen head of cattle had been attacked, and nobody knew who or what had done it. We rode over to where the problem was, behind a hill south of the ranch house.

The cattle's eyes was wide open and rolled back in pain. Great chunks of meat had been torn off the flanks and ribs, and the scary part was, it looked like some giant hand had done the tearin'. Four marks in a row looked just like fingers, with a fifth lower down and scraping up toward the four. 'Spite of the wounds, the cowhands what found 'em said that the poor beasts was still alive, but barely. Young Prescott, spoon-fed mother's boy that he were, got green around the gills and run off behind a tree. I reckon all that carnage was too much for his genteel nature.

Well, sir, I resolved then and there to find whatever had done this to the cattle. Prescott wanted to chase down the attacker right away, but I pointed out to him that if we had the three wishes from the jinni, the task would be loads easier. Yessir, I guess that kind of thinkin' don't come natural to most folks, just to us real cowboy-type fellers...

The sight of the butchered cattle was gruesome, to be sure, but I'd seen far worse things while practicing medicine. Wild Bill, on the other hand, showed his softer side upon seeing the first injured beast, its blood painting the prairie crimson. The poor man turned positively green. For a rootin', tootin' cowboy, he had no stomach for blood, and I was more sure than ever that he hadn't actually shot at anyone before, let alone killed them.

When Bill had regained his composure, he said it was a terrible shame about the cattle and that he wanted to help find what did it, but he had a score to settle with the jinni first. I was beginning to suspect what had actually happened to the cattle, but did not want to frighten Bill any further. So I mentioned casually that if we did find the jinni, the three wishes could help protect us from whatever odious beast had savaged the herd.

Bill W. thought that was a marvelous idea, and we packed our saddlebags with jerky and water (I convinced Bill he didn't want to take any more chances on liquor bottles just yet), stocked up on bullets, and set out...

Well, sir, we tracked that jinni for the better part of a day before we found him again. Meanwhile, Prescott was jawin' about makin' amends to people I've wronged when I had too much to drink and that.

He said I likely felt guilty about cheatin' folks out of money, takin' advantage of weaker folks to get money for drink, and threatenin' to kill folks when they crossed me. I reckon he were almost on to something there. Truth is, I did feel bad for them folks. It must be pretty humiliatin' to be taken advantage of by someone who, like as not, don't remember how good a job he did swindlin' a feller the night before. But then, 'tain't everybody what can hold their own against a man such as myself, in the drink or not.

We knew we was on the right track when we come across some more ripped-apart cattle. We was even startin' to see tracks in the sand every so often, like some varmint jumpin' great distances. But the strange thing was, the tracks themselves were big. And I mean to say *big*. They looked almost like people feet, but about twice the size.

I remarked on this to Prescott, who just nodded. I don't think he had yet realized what we was chasin' after, and so he didn't realize what it meant for the tracks to be so *large* and so *far apart*.

We was huntin' a monster, sure as shootin'...

We went nearly a full day before reaching the next bovine victims. I took the opportunity to teach Wild Bill the importance of making amends for one's trespasses made in the name of liquor. I explained to him the depressing weight of guilt one carries around with knowledge of such trespasses, and the difference in one's outlook that getting that guilt off one's chest can make. I'm not entirely sure if Bill took me seriously. I don't know that he'd ever apologized to anyone in his life, or had someone apologize to him. Still, I was resolved to see him through.

We caught up with the jinni, or nearly so, at the scene of his next crime. Four slaughtered cattle were breathing their last when we rode up. Their flesh had been clawed away, as before. But this time there were some tracks in the dust, and they were enormous. My suspicions were being confirmed.

Looking to the west, I saw a large reddish shape against the setting sun, half-floating and half-bounding away. The jinni, it appeared, was making himself a real body - the one thing all humans take for granted. But it seemed his powers were changing in the process - he was no longer flying. Instead, he would spring up on his beefy legs for great distances, sailing through the air, thus outpacing us. However, it would take him time to catch cattle and steal their flesh, and that was time we could use to our advantage.

"It will mean no sleep for us to catch him," I told Bill W. "The jinni is building himself a body, but he is still far from finished."

Bill made a few questions about how much it would hurt to have our flesh torn from our bodies, and danced around the issue of calling off the chase, but he mustered what courage he had and rode on.

For all his thousands of faults, Bill had a good heart, and it infuriated him to see cattle treated so wickedly. That, and he wanted his three wishes. I only hoped he wouldn't waste them on drink...

Well, sir, we rode all night long after that jinni, and poor Prescott was like to fall asleep in the saddle. I reckon he didn't know from hard work, not with them lily-white hands of his. He put up a brave front, though. Despite my warnings of the danger ahead of us - if the jinni could do that to cattle, he could do the same to us - he insisted on pressing on. I gave him a few chances to call off the chase if he were scared, but he rode on.

We finally caught sight of the jinni again just as the sun was risin' behind us. He was makin' another killin', and we pulled up behind a knot of scrub brush to take measure of our enemy. The jinni was rippin' the flesh from a young angus, ignorin' the pitiful cries of the poor heifer. It like to made me tearful, it did, to see a helpless animal in such pain.

The jinni, he took and formed the meat around his torso, makin' for himself a patchwork belly. His legs was already formed from the cattle he'd killed already, and they were six feet tall if they were an inch. Above the meat, though, he weren't quite so well-defined, and he kind of swirled around and that.

Well, sir, I weren't about to stand there and watch him slaughter more cattle, so I steadied my Winchester against the side of a tree and aimed into that jinni smoke for where I reckoned his heart would be. Prescott started blabbering some fancy talk, but I didn't pay him no mind - I had shootin' to do. Takin' a deep breath and lettin' it out slow to steady my finger, I pulled the trigger...

I warned Bill that any shot at the jinni's incorporeal form would have no impact. In retrospect, I should have chosen another word.

"Incorporeal" probably meant about as much to him as "don't drink." From what I could see, Bill's aim was true (despite a mild case of the shakes - he hadn't had a drink in more than twenty-four hours), and the bullet hit the monstrous jinni in what would have been the middle of his chest. There was a small swirl of smoke there, and the jinni straightened up from his grisly task and turned toward us.

"What is this?" he boomed. "Am I a mere mortal that you come at me with such pitiful weaponry?"

Bill levered another round into his rifle and fired again, now aiming lower. This time the jinni squealed as blood sprang from his newly-formed belly. I don't suppose he had ever felt pain before.

"Fools! The flesh you rip I can easily repair. Do you not think that I, who can create flesh for myself from these beasts, am able to heal my wounds as well?" Then the jinni smiled - an evil, curling leer. "But you, foolish ones, have no such ability." He made a swift hand gesture in our direction. The brush on our right caught ablaze, and we barely controlled our horses from bucking us in panic.

The jinni looked puzzled, and studied his misty hands for a moment or two before trying again. This time a tumbleweed to our left burst into flames.

"We're in luck!" I yelled to Bill. "His corporeality is affecting his aim."

"You cannot stop me!" the jinni cried. "Soon I shall have a real body, and no force will be able to put me back in any bottle!"

We dug our heels into our horses. The jinni continued to rant at us as we rode off. "How I will enjoy the delicious pleasures of the flesh! Why, I will be able to taste your hearts when I rip them from you and eat them!"

Once we were at a safe distance, we stopped to catch our breath. Eventually that jinni would figure out how to adjust his aim. And we would need more than bullets to take this monster down...

Well, sir, I reckon I plugged that jinni clean through whatever he had for a heart, but that only made him mad. Then I figgered that varmint had an appetite for evil, so I thought I'd target that next. He was hollerin' some nonsense when I sent a bullet through his belly. That just made the critter even madder. He sent a fireball our way and caught the brush blazin' beside us. That seemed to confuse him some, and he next hit a tumbleweed to the other side.

I realized that his aim was off, said so to young Twelve-Step, and we lit out like who flung the chunk. We needed to rest up once we were out of harm's way, so we sat under a tree for a spell. Young Prescott was deep in thought - them moody city-slickers, they're like that - so I picked up a sturdy old branch that was lyin' around and started whittlin' on it. Whittlin's good for puttin' thoughts in a man's head...

Bill tried to make conversation, but I shushed him so I could think straight.

He got a bit sullen - in that rural, uncouth way of his - so he picked up a long branch and started sharpening the end with his knife, as simple folks do when they were bored. 'Whittling,' I think they call it.

Then it hit me.

Making holes in the jinni's new body with bullets was reparable. But what about destroying the flesh outright...?

With my guidance, Bill was able to turn that branch into a fine weapon to use against the creature. What we needed next was a big fire, and we'd seen a way to do that...

Once I came up with a plan, it was all gravy. I whittled that branch to a fine sharp point, and even put some barbs on the shaft for keepin' our prey put once we caught him. Prescott marveled at my craftsmanship, but I'm a jack of all trades and all, and 'tweren't no big thing to me.

We set out after the jinni again, me carryin' the branch and Prescott ridin' ahead. We found the jinni two hours later, and he'd turned one of his arms into flesh at the expense of another cow.

Well sir, Prescott dug his heels into his horse and headed for the jinni at a fair clip. He was careful to stay in the dry brush, because that was part of our plan. I, meanwhile, circled 'round to the other side, all quiet and stealthy and that. When I cleared the rise on t'other side of the jinni, I saw Prescott was fillin' his end of the bargain perfectly.

I readied the branch, said a quick prayer for Prescott and threw my own name in - just in case - and charged...

As I rode toward the jinni, I started yelling all manner of curses at him to get his attention. Fortunately, he was still having problems with his aim. He set the trail of scrub brush behind me ablaze, and then decided to switch to tempests. He started one or two small tornadoes, but they only served to spread the fire around.

It was then that Wild Bill W. came riding over the ridge behind the jinni, his sharpened branch lowered like the lance of a knight. The jinni never saw him coming.

Bill speared the jinni right through the midsection, and the jinni screamed just like the cattle he'd slaughtered. He struggled to twist himself off, but the barbs carved into the branch held him fast. The jinni tried to bend his arm around to incinerate Bill, but that wily cowboy kept himself behind and out of reach.

How Bill had the strength to hold that branch while the jinni writhed and cursed and screamed, I'll never know. I can only guess that my own brave actions had inspired him to previously unimagined heights of manly heroism. I jumped off my horse and grabbed the branch so that Bill could dismount. Then, together we maneuvered the branch - jinni and all - over to the fire. I must admit, the smell of all that roasting beef was tantalizing, for we'd only had stale jerky to eat for quite a while.

As the flesh cooked away in chunks, the jinni's power escaped him, until at last only a misty arm and turbaned head were left, hovering exhausted above the flames.

He was beaten and he knew it, and he obeyed meekly when I ordered him into a small flask I had brought along for the purpose. The flask we would open again after we'd decided what wishes to have granted. As it turned out, their scope was limited according to the jinni's newly *reduced* state...

But even limited results are better than none at all.

Well, sir, I reckon there ain't too many wishes that could beat the barbecue we had that night. It was steak, all right, but with a tasty hint of spice you just don't get from plain old cows. Yessir, the only thing that would've made it better was a good jug of whiskey to wash it all down. When Twelve-Step Prescott had bedded down for the night, I pulled out my flask and toasted his health. I'd been chasin' jinn for the last two days. It was time for some whiskey to chase me.

Later, there was the matter of Big Old Vonda and of course, those three wishes...

But that's another story.

WEIRD TRAILS

Now not meanin' any offense to 'em, but you and me both know there's some folk as are just plain weird all on their lonesome. The lamebrain things some of us take into our heads to do, why, a body wouldn't believe it even if he'd just up and done it his ownself!

And there's some as do that sort of thing regular-like.

Now when I'm done with this next one, you can call me a liar if you've a mind to and I'll take no offense on it. But this here tale is jus' too dad-blamed stupid not to be true!

SHOWDOWN AT IDIOT'S ROCK

BY
KEITH HERBER

Folks around these parts are all familiar with that big rock that sits high atop the bluff just south of town; and they all call it by its old Indian name, Eagle Rock. But for a few years it was known to everyone as Idiot's Rock, site of a long ago showdown between two of the biggest lamebrains the West has ever known. Atop this rock, two of the stupidest ninnies that ever was laid it all on the line, both out to prove once and for all who was the dumbest of the dumb.

Although long ignored by historians, the 'town jackass,' or 'local ninnie' (an American counterpart to England's 'village idiot') was a vital part of the country's westward expansion. For a few short decades every sizeable town west of the Mississippi had its own jackass – an individual capable of tripping over every loose board, losing his shoe in every puddle; one whom could be counted on to entertain the townsfolk with his dunderheaded mistakes, excite them with hare-brained stunts, and brighten their otherwise dull and cheerless lives.

Perhaps the greatest idiot of them all was a man called Stupid Luther. Personally responsible for some of the most excrutiatingly nitwit screwups of all time, Luther's name was synonymous with imbecility. Famous for his flying cow pie dives, he was also a master of such classic western fuckups as 'unknowingly drinking from a spittoon' and 'accidentally sitting on the hot branding iron'.

Stupid Luther spent most of his life stumbling and bumbling his way from town to town, parading his dimwittedness before thousands over a long and glorious career. Santa Fe had collapsed in laughter when Luther was chased through the streets by an angered Billy goat; shortly after Luther had unthinkingly introduced the goat to Mama Guadalupe's tamale sauce. And Luther had been the talk of the town in Dodge City the day he got caught on the blades of a rotating windmill and spent several hours whirling around before anyone was able to get him down. Enhanced by the dizziness, Luther's achievements over the next few days became legendary. Falling off roofs in Abilene earned him such fame that he returned again and again for repeat performances. In Laramie they still talk of the day Luther was struck by lightning while holding onto the handle of Widow Johnson's water pump.

Of course this kind of reputation was bound to attract a certain amount of trouble, and hardly a month went by that didn't see some young dolt, armed with a pitiful battery of hackneyed pratfalls and cliché silly faces, come looking for Luther. These hotshots would give it their best but in the end Luther would always send them scurrying away, tails tucked between their legs. After all, who could face up to a man willing to drop an anvil on his foot, just for a laugh?

The challengers all moved on quickly, some eventually finding permanent homes in small, out of the way towns that had need of a local fool. Others were so completely crushed that they left the profession altogether, many turning their talents to politics.

Luther out-clowned them all, and his praises were sung from St. Joe to San Francisco, from Butte to Nogales. But the strains of the road began to take their toll; Luther could feel himself slowing down and, wishing to leave the business on top, decided to quit his active career. For his retirement he chose the town of Spud City, Idaho, population 398.

The folks at Spud City were thrilled to learn that Luther was moving in. He had swung through town once, years ago, had stayed two weeks and left them laughing with tears in their eyes. After all these years people still loved to tell the story of the day Stupid Luther got his head stuck in the rabbit hutch and got all his hair chewed off. To a town like Spud City, where entertainment was normally limited to what you could do with a horse and a potato, Stupid Luther was a Godsend.

Potatoes were, as you might have guessed, the mainstay of Spud City's economy. The local ranches harvested them by the hundreds of thousands. Once a week, during the picking season, a train from out East would arrive; this train would be loaded up with tons of Spud City potatoes and then, with steam engines straining under the immense load, carry off its precious cargo back to places like Boston and New York, where the potatoes would be served in fine gourmet restaurants.

While awaiting the arrival of the train, the potatoes were stored in a huge potato silo constructed and maintained by the Lewis Potato Combine, a company formed and operated by Eldon Lewis, who, quite frankly, controlled most of the potato industry in Spud City. This silo, which was loaded by a steam-powered potato elevator of Lewis' own patented design, was accessed by a rail siding that ran up next to the foot of the mountain. Parked by the silo, the train could be quickly loaded, then sent on its way.

Spud City welcomed Luther, and soon after arriving he was given a job cleaning the stables at the Silver Horse Saloon. His pay included free meals and a stall to sleep in along with enough money to keep his hair cut and provide him with a change of clothes every year or two. Luther adjusted quickly to his new, homey lifestyle, and soon grew to be quite comfortable. This idyllic situation, however, was not destined to last.

In his time Stupid Luther had made his reputation simply by being extremely stupid. But now the West was changing, modernizing, railroads connecting everything and bringing with them sophisticated entertainments from the East; strippers and juggling bears. The town jackass was rapidly becoming a thing of the past, and only those few fools who were well known, those who were almost pathologically moronic, stood a chance at making a living.

Regardless, there were still a few young dipshits out there who thought they could make their living the old way, relying on little else than a dull wit and a vacant grin to earn their keep. But a young lamebrain soon found out that without a reputation, work was hard to find. And there was really only one sure way to make a fast name for yourself, and that was to 'outgun' some man who already had one. It only stood to reason that sooner or later one of these young dumbbells would come alookin' for Luther.

He called himself Screwloose Rubin, and he bounced and geeked his way into town one quiet, sunny Sunday afternoon in the midst of the harvest season. His face and clothing were caked with the dust of the trail and he looked as though he had traveled many a hard mile before reaching Spud City. Townspeople in the streets stopped to stare at this brash young stranger, this unknown jerk, but he paid them no attention and, ignoring the boardwalks, splashed his way along the muddy, rutted street, headed for the heart of town.

Humming tunelessly to himself, Rubin turned into the Silver Horse Saloon, stumbling over the edge of the boardwalk as he did. He pushed against the swinging doors which then promptly swung back and slapped him in the face. On the second try he made it through the doorway and disappeared into the darkness beyond.

Less than thirty seconds later Rubin reappeared through the doors, this time suspended face down in mid air by two cowpokes holding him by his arms and legs. It seemed it hadn't taken long for Screwloose to spill someone's beer and then, while backing away trying to apologize, fall over a poker table, scattering everyone's chips.

The two cowboys swung Rubin back and forth a couple times and then, with a "Heave-ho!" flung Screwloose out over the street. With a tremendous splash he landed face first in a muddy wheel rut, arms and legs spread-eagled about him. The people who had gathered to watch broke into peals of laughter and Rubin lifted his head to grin appreciatively, and blankly, to his audience.

Meanwhile, around the corner of the saloon, unbeknownst to almost everyone, stood Stupid Luther, leaning on his shovel and taking in the whole performance. He watched as two passersby, Good Samaritan types, stopped to pry the stranger up out of the mud. The two got him on his feet, but as soon as they turned their backs, Rubin slipped again, this time landing in the mud on his backside. The crowd roared their approval. Rubin grinned mindlessly to the cheering townsfolk, but when he turned his gaze toward the distant Luther, his expression changed. Recognition lit his eyes and a subtle sneer twisted his lip. Luther met the young man's stare unflinchingly but then Screwloose was surrounded by the crowd and Luther lost sight of him.

The gauntlet was down, the challenge in. Stupid Luther knew he would have to either take a stand against this young dunderhead, or pack up his bags and get out of town.

Two hours later Stupid Luther struck back. With his one arm hopelessly entangled in the trailing harnesses, he allowed himself to be dragged the entire length of Main Street by a pair of carriage horses he was supposed have been preparing for a customer. Pounced and pummeled by the rutted road, he hollered and screamed as he was mercilessly hauled along, drawing the excited attention of a good one-third of Spud City's entire population. Luther was nearly a quarter mile out of town, well past the city limits, before he finally managed to get himself free. Later, returning to the city battered and bruised, he received not only much well-earned laughter and many taunts but a good deal of honest sympathy as well - along with the necessary medical care his injuries required.

The town had never been treated to quite the spectacle they had seen that day and when they went to bed that night their stomachs were still sore from laughter. Smiles traced across their lips as they slept peacefully. No one had any idea of what was to come.

Rubin was at it early the next morning. He had procured himself a one-time job at Pritchert's General Store cleaning up the floors and stocking the back room. In return, Rubin had been promised a hot breakfast.

It was while lifting a box of stationery supplies that a bottle of mucilage happened to roll out, fall, and break squarely over Rubin's head, covering him with the sticky glue and knocking him unconscious. He fell backwards, landing in a bale of eiderdown that Old Man Pritchert had ordered for Mrs. Lewis who was having her maid make new pillows for the Lewis children. The bale burst open, covering the gluey Screwloose with a thick layer of the soft, downy feathers.

It was but a short time later when Rubin awoke to find the glue had already begun to set and the coating of feathers was securely stuck. He couldn't, of course, comprehend what had happened to him and, in fact, he couldn't even see. Worse yet, he suddenly realized, he could hardly breathe. Rubin panicked. Bursting from the backroom he screamed desperately: "Mmmmmfl Mrnrrmpf!.." Pleas for help.

The widow, Mrs. Sykes, plumpish and fortyish, was standing down by the china display considering the purchase of a new pair of salt and pepper shakers when the feather-coated Rubin suddenly burst on the scene grunting and hollering, gesticulating wildly with his down-covered arms. Mrs. Sykes, who was quite religious and in fact taught Sunday school to the children of Spud City, was sure she was being visited by an angel sent to her from heaven, responding accordingly.

"My time has come!" she cried. "Lord take me away!"

Overcome by the emotion of her own impending death, Mrs. Sykes fainted away and, with the salt and pepper shakers falling from her nerveless hands to shatter on the floor, she flopped backward into

Pritchert's china display, collapsing the entire table and scattering crockery everywhere - leaving Mrs. Sykes sprawled on the floor amongst the ruins, her dress flopped back over her face.

Mr. Pritchert, standing near the doorway, took a different tack and, not knowing what to make of the sudden flapping, snorting apparition, yelped out loud and swatted Rubin over the head with his broom. Rubin yelled again, this time something like:

"MMMfffttph! Arrgghl" and then ran straight down the store's main aisle, out the front door and into the street, destroying a canned goods display and a wall thermometer that had both gotten in his way.

This was a 'golden moment'. Rubin here had the opportunity to achieve something truly beautiful. He was in a position where he could have stampeded a corral full of horses; or he might have fallen blindly headfirst into an outhouse; or he might have even stumbled into the Chinese laundry, terrorizing the owners and getting half the town's freshly washed clothing trampled in the ensuing panic. The potential here was truly unlimited.

But it was raining.

The instant Rubin hit the street the rain began dissolving the mucilage and his feathers fell away in wet globby clumps. But that's how the business was. One minute you were on top; the next, in the dung heap.

People still heard about it though, and they laughed heartily to think of stuffy old Mrs. Sykes with her dress pushed up over her face screaming and rolling around in Pritchert's broken china, hollering: "Take me Lord. Take me now!"

But it was all soon to be forgotten. That afternoon, Luther, who of course should have known better, said "Aw gee, okay, I guess," when one of the Ratt brothers, Mean Matt (the Ratt brothers being the three dirtiest, lowdownest, most good for nothing varmints in town) invited him back behind Miller's blacksmith for a drink of some moonshine. Of course Luther got drunk in no time at all and then the Ratt brothers beat him up, stripped him of all his clothing, painted him with shellac, and rolled him around in the dusty streets before finally tossing him into the horse trough. As if this wasn't enough, Luther was then arrested by Sheriff Carter for public drunkenness - and lewdness - and ended up by spending the night in jail. By nightfall Screwloose's performance at Pritchert's General Store was old news.

Things started to get serious on Tuesday: Rubin broke the Heywood's pump when he got his thumb stuck in the handle, then Luther blew the door off the saloon when a shotgun he had picked up accidentally went off. Later, Luther caused additional mayhem when he had to let loose all of Sven Olson's horses from their corral after accidentally setting off a raging brush fire.

But Rubin caused the greatest panic when, while aimlessly wandering around up inside the church steeple, he got his foot entangled in the bell rope and fell off the edge of the balcony. With Rubin dangling precariously inside the steeple, hanging by a single foot and screaming his head off, the bell swung wildly back and forth, ringing for all it was worth and convincing half the townsfolk they were under Indian attack, while leading the other half to believe that Judgment Day had finally come.

They managed to get Rubin down safely and the horses were rounded up and put back in the barn. The grass fire was quickly put under control and the saloon door was fastened back on its hinges. Parts were located for the Heywood's pump and that was back in working order before bedtime.

But a sense of uneasiness pervaded the town of Spud City that night and people rested uneasily in their beds. A sense of dark foreboding seemed to permeate the very air.

Dawn broke gently, without a hint of the awful things to come. Morning passed by uneventfully and no one saw hide nor hair of either of the jackasses. People began gathering in the streets in small groups, whispering softly among themselves. They seemed afraid to speak out loud.

Then it began. From out of nowhere Rubin came running down Main Street. His face was covered with ink and the seat of his pants engulfed in flames. No one was ever sure how this had exactly come about but it is enough to know that it did. At nearly the same instant, traveling at a right angle to Rubin on Simpson Street, came Luther at the reins of a runaway buckboard loaded with sacks of feed. It was obvious to anyone that this time both men were going all out. No quarter was being asked or given.

They met - the flaming man and the runaway wagon - at the town's main intersection. The horse, at the sight of the infernal ink-stained Rubin, screeched to a halt and reared up before bolting north up

Main. Luther, taken by surprise, was thrown from the wagon and landed squarely atop Rubin extinguishing the fire and knocking the wind out of the both of them.

The runaway horse and wagon galloped out of control up Main Street, soon passing out of the city limits and heading toward the mountain. The townsfolk watched helplessly, the two idiots temporarily forgotten, as the runaway wagon, loaded with at least a ton and a half of horse feed, bounced up the twisting road that led toward the great potato silo. The crowd gasped as the buckboard, hitting the railroad tracks, flew high into the air and then broke loose from the maddened, foam-flecked beast. The horse turned to the west, galloping across the foot of the mountain; but the heavily laden wagon, as though guided by some diabolical hand, continued on toward the silo.

With a sound like a cannon shot the wagon crashed directly into one of the silo's main supports exploding into kindling wood. Nothing happened for a moment but then, almost imperceptibly, as though in slow motion, the giant silo began to lean forward, emitting a horrible groaning sound as the damaged support began buckling inward. Rivets popping loose, the silo's seams began to split open. Potatoes dribbled out to rain thunderously upon the ground.

The silo continued to lean toward the city, twisting as it did and breaking loose its remaining supports. Then all it once it fell, smashed to the earth and burst open. With the sound of an avalanche a hundred thousand russets exploded forth to pour down the mountainside toward Spud City.

The townsfolk stood as though paralyzed with shock, unmoving. Then a woman screamed and the spell was broken. A full-scale panic set in and people ran hysterically every which way trying desperately to save themselves from the onrushing tidal wave of tubers.

Despite the confusion, everyone was clear when the deadly churning wave of fresh-picked vegetables pounded down on the helpless town less than a minute later. Hoslip's Feed Store was the first to bear the brunt of the surging wall of spuds, and it collapsed like a house of cards. Bargain's Dry Goods followed and it hardly slowed the potatoes at all. Six more buildings were totally destroyed before the rampaging spuds finally ground to a halt.

Then the fires broke out.

It was nearly nightfall before the last of the flames was put out and things seemed under control. The brisk winds had quickly spread the conflagration, and when it was all over most of the buildings east of Main Street had been destroyed either by fire, by potatoes or a combination of the two.

During the last stages of the fire-fighting Sheriff Carter had taken time out to put together a posse of deputies. Trying to beat the setting sun, they went out looking for the two desperado simpletons. It was plain to Sheriff Carter that something would have to be done about these two idiots.

Luther was discovered hiding in the Jones's barn, shivering under a horse blanket and a pile of straw. Screwloose they found somewhere outside of town about a half mile from the city limits, whimpering under a bush. Unwittingly he had chosen a spot atop a large anthill, and by the time they rescued him he was near covered with insect bites. The two outlaws were brought back to town and Sheriff Carter, securely backed up by his numerous deputies, laid it on the line:

"Look you two," he began. "We got a nice quiet little town here; at least we did until you two got to acting up."

He turned to Luther.

"Luther, I've known you for a couple years, and up 'til now I ain't had no real complaint with you - but this kind of shit, like what happened today, is what I've been afraid of all along." He spit out a chaw of tobacco and then went on: "You know it as well as I do, Luther. A man like you can retire if he wants - but there ain't no way he can retire his reputation."

With that the two idiots were supplied with pistols and belts and told to meet each other at sunrise on the summit of Eagle Rock. (Sheriff Carter had insisted on a location far from town).

There the two were to settle things once and for all.

The sun rose bright and clear the next morning, casting long shadows from the two figures that stood facing each other atop the high rock south of town.

Stupid Luther, stained felt hat shading his eyes, one strap of his dirty overalls falling off his shoulder and a deadly Colt .45 strapped to his side, stared into his despised rival's eyes.

Screwloose Rubin, perpetually dusty and now covered with dozens of itchy ant bites, stared right back at Luther, trying to break his opponent's concentration with a series of silly grins and dumb looks. He, like Luther, was also armed.

A Gray-Tufted Dust Finch awoke in a nearby Scraggly Pine and hopped out on a limb. It lifted its head and greeted the morning sun with its song, catching Rubin's attention. He glanced up toward the tree, trying to get a glimpse of the bird.

A few feet away a lizard scampered up on a rock to sun itself, distracting Luther from what he was doing.

Rubin's mouth hung open, a little trickle of drool appearing in the corner as he watched the bird hopping from branch to branch, twittering and flapping.

Luther, his adversary now forgotten, began creeping silently toward the lizard, his hands outstretched in the hope of catching the little critter.

"Goddamn it! That's about enough!"

Sheriff Carter, standing up from behind the fallen tree he had chosen for cover, was red in the face. "You two get on with this thing right here and now! I ain't got all goddamn day!"

Apologizing profusely, the two dumbbells scrambled to retake their positions. Facing each other again, the showdown recommenced.

It was Rubin who made the first move, going for the six-shooter strapped to his side. Luther, almost simultaneously, grabbed for his.

Rubin got his weapon out first but it spun loose from his hand and got away from him. He tried to catch it but bobbled it again and it fired off a shot when it struck the ground.

Luther got his gun stuck somehow and, pull as he might, could not get it loose. When Rubin's fallen pistol hit the ground and went off, Luther, startled by the sound, accidentally squeezed the trigger on his own pistol and fired a shot into his foot.

Rubin, trying to pick up his fallen weapon, chased about the rock but somehow managed to keep kicking the gun out of his own reach. Luther, holding his foot off the ground, hopped wildly about, howling with pain.

Sheriff Carter, once again standing up from behind the dead tree, covered his face with his tanned, weathered hand and gently massaged his temples. muttering something under his breath. The idea of having to put up with these two much longer was more than he really cared to think about.

That was when Stupid Luther played his final ace, the masterstroke joke that ensured he would, for all time, be remembered as the biggest jackass the West has over known.

He accidentally hopped backward off the edge of Eagle Rock.

They buried him up on the hill, in the town cemetery, and for awhile people remembered Stupid Luther; flowers would often appear on his grave, particularly on the anniversary of his death.

Screwloose finally chose to settle down in Spud City and took over the now-vacant jackass position. For a few years he continued to provide the townsfolk with a good laugh now and then, but it never seemed quite the same after Luther passed on.

A short time later, Old Man Pritchert bought a machine from out East and started showing movies on Friday nights at the General Store. Then the saloon began bringing in more money and they started having live entertainment. Between the two of them, the jackass trade was just about put out of business.

Potatoes had become big business by this time, and that's when they changed the town's name to Lewiston, thinking that the old name wasn't quite respectable enough. Then some people started saying that having a town jackass wasn't anything to be particularly proud of either. The City Council soon after gave Rubin his walking papers and he was forced to look for other work. Even Idiot's Rock, once remembered for its great showdown, was once again being called Eagle Rock.

At Rubin's age another man might have folded up, or started drinking, or just said the hell with it and put an end to it all. But not Rubin. Nope, he took it all in stride and before long, with a couple of loans and a lot of work, he opened this own newspaper, providing Lewiston with its first local press. The paper turned out to be quite successful and Rubin was happy in his work. But he always attributed his success to the years that be had spent thinking like a complete fool.

And he never forgot Stupid Luther, either. He always remembered that day on Idiot's Rock - the day he learned that, try as he might, he could never hope to be anything other than the second biggest jackass in the West.

-PUBLISHED IN HAYES,1982

Takes all kinds, don't it? Well, everybody pulls a lamebrain stunt at least onct in their lives. Ifin' you ain't dine such a thing yet, pard, that there means you got somethin' to look forward to.

A'course there's them as gets involved in such shenanigans through no fault of their own, 'ceptin' maybe what ya call an error in judgment. Yep, that there phrase covers a wide territory, don't it?

Then there's them as do the right thing fer the dumbest reasons, 'r blunder their way through life like this here fella one time....

DEATH'S DOOR
BY
MARK SIEGEL

Hubbard thought he probably was dying of thirst when he saw the river-greened valley below. Yet the thought that preoccupied him as he picked his way through the rocks along this inexplicably lifeless mountain trail was something like, "Lost Dutchman, my hairy red ass. Lost Moron, wherever he came from. How smart can you be if you lose a gold mine?" As he moved down the slope, the forked river flickered like a serpent's tongue among the boulders and vanished completely when he turned the corner that Hubbard guessed would be the last difficult pass before he escaped this hell.

He found the skeleton still clutching the key ring a few hundred yards from the huge metal door. The door was set in the side of the sheer rock face that ultimately blocked his way. A single enormous key hung from the ring.

As he stared at the remains of what must have been a seven-foot man buried up to his waist, the key dangling from a desiccated arm still upraised well above normal eye level, Hubbard felt his thirst hit somewhere in the back of his brain, and he knew two things immediately. Nature was making its message simple, he thought, so even he couldn't miss the point for once. The first thing he knew was that he was going to die if he didn't make it through that door and down into the valley. The second thing was that the key unlocked that door.

Still, he sat there theorizing for a moment, if only to imagine his wits had something to do with what anyone else would have assumed was blind luck. The only time you put a single key on a key-ring was when you were going to hang it somewhere – like next to that door over there. He didn't see a spike or anything like that on the cliff wall, but he was still some distance away, and the afternoon sun cast flag-shadows that furled in the heat rising from the rocks. Perhaps the dead man had lived in a cave on the other side of that door, a cave that opened out onto the valley below, where he tended his livestock, safe from marauding neighbors. Or maybe there'd be treasure of some sort in the cave; that would be an even better reason for protecting yourself with a locked door. Or – *just get the water, Hubbard.*

He approached the skeleton, its stiffened ligaments tanned and dried in the moistureless mountain air. The big guy looked as if he had been half-buried and left to die just before . . . throwing something. Long black strands of hair drifted in the dry wind. There wasn't a seam in the dirt that had closed over his lower half. Hubbard prodded at the skeleton with his foot, just to make sure the giant hadn't been cut clean in half and only looked buried. The key swayed in the arm over Hubbard's head, but the skeleton remained firmly planted in the dry, hard-packed earth. Swinging his empty canteen by its strap, Hubbard attempted to knock the key from the bony hand. Enfeebled by his exhaustion and thirst, he had to do it a second time, as hard as he could, before something cracked and the key-ring fell to the ground a dozen feet away. The entire forearm had come off with the blow.

As he stooped to pick it up, Hubbard heard something - maybe dislodged rocks - from the direction of the door. He straightened up quickly to look, but was overcome with dizziness, reeled, and fell to the ground. He closed his eyes and breathed deeply, but the dry, hot air burned his already parched throat. Forcing himself to inhale through his nose, he gradually calmed himself. When he was no longer panting, he heard the footsteps close to his head.

Too tired to leap to his feet and defend himself with his empty canteen, Hubbard merely opened his eyes. An Indian, a big, naked Indian, with a vaguely green cast to his skin, was reaching down to take the key from Hubbard's hand. Either that, or he collected empty canteens from people who had died of thirst.

Hubbard rolled from his grasp and scrambled to his feet, grabbing the only weapon he could find. He swung the canteen around his head like a mace while jabbing the skeleton forearm at the green giant. He screamed and hissed and danced back and forth in what he imagined was a fighting stance. The big Indian blinked at him once, then turned and walked back into the rocks. Hubbard stopped congratulating himself when he realized the skeleton claw in his hand no longer held the key-ring, that it wasn't on the ground around his feet – that the Indian must have walked off with it while Hubbard whooped and hollered like a savage.

He sunk to his knees, exhausted and gagging. If he didn't get the damn key back, he'd die. He had to follow the green man. Even if he couldn't get the key back, the man might lead him to water. Savvy savages must drink to survive. Hubbard struggled to his feet. Dusting the new dirt off his already filthy britches and shirt, he stopped in mid-gesture when he saw the skeleton of the giant was no longer where he remembered it.

People said Hubbard had a vivid imagination, and not just about his own financial prospects. He staggered back across the small flat space where he had been wasting his last ounces of perspiration and studied the ground where the skeleton had been half-buried. There wasn't a sign it ever had been there. Hubbard scratched his red hair with the skeletal hand.

Something on the other side of the door, the promise of water, he supposed, told him to get his ass in gear. He struggled up the rocks in the direction he'd seen the green man take.

Hubbard climbed for half an hour, ever upward. Tracking was easy, because the giant Indian left big, somehow moist, footprints in the hard-pack. Hubbard wasn't sure now he'd be able to find his way back to the door in the deepening shadows of late afternoon, but he simply had no place to go except after the key. As he climbed through the terrible desolation, it occurred to him that, even if he never found the key, this path might lead him over the rock wall and down into the fertile valley on the other side of the door.

Hubbard imagined himself hustling that laggard George Donner over the Sierra Nevada. "Piece of cake, really, George, for the experienced adventurer. No it never snows up here this early in the season. . . ."

The trail led him to a sheer bluff overlooking an Edenic paradise. His thirst had passed being merely intolerable. If the river had been directly below him, he'd have thrown himself at it despite the fatal height. He thought of Moses on Sinai looking out over the Promised Land, knowing he would never enter, but Hubbard couldn't help imagining the white-bearded prophet with his staff in one hand and a rum punch in the other, the brave little paper umbrella raised to shade the icy glass from the desert sun.

He looked straight down. A silver fog, resolving into something like a small black thunderhead below in the slightly thicker air, drifted beneath his feet, obscuring the five hundred foot drop to the valley. Hubbard hallucinated for a moment that, if he were to step out onto it, it would bear him magic carpet-like to his intended destination. He actually had one foot half-off the ground when he saw what was left of the Indian.

Like the first skeleton, he was half-buried in the dirt, his arm outstretched in what was an even more obvious throwing motion. Although he looked as if he had been dead for weeks, his skin and sinew well on the way to becoming leather to match his twin's back by the door, Hubbard assumed it must be the same Indian who had taken the key from him, because it now dangled from his upraised arm. In fact, Hubbard discovered, it was firmly clenched in his fist, so that he could not pry it loose. With a sigh, Hubbard stepped back and swung the empty canteen around over his head.

As Hubbard struck, the Indian opened his eyes. The Indian's arm cracked and the key fell to the ground, but Hubbard let go of the canteen in shock and stumbled backward. The canteen flew off over the cliff, and as he spun and slipped, Hubbard found himself on the very brink of the precipice, madly waving his arms as he teetered between life and death.

An enormous hand clutched his shirt collar and dragged him backward onto firm ground – or what looked like firm ground, at any rate. Hubbard wasn't positive because his feet weren't on it, but dangled ten inches above. Slowly the Indian, again fully fleshed in his greenish hue, rotated Hubbard by the top of his red head until the two men were face to face. "You stay here. Throw key over."

"It speaks!" Hubbard squawked to an imagined audience. When he was really scared he found it helped to imagine his life was a dime novel.

"Must no open door. Throw key over cliff."

Hubbard managed to sputter, "Why the hell don't you throw the damn key over yourself?"

The Indian simply looked at him fiercely. Although choking on his own shirt and nearly hallucinating from thirst (nearly?), Hubbard responded with a clarity that surprised even himself. "You can't, can you? Every time you try, you get sucked into the earth and die, don't you?"

The Indian communicated with his all-purpose glare.

Hubbard was thinking of refusing the request anyway, because he was not altogether sure he himself would not turn into an ivory planter if he tried to pitch the key; but getting enough air was becoming an even bigger priority than getting water. Maybe he could kick the key over the cliff, or poke it there with a stick, if he could find a stick in this desert. Hell, he could wait until the Indian stiffened up again and use one of his bones. "What if I do?"

The Indian opened his hand and Hubbard hit the ground like the sack of sand used to test a gallows trap door. "Then Death cannot escape."

"Can that be translated into something like a beer?" he mumbled hysterically.

The Indian picked Hubbard up by the back of his belt.

"Look, I really need water," Hubbard croaked.

"No water." Even the Indian's words glared. He was swinging Hubbard gently back and forth over the edge of the cliff for emphasis.

Hubbard noticed a hawk floating in the mist below him. On its back. The bird flapped listlessly, and appeared to be crying out, although no sound spanned the twenty yards between them. If *the cloud is some kind of gravity-defying magic,* Hubbard thought, *I can let the Indian throw me and give him the finger as I backstroke to salvation.* But the bird did not look happy. It seemed to be molting, big time. "OK, OK, I'll get rid of the key for you."

The Indian carried him like a suitcase back to the key and dropped him on it. Hubbard waited to be paralyzed by contact with the key, for it to burn itself into his belly or suck him into the earth. Nothing happened. He picked it out of his crotch and slowly stood up. It was just a key.

Hubbard hefted it in his right hand. He looked out over the valley like (he imagined) a Sioux war chief about to hurl his war tomahawk a hundred yards into the skull of that General Custer. He glanced back over his shoulder at the real Indian.

"Give me room, man. Back over there, where you like to bury yourself." Hubbard brought his hands together across his belly, went into a crouch, pumped, rocked back, and flung his arm up and around in an arc he imagined was more than three hundred sixty degrees. His open right hand hung at his side. He shaded his eyes with it, trying to track the key through the mist. Then he looked back over his shoulder at the Indian. "OK? Fini?

The Indian grunted, folded his arms over his chest, and closed his eyes.

Hubbard edged away from the cliff and back toward the pass.

The Indian opened his eyes and frowned.

Hubbard knew instantly what was going through his mind. The ground was not responding. Earth magic had not occurred. Hubbard switched the key he had hidden in his left hand back to his right so that he could point over the cliff with his left. "Oh my God! Look at that. I think that damn hawk caught the key!"

The Indian walked to the cliff edge and peered over the edge. Hubbard slammed him in the spine as hard as he could with the fist that held the key.

The Indian teetered on the edge of the cliff and Hubbard slammed him from behind as hard as he could. The giant spun in the air, reached around for Hubbard – and lost his footing. With a howl, he went over the side, clawing at the rock-hard ground, his fingers leaving deep gouges as he slowly slid away. Then he stopped sliding.

Hubbard jumped up and down on his fingers with no apparent effect. The Indian's head reappeared over the cliff-face, and Hubbard dealt him a terrific blow to the skull that fractured several small bones in his hand. And then, just as the Indian seemed about to hoist himself back onto solid ground, something happened. He let out a scream of anguish and began to slide backwards. Lying in the dirt several yards away, Hubbard peered over the cliff.

What looked like tentacles of cloud had wrapped themselves around the Indian's right ankle. His entire leg had turned black.

The Indian's struggles grew more feeble, and a minute later he disappeared from sight. There was no receding scream, no crash of rocks dislodged by the heavy body. He was simply gone.

Hubbard heaved himself to his feet with a sigh of relief. He loosened his collar with his right hand as he headed back down the trail to the door he had been forced to abandon earlier. He could make it, he thought, broken hand and all. Downhill would take him less than twenty minutes, and the heat of the setting sun was already dulled. He hefted the key in his left hand. Death locked up in the valley, good Lord. He'd told a few whoppers in his day, more than most, and he knew one when he heard it. Sure he'd stay away from that cloud if he had a choice, but it obviously did its damage up at these higher altitudes. What else explained the green valley and all that cool, cool water below? He could practically feel the key grating in the lock of that door. The treasure on the other side – probably the Dutchman's treasure! How else could it have stayed lost all these years? The Indian had protected it!

Hubbard felt a prickling on his neck and spun around. There was nothing there. The silver-black cloud had begun to drift back down the cliff face toward its door. It's door? Where had that idea come from? *I've got to get something to drink*, he realized.

There was no evidence that it had rained in this place for a thousand years; no sign of life, not a weed or a prairie dog to eat it. Staggering by the time he reached the door, Hubbard fumbled to fit the key into the lock. He could barely stand by now, and when he finally scraped the key into the key hole, he slumped to the ground, leaning against the door, trying to muster the strength to turn it with his uninjured hand. Only as his own breathing calmed did he hear the breathing on the other side of the door. "Who's there?" he croaked.

The breathing stopped. There was absolute silence.

Could it be the Indian again? "I know you're in there," Hubbard gasped.

Suddenly someone was pounding on the other side and Hubbard scrambled away from it on all fours. He sat on his butt, legs outstretched in front of him, staring back at it. "Open the friggin' door!" someone yelled from the other side.

It didn't sound like the Indian. "Who are you?"

"Name's Jakob Waltz. Let me out of here."

Waltz? The Lost Dutchman?"

"Do I look lost? I'm locked up!"

"You're the Locked-Up Dutchman? Not the one with the gold mine?" Hubbard's brain was barely functioning. Without water, he felt his little wheels grinding to a gritty halt.

There was a pause on the other side. "Let me out and I'll tell you all about the gold mine," came a calculated response.

Normally Hubbard would have bargained, but he was as desperate to get in as the other man was to get out. But why was he so desperate to get out? "Do you have water in there?"

There was another pause. "Sure."

"Really?" Hubbard was in no position to doubt it, but he also needed time to struggle back to the lock and turn the key. Might as well make this Locked-Up Dutchman think he was still capable of walking away.

"Sure, sure. Listen."

As Hubbard began to crawl up the side of the rusty metal door, he heard a vague sloshing sound from the other side. It was enough to trigger his reflexes to turn the key in the lock. There was a whooshing sound as the door fell open against his weight, and he fell across the threshold.

He found himself staring up into darkness. Instead of the green valley he had imagined, he was in some sort of cave, about ten feet in diameter, closed off by a second metal door at the opposite end. There was a rag stuffed in that keyhole, something that looked like a ragged old bandana. The bandana's owner was standing over him, peering out the door. He did not look entirely human, although Hubbard's brain was too befuddled to tell him exactly why.

"Where's Geronimo's big brother?" the Dutchman asked suspiciously.

"The Indian? He . . . fell," Hubbard gasped. "Where's the water?"

The Dutchman pointed with the stump on one wrist toward the still-locked door. "In there. You just got to go in there. What do you mean, he fell? Is he out here or not?

"Fell off the cliff."

Waltz's eyes narrowed. Actually, one of them narrowed and the other, in which a cloud appeared to have replaced the pupil, seemed to stare right through him. "That Indian was not the falling type."

"Well, he partly fell, and then the cloud grabbed him. I need water."

Waltz rubbed his grizzled chin with a hand where the stump had been a moment ago. The hand was misshapen and had only three fingers, as if it had been hastily sketched in, yet there was no visible scarring. "Told you, the water's on the other side of that door. The thing is, you can't open that door while this one's open. It's sort of like one of those, uh, secret Chinese lock things. This door you came through has to be locked from the outside before you can unlock the other door from the inside, but you have to use the same key for both, because I lost the other key in the valley. Follow me?"

Hubbard was in no condition to follow anything, but he wasn't about to admit he'd never heard about these Chinese locks. "What have you been drinking if there's no water in here?"

He didn't respond, but ducked his head around the outside door again, as if to make sure the big Indian wasn't sneaking up on them.

"There's nothing in here to drink. You gotta go through that door after I go through this one."

"Then what's that?" Hubbard gestured toward a large ceramic jug, apparently the only object in the cave, crammed into one corner. There was a familiar label on it.

"Jack Daniels," Waltz told him matter-of-factly.

Hubbard crawled over to it. The familiar black and white label of the Tennessee whiskey manufacturer in fact was etched on the ancient jug. "Cask 666. This must be pretty old stuff."

"Right," Waltz confirmed. "But I wouldn't open it just yet."

Hubbard looked at the label again. It must be first rate firewater. Apparently, back in those days, they'd said "spirit" instead of "spirits." He shook the jug, and there was a rattling sound, followed by a faint cursing.

"I wouldn't do that if I were you," Waltz told him. "Jack don't like it."

This seemed hilarious to Hubbard, but his throat was too dry to laugh. "Waltz, I'm dying. Just tell me, are you an hallucination?"

"You can't die in here. Not entirely, anyway."

Hubbard noticed that some of the old miner's whiskers wriggled like thin white worms. "I'm going to open that other door now. I'm gonna die if I don't get something to drink."

"Next to letting Jack out of that jug, that would be the biggest mistake you could make." Waltz shifted from boot to boot, which made a peculiar squishing sound. "See, the thing on the other side of that door, the cloud thing, will eat your sorry ass, like it started to do with me before I locked myself back in here. It absorbs every living thing it touches. That's why the Indians locked it in here and left their spirit champion to guard the place."

Uh oh, thought Hubbard. "And now that there's no champion?"

As if in answer, a pounding started on the other side of the still-locked door. Waltz jumped back, and Hubbard heard the sloshing sound again.

"You've got water hidden in your pants!"

"It's not water," Waltz protested. "It's my blood. I got no circulation, and it's all settled in my legs. Can't take my damn boots off because my feet'll swell up so bad I'll never be able to get 'em back on."

The pounding grew louder.

"Grab the jug," Waltz told Hubbard, "but be careful."

Hubbard staggered to his feet with the jug in his arms and Waltz ushered him out the door; not out of politeness, Hubbard realized, but to make sure the Indian wasn't somehow waiting in ambush, ready to sever the first head he saw. Waltz locked the door from the outside and pocketed the key. "Hey," Hubbard protested.

Waltz looked at him and then slung Hubbard's free arm over his shoulder. With a last admonition not to drop the jug, Waltz helped Hubbard stagger back up the path he already had traveled twice that afternoon.

The sky was darkening now, and the muffled pounding on the great iron door was echoed in a low rumbling that evoked the restlessness of the entire valley below. Hubbard tried not to look at Waltz at this close proximity. The arm that supported his pack shifted like a python as they walked, and when Hubbard glanced up and found himself looking into Waltz's ear, he swore he could see something moving inside the man's head. Only his incredible weakness and his complete lack of options kept Hubbard stumbling along in the Dutchman's grasp.

By the time they reached the cliff over which the Indian had disappeared, the sun had set behind the mountains; but in the glow of dusk Hubbard could see the cloud roiling angrily at their feet, licking at the edge of the cliff but, like water sloshing in a tub, not yet spilling over.

"Now," said Waltz, steadying Hubbard so that he might stand alone for the moment, "give that jug one last shake, pull the cork, and toss him over the side. But be quick about it."

"What?"

"You got to do it," Waltz reprimanded irritably. "Now."

"But..."

"Shake, pull, and throw!" He backed away from Hubbard a few steps, maybe to give him room, maybe to get a running start.

Hubbard sighed, then turned back to look at the cloud, which seemed to have crept fractionally closer. He shook the jug as hard as he could, and, as he ripped the ancient stopper from its mouth, a terrible scream twisted from its mouth. Hubbard swung the jug in a wide arc and watched it sail down into the cloud.

"You might want to step back a bit," Waltz informed him as a blinding flash erupted below them. Hubbard fell backwards, and lay in the dirt completely without strength, staring up at the sky. As the explosions continued below, ribs of white cloud formed on all four horizons and quickly moved toward the center of the sky, where they locked and wove into an enormous nimbus. Then a huge bolt of lightening burst from the center of the rain cloud, ripped by the cliff edge, and smashed into the valley below. "Now that's what I call white lightening," Waltz laughed.

And that was the last thing Hubbard remembered him saying, because he was completely distracted by a tiny, wet blow from the heavens. For a moment he thought he might have imagined it, but then came another and another, and, within seconds the rain was pouring down. Hubbard closed his eyes and lay still with his mouth wide open.

When his eyes opened again, it was early morning. Hubbard was unable to move his arms, legs or head, and realized he was buried in the earth with only his head and his toes poking out. *I am nobody's spirit champion*, he thought, rocking himself from side to side. *If this has proven anything, it's proved that.* As if in response, the still damp mud began to break away with his rocking, and in a few moments he had freed himself. His clothes were soaked and filthy, but as he flicked off mud he couldn't help feeling grateful that he hadn't drowned like the proverbial turkey who couldn't help staring up during a rainstorm.

There was no sign of Waltz, or of the Indian for that matter. Hubbard crawled to the edge of the cliff and looked over. The valley below was virtually unrecognizable from the day before. Gone was the rushing river with its tree-lined bank, gone was the green plain of grass - and gone was the cloud. What remained was a brown, rocky desert, much like the desert Hubbard had tramped through the entire previous day.

Hoisting himself to his feet with a sigh, Hubbard swayed briefly before regaining his equilibrium. He turned away from the cliff and toward the path back down the mountain. *I can make it*, he thought. He supposed he could ring out his filthy clothes and suck up the extra moisture, no matter how vile; but as he started down the path, Hubbard saw little pools of water cratered among the rock formations. Little shoots of green were already poking up through the red earth.

WEIRD TRAILS

Wellsir, it's gettin' on early, an' all this jabberin's plumb tuckered me out. Think I'll be turnin' in now, ifin' that's all right with yerself. Say there, pard, you don't look so good; little green around the gills, as they say. Get aholt of some bad grub, did ya? No? Well mebbe it's the coffee, then. A good pot of cowboy coffee'll stand up in the pot an' curse yer mother afore it jumps down yer throat to commence it's mischief in yer belly.

Whatever it is that's ailin' ya, it don't look too likely that you'll be sleeping much right off, so why don't you take the first watch? You can wake me when ya find yerself gettin' drowsy. It's a right nice evenin', don'cha think? Fine, full moon up there in that cloudless sky. Why, there ain't man ner beast as could sneak up on this here camp without bein' seen like it was broad daylight.

'Course, if ya take any of them stories I told ya into account, well then that sortta changes things a mite, don't it? Think there cud really be a giant rattler prowlin' around out there in the grass? How 'bout a wolf that ain't necessarily a wolf? An' ifin' ya hear the sound of wings a'flappin' up above, who's to say how many of them there stars them wings'll block out, eh?

Ah, but them was all just stories, told to pass the time around the campfire on a lonesome night in the wilderness. You can pay them no nevermind, have another cup of coffee and enjoy the evenin', that's up to you. I never did mention which of them tales was true, 'r if any of em' was. Well, that can wait till mornin' I 'spect; no use goin' over it now, with me half asleep an' ready to snore. Give us somethin' to jaw on over breakfast.

Now, don't you go an' get all jittery on me an' commence to shootin' up the countryside every time ya see a shadow that don't move like ya think it should. Ammunition is hard to come by in these parts, an' ya never know when ya might find yerself desperate needful of that one last cartridge...

'Sides, ifin' any of them stories was true, it'd take more 'n a sixshooter to discourage any of them critters I tolt ya 'bout. Anyway, if somethin' did come our way, it's best to make yerself as small as you can an' jus' let it pass on by, right, pard?

Gol dern if you ain't the palest fella I seen in a long spell! Hope ya get over whatever all's ailin' ya afore mornin', on account of it's a mighty long ride from here to anywhere fer the both of us, an' it's no good startin' off dead tired. Mornin' comes quick around these parts - at least, fer some.

G'night, pard.